ALIVE IN '95

For Pete – *WGLF!*

►►

Cover Design by Molly Burch

Radio City Music Hall Photo © GoCardUSA, used under Creative Commons license (flickr. com/photos/gocardusa/3752216239). *Image edited for book cover design.*

Library of Congress Control Number: 2025911802

ISBN: 979-8-9989996-5-9

eISBN: 979-8-9989996-8-0

FIRST EDITION: LIVE IN '25!

INTRO

AFTER A CARDIAC ARREST took out the bum heart of her boss, Bobbi Rollins became the unlikely successor of Bewilder Records. Despite her passion, prowess, and the shorter male lifespan, it still seemed a little suspicious for a woman with the voice and gait of a cartoon sailor to rise to the top. Most of the music industry was run by men with receded hairlines and souls. What they had in common was a proclivity for women and wearing suits, although Rollins' get-ups were best described in *The Face* as "what Elvis Costello might wear to the dog track."

Some speculated that she'd leveraged notorious family ties to make her ascension. Allegedly, Rollins came from old money on one side and a criminal ring of connections on the other. She was known to say she had "a key or a lock pick" to any door in the city. Why wouldn't she hype her own mythology? The sport of selling records was played on a minefield of grifts and chancing. As such, Rollins would do the maximum of both on the day of her most unexpected and legendary deal.

▶▶

March 16, 1994. The same day Tonya Harding was being charged with conspiracy, Bobbi Rollins incited a conspiracy of her own. She signed a new band. A band helmed by two electric brothers more capable of calamity than metal in a microwave. A band that would wake rock'n'roll from its smack nap and save them all before the year's end.

None of this would have happened if Rollins wasn't both desperate and defiantly committed to luck over logic. Bewilder Records would be bankrupt by the year's end. Like many women before her, Rollins had been set up to take a fall. She'd known their main act, The Reverie, was underwater on the follow-up they owed the label, but that was chump to what Rollins had learned the label owed everyone else.

If that wasn't enough in a world injecting junk, Rollins' live-in lady friend shot up with a turkey baster! With financial doom and a baby on the way, Rollins took off on a bender to course correct. Her quickest fix was to get The Reverie back in the studio, if only she could find them. The band's hobbies had become so polarized, Rollins didn't know whether to search for them in Buddhist temples or opium dens. She scratched her signature electroshocked hair and thought, Chinatown?

In fact, Chinatown would have been close. The Reverie's singer had surfaced at a club down on the Bowery, some gig of no names. Rollins' intel had come from the doorman. He'd been a reliable source, though he was about as legit as his knock-off Kangol. Even the kangaroo on his cap looked more like a rat.

Rollins spotted her doorman checking IDs in a cloud of smoke underneath the club's buzzing sign of a beehive. This guy wasn't law-abiding so much as he was hustling to sell the underage kids fakes from his Kwikprint truck operation around the block. Everyone was scamming today's youth; only Bewilder Records wasn't doing as well yet to cash in.

"Will Hawking still here?" Rollins asked him, forking over a denomination that had nothing to do with the $3 cover.

The doorman shrugged and coolly pocketed the cash.

"You're fucking chatty tonight," she replied.

Inside The Hive's lobby, booths showcased wilted cardboard boxes stuffed with DIY merch slung by girls more interested in sizing each other up. Rollins followed the cacophony downstairs into the ballroom. Spotlights flickered on a band called Girlcrush. Their red and yellow logo displayed playmate silhouettes often seen at strip clubs or on a truck's mud flaps.

Rollins joined the showgoers who were more interested in crowding the bar than the stage. She kept her cool not to grimace when the wet, pleather-rimmed bar top soaked through her houndstooth blazer, but howled after evaporated perspiration reformed and dripped from the ceiling pipes into her mouth. Rollins ordered an antiseptic double vodka from the bull-nosed bartender and then swiveled to scan the room. None of The Reverie guys were in sight, so she amused herself by undressing Girlcrush's singer, a Blondie archetype erotically kneading a Moog. Unfortunately, their sound was the antithesis of the *wu wei* Rollins loved about music. It'd been so long since she'd encountered that intangible, authentic sound and spirit of a true rock'n'roll band that's working hard but hardly working.

After the set, equipment shuffled on stage for the next act. The Reverie's faded first single began to play over the PA, as if to soundtrack Rollins' failed effort to find them. Girlcrush's singer slid next to her at the bar.

"I know you," she said to Rollins, licking her teeth encircled by pin-up lips.

"Yeah? I know your type, too, Debbie," Rollins said.

"It's *Diana*." The bartender lit her smoke as if on cue. "You're from Bewilder Records, right?"

"I'm looking for Will," Rollins said. "You know, Will Hawking from The Reverie?"

"Yeah, duh. He was here to drag out their bassist. Totally strung out," said Diana.

"Brilliant." Rollins pushed off the bar to walk away, but Diana stuck out her fishnet leg like a boom gate.

"You should stay," Diana said.

Rollins leaned towards Diana and palmed the slick heat of her exposed lower back. "I'm not signing you."

She was close enough to feel Diana's breath hiss when the ballroom went black.

A rattle from a tambourine signaled the crowd. Bodies condensed towards the stage. Blue lights illuminated a five piece under no banner. The singer in streetwear swaggered forward. He flaunted a look that money couldn't buy, but could be sold. He adjusted his mic stand low for his height, which was auspiciously taller than the rest of the band in formation. A buzz from the PA preceded a waking riff of common chords. Then, a beat, washy hi-hats outpacing a jammy bass drum. One guitarist stepped forward to assert himself as the lead, weaving his strings around the rhythm like a loom. His expression was placid but for a side mouth curl that seemed to promise something. That something was delivered after the singer swept the mop-top from his brows and bent down to mouth up the mic. What came out was unsettling. A voice of psychedelic sheen crackling with punk, on key. It was the audio equivalent of what the Japanese called *umami*—you either lust for it, or you're allergic to the MSG.

Rollins spat out her drink stirrers, then bulldozed forward to reckon with this phantasm on stage.

The kid never touched the mic, like his hands were cuffed by the tambourine behind his back. His big doe eyes hovered above the crowd as though he saw beyond them. The whole band barely moved, whereas Rollins submitted to the crowd's enthusiastic shoves, shifting her left and right. The opener seemed to end only after there was mutual consensus—a feeling as though they'd escaped onto the better side of a border, leaving behind a spun-out squad car to sulk in the dust. And now it was time to launch a victorious anthem.

OOMPH CRACK OOMPH-OOMPH HISS
OOMPH CRACK OOMPH-OOMPH HISS

"This is 'Muse Box,'" the singer announced in his guttural rasp, and the lead guitarist stepped into the cyanic spotlight to introduce a rollercoaster riff. It was then that Rollins noticed their obvious genetic likeness. They looked like brothers. What could go wrong? Rollins guffawed, thinking of her own sister who was uptown going down on Will Hawking's ex-girlfriend. Rollins felt a flash of responsibility for The Reverie's current state of ruin, but was set free by the devilish charisma before her. Nevermind the grunge! These boys were forged from the blood of a barroom brawl between Pete Townshend and The Sex Pistols. They were a clash of nostalgia and the future.

They were now.

They were—who the fuck were *they*? Still, no one had said!

▶▶

Before the lights turned on to flood out the herd, Rollins sprinted back to The Hive's payphone. She fogged up the booth, fumbling through her black book.

"I just heard some pinnacle shit!" she said, sweltering into the receiver.

"It's too late, Bobbi," the man said. "Stick to the playbook."

"This band shot the head off a snake. Fuck the playbook!"

1

NAT

NAT DEMPSEY HAD ALWAYS been the early bird in a crowd that barely woke in time for their nooners. His doggedness dragged him out of bed and came alive in chords. Nat had a smart mouth but needed music to communicate his vision. At first, Nat's vision was obstructed until he broke down and recruited his younger brother Jamie to start Bolero. Why Bolero's musical aspirations hinged on each of the brothers was contentious. Jamie claimed Nat wasn't enough, whereas Nat accused Jamie of being too much. Even when Bolero was nothing, Jamie had such conviction that they were going to be something. Meanwhile, the shot at becoming anything relied on Nat's songs and discipline.

The Dempsey brothers had a way of bickering even when they agreed. They agreed most that Bolero could reach way beyond the handfuls they were playing in dusted barrooms across the Tri-state area. Bobbi Rollins at Bewilder Records knew it, too. Two months ago, Bolero was loading out of a last-minute gig at The Hive when she approached him and Jamie, sweatier than they were.

"You have a demo?" she said.

"No."

"You brothers?"

"You can't tell?" Nat said as he often did. His tone revealed a sting that, despite their resemblance, it was like his younger brother had been perfected in Nat's image. They both had sandy hair at birth that'd since grown taupe, but Jamie was taller with rounder eyes, without the slightest hook to his nose or crook of his front teeth.

"You take drugs?" she asked.

"Only the fun ones," Jamie said, and Nat shoved him.

"I want to sign you," she said.

"Let me think about it," Nat replied, and Jamie returned the shove.

Jamie pulled Nat by the collar to argue that there was nothing to think about. Nat claimed that was because Jamie was incapable of thinking, to which Jamie countered, "You don't need to think when you fucking know."

What Nat knew as the ink dried into his left hand was that his brother was right. Nothing about their band would go unnoticed with Jamie's infectious hubris.

After that, things moved quickly, which was a welcome transition for the band who were barely aware of how hard they'd been working to run in place. Rollins fast-tracked Bolero to record their debut album at Lockstock, an upstate campground some bankrolled hippy had converted into state-of-the-art studios and residences. The band invited an entourage including Girlcrush and a few hometown friends. Almost everyone was from Hillside, a proud but unpretentious town along the jagged border of Queens and Nassau counties. Nat was concerned about the distractions, but wanted to involve Eleanor. He couldn't understand why she was low-balling her talents to work as a tormented lackey in TV production, so Nat took it upon himself to sell her photography credentials to Rollins. The label agreed to hire her to shoot Bolero's studio sessions before taking her next job abroad.

Nat rode along to pick Eleanor up from the train station. On the ride back to Lochstock, she leaned on him the way every one of his girlfriends complained about, present one excluded.

"Look familiar?" he said when they passed the area's landmark covered bridge.

"Not really," Eleanor said.

"Interesting."

"What?" she said.

"Nothing," he replied, electing not to mention her postcard of the covered bridge since she didn't seem to remember the harsh, preteen summer she spent up here before her dad got discharged. Nat kept Eleanor's postcard in a cigar box with other treasures—portable pieces of his past and things that once belonged to others. Like the war-time letter his pops had written to the woman he'd spend his life with—that he loved her, but didn't expect her to wait for him. Maybe there'd been someone else, or maybe it was the expectation that death awaited him on the western front. Somewhere in all that was a great song that Nat hadn't been able to write yet, and not one that he envisioned Jamie to sing. Nat would need to do that himself.

After Nat gave Eleanor the grand tour of Lochstock, she was quiet.

"What's up with you?" Nat said. "Why are you holding out on me?"

"No, it's impressive, but I mean, it's no R-STUFF," she said of the local storage facility where Bolero used to rehearse.

"R-STUFF?" Nat shuddered to recall the reek of forgotten hoards and weed growing behind purple death trap roll-up doors. "It's way too early to start romanticizing that shithole."

"Oh come on, it wasn't that bad," Eleanor said.

"What about the time we got jumped?"

"That was a misunderstanding."

"Yeah, they misunderstood thinking that we had any money!"

"Well, it's looking like those days of empty pockets are behind you. Let's hope it won't result in any loss of character."

"That's why you're here," Nat said.

Eleanor checked his hip. His response oscillated between too comfortable and slightly strained. "Look who's taking his legacy so seriously."

"You have no idea."

"You better let me get the picture, though," she said and snapped a candid of him pinching the 11 between his brows.

▶▶

In the mornings up at Lochstock, Nat'd whistle working riffs as the gravel crunched a beat on his walk towards the lake. He'd discovered the outdoor shower and kept returning, not because he was into its sulfuric smell, but to avoid everyone fooling around in the communal bathroom. Afterwards, he'd stop by Lochstock's HQ to check the messages and phone Karen, whom he called his 'lady' because she was too dignified to be his girlfriend. Then he was the first to arrive and last to leave the Balmaha studio.

Nat found Will Hawking from The Reverie already occupying the phone at HQ. He had his bare feet on the old infirmary desk and seemed aggravated by how he opened and closed its drawers, discussing something legal, like a contract or a lease. Nat poured some of the mysteriously infinite drip coffee and waited outside. The label had booked The Reverie to record at Lochstock's Conic Hill studio, a few football fields from Balmaha. Nat suspected Rollins was putting the pressure on, having both bands scheduled simultaneously. But Nat viewed The

Reverie less like a threat and more like a cautionary tale. That band was one fuck up from being forgotten. Maybe *that* was Rollins' message.

"Hey man, sorry about the wait," Will said in his baritone voice, stepping out onto the covered porch. "Didn't expect anyone to be here so early."

"It's not that early," Nat said. "Looking a little early for you, though."

"Yeah, well." Will stretched his arms above his head and squinted at Lochstock's lush grounds. He looked straight out of a seventies time capsule. Girls loved this sedate Jaggerish fucker.

Nat thought Will was arrogant and dull unless he was on stage, crawling around shoeless. Nat's brother, Jamie, couldn't have been a more different frontman, almost impervious to movement. Yet Jamie and Will were both captivating. There's no one way.

"Getting some affairs in order," Will said.

"I wouldn't know by your lyrics, but you've got a way with words," Nat said, taking a sly dig at the recent affair between Will's ex-girlfriend and Rollins' sister.

Will sighed. His lack of reaction was shocking. Nat would kill to have such pacifists in Bolero.

"Anyway," Will said, "I think we're gonna swing by for some festivities tonight. You know, create some rancor to 'spin heads' about, or whatever Rollins says."

"Well, BYOB," Nat replied, regretting the bluff of his extended invitation.

"That won't be a problem," Will said before strolling off.

▶▶

Back inside HQ, Nat pulled a fax that responded to yesterday's incident report. Bolero's producer, Remy, had cranked one of Balmaha's speakers beyond the sound barrier. It'd taken off like the Challenger. The reply was brief:

GOOD SIGN!

YOU MADE IT TOO FAR WITHOUT A FIRE.

LIGHT UP & SHINE ON, SONNY.

- ROLLINS

Nat smirked when he dialed Karen, who was already known to refer to his bandmates as baby pyros. Karen was a stoic by comparison, even with her hazards of single motherhood. She had a daughter named Julia. The kid wasn't Nat's, and that familial boundary was firm.

When asked about Nat, Karen made it sound like she was clairvoyant. "I knew what I was getting into," she'd say.

Well, yeah. Nat was much younger, and they started dating after she fired him from Guitar Center for immediately abusing the discount policy. Nat thought he knew what he was getting into, too. But as time passed, he was stalling to accept what to do now that he knew better.

Karen answered his call on the second ring.

"How's the house?" he asked.

"Still in order."

"Julia?"

"Lovely and oblivious."

"You?"

"Oh, lovely and aware."

"Aware?" Nat said.

"You know what I mean, of this courtesy rundown." Karen paused. "It's really not necessary."

"Well, neither is the cat, but how's Groucho?"

"Still a dick. And you?"

"Still a dick," Nat replied. He could visualize her slowturn grin.

"How'd it go yesterday?"

"Pretty sick. Remy's rigged up some tambo on the snare so KP's kit is sounding more splashy. Got away from it a bit late night. There was a minor explosion..."

No reaction, then, "What's on today's task list?" she asked.

Nat lived by the task list. Karen believed this had something to do with him being a Virgo. Nat believed this had to do with the band being prone to the type of horseplay that could escalate to violence without a task list.

"Gonna rework some of Sulky's bass tracks, probably lay them down myself," Nat said. "Then get a guide going for 'She's Leaving.' Might do a singsong fade out for 'Whatever Tomorrow' with the whole crew."

"Sounds kitsch. Don't do that," Karen said.

"You're probably right."

"Is 'She's Leaving' new?"

"Eh. I think you know it," Nat lied. "Oh, and tonight's Eleanor's send off." He coughed.

"Right. Give her a hug. Or better, tell her *auf Wiedersehen.*"

2

ELEANOR

O N HER LAST NIGHT at Lochstock, Eleanor pregamed in Girl-crush's cabin, provided by Bolero as a thank you for sleeping with them. It stunk of designer imposter perfume and menthols. She took a half hit of E, regretted it, and then committed because nobody wins the fight against a high.

"Shit. You really duked my daisies," Eleanor said, holding up what little remained of her favorite jeans.

"I can crop that top, too," Diana suggested, Girlcrush's singer still looking eager to do something with the scissors.

Eleanor fingered the faded outline of pyramids on her chest. "No way, this shirt is a classic."

An adolescent Eleanor would've let Diana cut it up. Eleanor was an only child who grew up too unpolished and appealing not to have fallen victim to makeovers from girls at school with ulterior motives. She'd incurred mutilated bangs, a partially pierced ear, and razor burn from an inane expectation to shave her big toes. Girls often wanted to pry about the Dempsey brothers who lived on her block. In that way, now was no different. Diana's agenda was to ride Jamie, and for Girlcrush to ride Bolero's coattails.

"A classic? *That* looks like a stain," Diana said, pointing to David Gilmour's forged signature on Eleanor's shirt.

"It's a fake," Eleanor tried to admit without laughing and pulled on her shorts. She fell back into the bunk, not having anticipated how weightless they'd be.

"A fake stain?" said Pam, Girlcrush's drummer, who talked like she was being tickled and lived life like a sex doll in a pool of musicians. It was currently Bolero's lesser guitarist, Greg's turn on the float.

Diana began reapplying what she believed was CK One, but Eleanor knew was a knock-off Jamie got for her on Canal Street.

"I need some air," Eleanor said, wafting out the shirt Nat once gave her as a faux souvenir after they missed Pink Floyd at the Meadowlands. Jamie had flaked on his turn to stand in line overnight at Tower to buy tickets.

Eleanor launched herself from the cabin towards a cat-herded circle of seating around a stone pit. The air was pure and intoxicating. After plunging into a captain's chair, she spun the raw edges of denim on her shorts, twirling threads up her thighs. The tall pines of Lochstock encircled the black canvas of sky above her. Eleanor gave them a wave. Her half hit had activated, bringing the trees to dance, but now they were retreating. They heard the rustling sound of an engine. Eleanor heard it, too.

It was Jamie. He was surfing the hood of a tractor plowing across the fields. Eleanor couldn't make out the other blurred figures operating the machine. Their encroachment dragged on, which must've bored Jamie so much that he jumped off. The tractor labored on towards the Balmaha studio. Jamie sprang up like Gumby, aimed his finger at Eleanor, and blinked one eye like a trigger pull.

"Blue 42!" he howled, then charged her with his arms flung wide.

Eleanor prepared as if Jamie were a butterfly planning to perch on her finger. His collision smacked the wind out of her and the chair to dust.

She wheezed as the weight of his body morphed her into the cool forest floor. Eleanor's pupils were stupefied when she noticed Jamie's knuckles.

"You're bleeding," she said, her voice strained under his weight.

"I don't see anything," he said before nestling his philtrum and twice-broken but somehow perfect nose against her neck.

Eleanor felt his hand slip under her shirt and breach the skin of her belly. Her eyes bulged. Did he bite her collar? Was he now giggling and licking the curve between her head and shoulder? Sensations swung from a plunge into hot honey to a night tremor. What the fuck was he thinking?

Eleanor palmed Jamie's face to shift their physical engagement into her comfort zone, a merciless wrestling match. Eleanor won by blowing a raspberry into Jamie's neck. The sound of forceful, rippling farts caused Jamie to submit and squeal like the deviant child he was. The effort left her lips pulsating and the rest of her body feeling like tube socks filled with jelly.

Still entangled, Eleanor gazed at the twinkling obsidian above. She asked, "How do you know if you are on the dark side if you can still see?"

"Close your eyes," Jamie replied, testing another grope slow enough for her to bat down.

"You're lucky I love dogs," she said.

"Why?"

"I don't know. Because you're the worst," Eleanor replied. "Wait, are we on the dark side of the sun or the earth right now?"

"Well, well, what's this?" Diana and Pam had interrupted them, pecking around like sexy hens, clucking in heat for their rooster. "Has Peter Pan returned to Neverland and found Wendy?" Diana continued to narrate in her husky, suspicious tone.

Eleanor confessed, "I think I'm more like Alice down the rabbit hole." She realized she needed to reconfigure everything that was disheveled underneath her shirt and was delighted to find a clove in her bra. The occasional aromatic smoke was a tiny rebellion against former life as an athlete.

"Nah. Ele's more like that crocodile trying to get us up to no good," Jamie replied.

"Please, babe. We all know Ele is too smart for that," Diana said.

"Not us," Pam said before Jamie used her and Diana like crutches to walk away while he rattled off a range of raunchy activities to do in the outdoor shower.

Mixed with the synthetic tingling in Eleanor's body, their departure crept in an unwanted feeling of being left behind. That feeling had been irking, even before Bolero got signed. Once they did, Eleanor felt the impulse to assert herself somehow. Rather than be patient for the next unscripted project with B&M, she took a job working on a documentary in a European city she'd never heard of before. Eleanor sucked the crackling black cigarette to its filter with her runner lungs, then forced herself to sprint into the next phase of the night.

There were other stragglers on the screened-in porch of Bolero's cabin, where she was lodging. Bolero's rhythm section was in a heated therapy session with Eleanor's former roommate, Lindsay. On her way to the bathroom, Eleanor kept her head down to avoid eye contact with them. The bathroom wasn't much more than a coffin with a toilet and a compact mirror. She could still hear them from inside. Lindsay and Bolero's drummer, KP, were attempting to deescalate Sulky, the bassist, using their combined strengths: Lindsay's psychology degrees and KP's cooling techniques from when he was a bouncer.

"Relieved!" Sulky screeched. Apparently, Nat had relieved Sulky from his bass playing earlier.

Eleanor wondered how different her world might be if Greg and Sulky, the charmless Sullivan brothers, had lived across the street instead of Nat and Jamie Dempsey. Maybe she would've stayed on track instead of having an identity crisis at 23. Eleanor relieved her bladder, then applied someone's red stick deodorant and attempted to fluff her mid-length waves. She didn't know what to do with her hair when it wasn't in a ponytail. Like her eyes, the color of her hair was hard to pin down. Somewhere between tea and honey, depending on the light.

Before leaving the cabin, Eleanor dug through her duffel bag to grab her camera and a fresh roll to accomplish her official purpose for coming to Lochstock. She needed the money and gasped at how handsomely Bewilder Records was willing to pay her, even though her CV was limited to two lines from wrap-party photos she'd taken as an intern on *The Reel World*. Nat said he sold them on her "familiarity and command" over Bolero as her subjects. That really cracked her up, even though it was kind of true. She had taken so many photos of them over the years. Rehearsals at R-STUFF, live at the early but earnest gigs, and around Hillside's industrial park to use for promo flyers.

None of those times compared to what she saw through the lens at Lochstock. Eleanor did not expect to be captivated, particularly with Nat, whose emotions were often under a blanket of elusive moodiness. She felt closest to seeing how his brain worked in the studio. His quiet moments behind the glass, his sitting Indian style on the floor, tuning and noodling. Even Jamie behaved more like a savant than an idiot. He obediently absorbed the material, then delivered these electrifying, incredible vocals. Songs done in a few takes. She could tell by Nat and Jamie's shared eyelines and grins that they were aware of their synergy and how much it promised. Eleanor admired their achievement, and she envied it.

"Anybody indecent?" Eleanor announced while tiptoeing back to the porch.

Sulky had left, and Lindsay was now cuddled on the wicker lounger with KP, the only member of Bolero without the trouble of a brother in the band. They had been in love since Eleanor's matchmaking last year.

"Closer to catatonic," KP said.

"Prove it," Eleanor said, and piled on the lovebirds. The splintering of the wood under their weight tickled Eleanor's ears.

"Are you okay if we don't make it back to Balmaha tonight?" Lindsay asked.

Eleanor popped back up to mime tucking the lovebirds into their wicker nest. "Totally. I probably wouldn't if I had the option."

"Oh, you have options," Eleanor heard KP say as she left.

"Ele is back!" Lara from Girlcrush and Greg shouted, crowding Eleanor in their dance like fighting rabbits, rolling barrel punches, and bopping around to "Golden Years."

Eleanor recoiled from the fuss of her entrance into Balmaha, even five types of high. In the future, she would ask a therapist if her need to show up early had nothing to do with her military upbringing, but to increase her chance of blending in like an unremarkable plant or a well-placed table. She took out her camera and snapped a few live ones before hopping over to Nat, who was also the type to stand in a corner.

He was excitedly slurring on about the production genius of Harry Maslin and George Martin with Bolero's producer Remy. Remy looked more interested in deejaying with his fingers poked through queues of discs. Eleanor swiped Nat's sunglasses off his face and put them on. They nearly blacked out her vision in the dimly lit room.

"Whoa! How do you see anything?" she said.

"I see everything," Nat replied.

"You can't see me." Eleanor turned like she was pulling a cape across her body.

"Wow. I thought we had you until tomorrow, but I think your head's taken off early, Miss Huston."

Eleanor felt hot and childish when he called her this and shoved him into the wall.

"Hey, take it easy." Nat signaled with an upward nod to look across the room towards recognizable outsiders, Will Hawking and one of his bandmates from The Reverie.

Eleanor got ogle eyes at the look of Will. His voice felt like what she imagined it'd be like to put on a cashmere sweater that had been sitting in the sun. After a recent event, she wondered if they'd had an unspoken thing. Eleanor gulped from Nat's Heineken. "Ugh, is this skunked?"

"No, you just don't like the taste."

"I was wondering who came back with Jamie," she said. "They nearly ran him over with that tractor."

"Trying to take out the competition, eh? Where is my prodigal brother?" Nat asked her.

"Why would I know?" she said.

"You just said—Why are you being defensive?"

"Is to be defensive to be guilty?"

"Guilty of what?" Nat's brows slanted. "Are you really that fried, *fraulein*?"

"Yeah, no. I was just relaxing outside with the trees when those guys from The Reverie came through, and then Jamie took me out. Look," Eleanor said, lifting her grass-stained knee into Nat's chest as proof.

"Oof." Nat keeled over. "You're fucking oblivious of your impact."

Eleanor winked under his blackout lenses. "Don't worry, though."

"Worry about what?" Nat said.

"Jamie," she said. "He's off with the usual suspects."

"Suspects?" Nat puckered his mouth and scratched the stubble that quickly grew back on his face. "So he's with Diana... and Pam?"

Greg groaned, embellishing that he'd overheard this by crushing a can between his fist.

"Don't look at me," Eleanor said to Nat.

"How could I? I thought I couldn't see you," Nat replied. No shades could shield that blue-eyed stare of the Dempseys. The golden dart that split Nat's left iris fully pierced her in moments like these. Eleanor returned Nat's sunglasses to his face just as Jamie burst into Balmaha. He wore a sex-spent grin and looked like he'd run through a sprinkler.

Greg chucked a fresh brick of lager at Jamie's face. Jamie showboated by chugging the can, fueling Greg to clothesline Jamie to the floor. Remy played "Disorder" by Joy Division to score the brawl. The chaos gave Eleanor the cover she needed to move onto the sectional with Will.

"Not a fan of assault?" Eleanor joked, acknowledging Will's uncomfortable reaction to Bolero's conflict resolution style.

"I come in peace," Will spoke in a neutral accent. Maybe Connecticut.

"I'm somewhat of a peacekeeper myself," Eleanor said.

"Weren't you responsible for that scuffle happening?" he said.

"No way, I'm–"

"Ele, right?" The peek of his tongue as it smoothed over the 'l' behind his exaggerated lips was like a strawberry she wanted to suck.

"Guilty," she said.

"You're the one who works on that show with seven strangers." He said this in a tone that Eleanor took to patronize her work, and possibly work in general.

"Yup." Eleanor looked down. She fingered *fuck off* in cursive on her camera strap around the same time Jamie had yelled it out loud. Nat and Jamie were now arguing about a backing track.

Will leaned over to her and said, "They look like they could use your mediation right now." She could almost taste the natural tobacco on his breath.

"I avoid counsel after midnight," she said.

"Better to resolve disputes over breakfast?" Will said.

"Yeah, no. Mostly, there's nothing to resolve after they sleep it off."

"Oh, that's convenient. Our band usually harbors things until the brink of death." Will thrust his lofty brown hair that curled away from his angular face. His eyes were like an abyss. It was hard to tell where his pupils began.

"Okay, time out," Eleanor said. "We know who we are, but since we don't *really* know, can we just start at like, 'Hi, what's your name?'"

Will kicked his feet up on the crowded table of empties and rested his hands behind his head. "I'll play along. I'm Moonstone."

Eleanor blushed and also scowled. She couldn't determine how to play this interaction.

"So, Ele, what brings you here besides your questionable peacekeeping? I don't think I've ever brought just a friend to record. Are you here for business or pleasure?"

"That question was pretty loaded," Eleanor said.

"Like most of our company," Will said.

Eleanor observed his Nalgene water bottle and said, "But not you?"

"That doesn't mean I don't know how to have a good time." Will graced her knee. His hand was bone dry. He had long fingers that wrapped deftly across her bare joint.

"Nice to meet you," she said.

"There you go again with that. I thought we already had a bit of a past," he said.

"What are you talking about?"

"You were at that show at The Zoo," said Will. Eleanor and Nat had gone, expecting to see The Reverie. Rumors floated that their bassist had OD-ed. Instead of the full band, Will performed a chilling acoustic set by himself.

"I was relying on you that night," Will said. "Are you familiar with Buddhism?"

"No. Are you familiar with The Jam?" Will didn't seem to associate that Remy was now playing "Ghosts," her favorite song by them, which began lulling her to sleep.

"Anyway," he said. "You were the person I connected with that night."

"Shut up. That's like a frontman fallacy," Eleanor said, wondering if she mispronounced fallacy. She was so tired.

"Shut up?" Will rubbed his clean, punctuated chin.

"I didn't mean it like that. I'm just—I have to shut up." She sat back and nestled into Will's side, then closed her eyes, intending to rest for just a minute.

"Do you want to leave?" Will said, or was it his voice in her head?

"Yo, Will!" Nat yelled, waking Eleanor from her shallow dream. "Remy's saying you guys are gonna poach him after we wrap. Is that true?"

"I don't think that really qualifies as poaching, man," Will said to him. "To be honest, we've been on a bit of an unruly sonic quest trying to produce this on our own for too long. I can't say anymore about it, other than it hasn't been good for anyone."

"Fair enough," Nat said. The two shifted their level of competition from a playoff game to a friendly.

Eleanor scrambled to leave, rejecting Will and Nat's help to get up from the couch. When Will stood up to say goodbye to her, Eleanor assessed that she couldn't fit into his jeans. He barely did either. She tried to make herself small in his arms for a goodnight hug.

"See you later?" said Will.

Before she could reply, Nat said, "Not gonna happen. You didn't hear? Eleanor's deserting us all."

Eleanor released Will and squared up to Nat. She lifted the one-hitter from his gingham pocket and exited before her expression revealed too much.

Outside the Balmaha studio, amber was gaining on the dusky tree line. Eleanor lifted her camera to take a last picture. This moment was how she felt—caught like the light between night and day. Her time at Lochstock hadn't ended in the arms of old or new, and in a few hours, she'd be gone.

3

JAMIE

JAMIE DEMSPEY OFTEN SLEPT through the morning, but a cop's maglite of country sun hit him harder than Greg had the night before—both brutal, if not familiar, sensations. Jamie yawned and cradled his ear. It throbbed like the rest of him. He glanced around the shadowy cabin at Lochstock. Everyone else was up and out except Ele. She slept across from him on Nat's top bunk, revealing a wedgie as impressive as her ass. Jamie hopped down and shook the rails of her bed.

"Ha-ha, I see your butt," he said.

"Fuck off, Jamie." Ele twisted herself into the sheet and rolled over.

"Yo. Who do you think you are, Ele? You can't be the first one into bed and the last out, man."

"What about KP and Lindsay?" she said, rubbing her eyes like she'd been crying.

"Couples don't count, man. Your shit is prime for insubordination."

"If you wanna talk about being insubordinate, you can start with sacking me into the dust last night. I think I bruised a rib."

"Don't remember that now." Jamie tee-heed.

"Also, insubordination? What are you in the army now?"

"Oh, fuck that." Jamie swirled his finger-length hair. "I'd rather die than get another one of them buzz cuts."

"Little Jamie. I would die to see you with another buzz cut."

"Yeah, you and your dad both. Big Mick Huston was always comin'
after us with them clippers." Jamie kicked around piles on the planked
floor to look for his shoes.

"What's up with your face?" said Ele.

"Bullshit, right?" He'd found his gum-soled Adidas and started lacing
up. "I didn't deserve that."

"Yeah, right. You are one of those rare people who deserves everything
they get," she said. "Be it a record deal or a beer can to the face."

Jamie let out his first of a thousand boisterous daily laughs. "When are
you out of here, then?"

Ele checked her watch, which she'd secured to the bedpost. "Shit. KP
and Lindsay are giving me a ride to the train station soon."

"Next time you see me, things are gonna be crazy," he said. "Bolero
will be famous and all that."

"Yeah, but you'll still be an idiot," she joked.

"And you'll still love me," he said. Ele dangled her long leg off the bunk
and swung a kick at him. "Alright, Ele. Well, knock'em dead in *lederhosen*
or wherever the fuck you're going."

"It's Leipzig," she said, but he wouldn't remember.

Jamie left Ele behind with a sense of humor and dread that her departure would make his brother Nat a much crankier bastard. Jamie knew
simply by the way his brother said her name that he had more reverence
for her than anyone else.

►►

Jamie dragged his ass through the bumblefuck of nature to the communal bathhouse. He didn't belong in the woods. He belonged to the noise
and bedlam of a city or an emergency room. After inspecting the shower

stall for spiders, he rinsed off last night's filth. Jamie flashed back to Diana and Pam, kissing in the outdoor shower, the snap of their wet bras before plucking them off. All three merged their slippery mouths and bodies and pulled each other's soaked hair under the spout and open air. His knees almost buckled when they took indistinguishable turns with him to the back of their throats, cackling and gagging. At the realization his dick was long enough to poke through Diana's thighs from behind and breach Pam's lips on the other side, he proudly came again.

Jamie dried off using someone else's towel. Unlike sexual exploits, practical matters were harder to remember. He relied on others and inherently wanted their attention. Now that Jamie was out of his mom's house, Sulky, his most loyal friend and bandmate, was the one who kept Jamie in clean clothes and supplied with his basic needs for OJ, cigarettes, and cereal. The only downside was that Sulky wigged out when Jamie stayed out or kept his door closed for too long. Then again, Sulky got his nickname because he was constantly bent out of shape.

▶▶

Down at the mess hall, KP and Sulky were smoking cigarettes and kicking a ball around out front. Jamie booted a few before heading inside, where some of the girls were picking at breakfast scraps, looking tired with undone faces.

"Damn, I remember you girls looking better yesterday," Jamie said.

"That line gets older every day," Lindsay retorted before collapsing onto her paper plate.

Lindsay used to be cool when she was Ele's roommate, who wore weird costumes and paid for everyone's drinks. Now she was smug as fuck, all wifed up to KP and always psychoanalyzing everybody.

Jamie bent over and kissed Diana's head, which he'd deny was a cheap gesture to show her top rank in his hierarchy of chicks.

"Stop getting me wet." Diana ducked and smoothed her white blonde hair, which looked kind of skanky but still hot when the roots grew out.

"That'd be impossible," he said.

"Don't be grosser than the breakfast," said Lindsay.

"Seriously. You're lucky you look like that, babe," Diana told him.

Jamie swiped Diana's toaster waffle. "I was thinkin' you're lucky I look like this, *babe*."

Lindsay said, "I don't know Jamie, your face is the one looking a little roughed up today."

"Haha! Touché." Jamie circled the mild yellow bruise above his eye. "Not my fault. I'm going mental out here in this fucking forest."

Lindsay cracked a laugh. "That's a new one. Blaming urbanicity for your behavior."

"Where is everyone?" Jamie asked mid nosh.

"Nat was over at Conic Hill with The Reverie, but if you bothered to look at the schedule, you'd know he's back in the studio waiting for you now," Lindsay said.

"Fucking old news, them Reverie guys," Jamie said.

"Not to everyone," said Lindsay.

"Lara told us Ele was looking cozy with Will Hawking last night," Diana said.

"Nah. I didn't see that. "

"Well, you're myopic," Lindsay said.

"That's a nice way of putting it," said Diana.

"What's nice about it? Fuck you guys, anyway. Here on our dime and talkin' this much shit."

"*Bewilder's* dime," Diana corrected, like that entitled her to be there. "Speaking of, you better get to Balmaha to make it worth their while, babe..."

►►

Jamie perked up when he entered Balmaha's live room with its ashy wood-paneled walls, white velvet drapes, and black foam egg crates. It was open and energizing, like legs spread for his showmanship. Unfortunately, it still smelled like burnt ass and flame retardant chemicals from the blown speaker. Everything was crowded around KP's drums. Jamie could see through to the control room where Nat sat next to Remy, swiveling in leather armchairs at the mixing desk. They were already stone-faced, like their brains were stuck in the middle of a whacked game of chess.

"You're late," said Nat, paging through the glass. "We've already tuned the room."

Jamie entered the control room to join them, sitting on the only couch he and Diana hadn't banged on yet because Remy and Nat were always working. Remy played back some of yesterday's session. Nat had pushed everyone to jam through too many melodic ideas. It was creative punishment. Nat usually presented at least a 90% baked song. No one else was expected to think. They sounded like dog shit! Jamie concealed his grin, knowing his bro was probably playing poker to test if Remy would shoot them straight.

"I've got to be honest with you—" Remy paused before admitting with the gusto of a bong rip, "This is unwieldy."

"It's dog shit," Nat said.

Jamie keeled over. "Dog shit is legit the only way to describe it! Our man Remy, we trust."

"Can I trust you to destroy that tape?" Nat said to Remy.

"Oh no, I don't destroy," said Remy.

"Oh yeah? What about that fuckin' casualty?" Jamie pointed to the speaker in the corner, now covered like a tagged corpse.

"That was sacrificial, man," Remy said unapologetically. "She was weak."

Instead of actually making music, Remy and Nat took off on a discussion about mental stuff like lateral thinking and music theory. Jamie's attention diverted to poking the squishy fill inside a puncture he'd found on the couch.

"I just don't want the studio time to end," Nat said.

"Listen, man. If you can be yourself and do what I say, you might have a career long enough to test that position," Remy said. "But never fuckin' ruminate when you've got the *mo*," Remy pleaded. "You gotta capture the bomb."

"The mo?" said Nat.

"The bomb?" said Jamie, as only an explosive could have recaptured his interest.

"The mo, man." Remy sighed. "The momentum. The kinetic shit that got you here. If that doesn't encapsulate on this record, we've all failed. Don't fuck off now or else you'll never—"

"Get to fuck off later?" said Nat.

"Are we gonna lay something down already?" Jamie asked.

Nat picked up his Martin and moved to a stool. "This is 'She's Leaving' from the top," he said before altering his clipped speaking voice into a soft drawl to sing.

Jamie accessed his superlative focus to scan the song's blueprint. He absorbed every tone and inflection and imagined where he'd embellish. When Nat finished, he handed Jamie his legal pad with the lyrics to review.

Now it was time for Jamie to step into the booth.

"Remember, Jamie," Remy said through the glass. "There's supernatural genius in filtering these songs through you."

Jamie yawned and put on his phones. "No shit, go on."

"Nat's the thinker. He thinks about the structure, the dynamic. Knowing what to riff off, that critical understanding of what's good. You feel it, man. Your guts and his goods. Go on now, transform that shit and make it fucking great."

Jamie rolled his neck and shoulders under the warm bulb above his head. He was almost ready. He lipped up to the pencil-thin AKG. "One thing though, Nat." Jamie glared into his brother's two-tone eyes on the other side of the division. He held up the pad, grinning and said, "There's just no fuckin' way this song's about Karen."

FOR IMMEDIATE RELEASE

BOLERO'S DEBUT ALBUM DELIVERS
ROCK'N'ROLL RESCUE

New York, NY - June 14, 1994

Bewilder Records is thrilled to an-
nounce the release of Bolero's highly anticipated debut album, "Light
Up and Shine On."

Led by the dashing and clashing
Dempsey brothers, Bolero has quickly
emerged as one of the most exciting
acts on the alt-rock scene. Their
music is fresh and loud, just like
their attitudes.

"Light Up and Shine On" showcases what no one else has: Jamie Dempsey. His singular voice elevates Bolero's deft songwriting, which is inspired by guitar music at its best, and gut punches its mediocre.

The album's first single, "Muse Box," is undoubtedly the record's core. The song will be a generational anthem sung in stadiums, just as it once was in small clubs before Bewilder plucked Bolero from an obscurity they'll never know again.

Bolero's breakthrough isn't all we'll be hearing from Bewilder Records this summer. The label's former heavyweight, The Reverie, releases its long-awaited follow-up next week.

Expect an epic showdown on the airwaves this summer…

4

WILL

A FTER THE REVERIE WRAPPED their long overdue second record at Lochstock, Will leased a cheap apartment for the band to move in together back in New York. His pitch was that they'd be able to rehearse more, rebuild their synergy to promote the new album, and get through the upcoming festival season in Europe. Dasuki was upbeat about it—that's just the type of drummer he was. Dave, the band's bassist and main songwriter, gnawed his calluses and said nothing. Dave had been too sensitive to handle the success of their debut album, and Will was concerned about what might happen to Dave if their second was a failure.

Andy accepted Will's deal but didn't buy it when Will said, "We're all in the same boat."

"Yeah, well, you're the only one with a fucking life jacket," Andy replied before he got too stoned to argue with his eyes open.

Even though Will kept his family money quiet, he carried a chip of wealth on his pointed shoulders like some carried poverty. Will wanted to quit, but didn't feel right about being the only one spared from ruin. As a result, he'd put up some of his personal trust as collateral against the band's mounting debts. He also vowed to quit all the substances that plagued Dave, as if Will's abstinence could cure Dave's slouch towards addiction.

Will had another motive to move in with the band and take a hiatus from his place on Sheridan Square. He needed space from where he had lived with his ex, Cath, who recently moved out after a betrayal too big to ignore. All she left was turpentine. Being that Cath was Dave's sister, the turpentine wouldn't be enough to strip her from Will's life. Cath was an obstruction to addressing Dave's drug use. Cath deflected, claiming that Will was addicted to missions that distracted him from emptiness and boredom. Cath was harsh, but her delivery and appearance were so pixie-like, so delicate and slight—anything unpleasant was too easy to ignore.

Will wouldn't deny his need to indulge in the occasional sabbatical, whether observing monks, hiking the French Alps, or living Costa Rica's *pura vida*. Being in The Reverie had kept Will's interest and felt convincing for a while. He'd even taken honing his craft seriously. Will had a deep voice that, with coaching, emulated soul. He felt natural performing and studied those who'd done it exceptionally. Janis, Jagger, James Brown. That said, Will's guitar with its mother-of-pearl fret inlays was more sophisticated than his playing, and he'd never written a song on his own. The Reverie relied on Dave to write lyrics and find the melodies on which the words landed. Creatively, the band crumbled whenever Dave did.

▶▶

Since moving in with his bandmates, Will's sleep had been terrible, and his dreams strange. He chalked it up to the adjustments of being sober and sleeping alone.

Dasuki was convinced their apartment had bad juju.

"What is that, a Nigerian thing?" Andy said what Will was too PC to ask.

"No, it's the chickens, man!" Dasuki replied, referring to the live poultry in the alley below. The band was living over a takeout spot called Noodle Garden, which was, along with the chickens, owned by a guy named Satan (pronounced '/si'tän/' by no one). This quirk went from amusing to unbearable after one night.

Satan's chickens had interrupted Will's afternoon nap like a distress signal for the night ahead. Rehearsal, followed by an insider party that their label was throwing to tease Bolero's debut record. Now that Rollins had firmly positioned The Reverie into this competitive dynamic with Bolero, Will's obligations to attend the events that repulsed him had tripled. Will was hesitant at first, but Rollins' scheme had also tripled The Reverie's airtime and pre-sales.

During these close encounters with the Dempsey brothers, Will's thoughts often drifted to Ele, Bolero's friend he'd met at Lochstock. Meeting her had upped his game during recording. Will speculated on the extent of her history with Nat, or maybe Jamie, or if she was the one that got away from all of them. Will romanticized the memory of his hands caressing her smooth legs and the quirky intimacy they shared the night they met. Surprisingly, this exercise in imagination had outranked all the other physical company he'd been keeping since finding out about Cath and Rollins' even cruder sister, Fran.

Will pulled on a well-worn raglan shirt and left to knock on the doors of his bandmates. "Lo Mein and Clay's in fifteen," he called on his way to place the order.

Clay's Tavern was where the newly cost-conscious Reverie practiced for free nearby. It was like the Alamo of Irish pubs, holding out from being absorbed by Chinatown.

"Make sure it's the Veggie this time," Dasuki said, appearing from his room. In solidarity with the alley chickens, the entire band had gone vegetarian.

"Are you coming to the Bolero thing at Rollins' house after?" Will said.

"Nah. I'm gonna stick back with Dave. Cool if it's just you and Andy?"

Will nodded. Dasuki was much better company than Andy, but the trade-off was that Dasuki was also a much better babysitter for Dave.

"For real though? I'm not up for a confrontation tonight." Dasuki rubbed the lines around his mouth that almost permanently grinned.

"You know this Bolero feud is mostly for show, right?" Will said.

Rollins had pitched her Beatles-versus-Stones dynamic while holding The Reverie captive on a midnight road trip to Philly to visit dueling cheesesteak joints, which, of course, none of the band could eat.

"Just a few lightweight jabs to generate a buzz..."

"Not sure anyone told that to Bolero," Dasuki said.

"Some people are just more naturally insulting."

▶▶

Long after practice concluded, Will and Andy arrived in one of those Brooklyn neighborhoods where it was unclear if it was entering a cycle of revival or despair. In front of Rollins' semi-detached townhouse, Will could hear a raucous of characters sunken behind overgrown shrubs. The first person they encountered was Bolero's expensive and shrewd manager, Joe Beck. He was a bloodshot mess, failing to punch through the wrought-iron gate at the edge of the property.

"Whoa, take it easy," Andy said, and gently lifted the latch for him to exit.

"Should we turn around now?" Will said, but he and Andy walked on, following the muffled but unmistakable laughter of Jamie Dempsey along with Sulky, Bolero's bassist.

"What was up with Joe Beck?" Will asked them.

"The likes of you," Sulky said. He blew noxious smoke to invite Will and Andy to be regaled by its aroma.

"I don't know what I'm supposed to be smelling here," Andy said.

Will opened his pack of American Spirits. "Can I offer you one of these instead?"

"No one wants your fuckin' wigwam cigarettes, man," Jamie said. "Everyone knows you've got no spirit."

Andy snickered.

"Where's the rest of Bolero, then?" said Will.

"Chained up to their women, no doubt. Unlike us, free birds soarin' down here." Jamie spread his arms to flap in his loose-fitted chambray shirt.

"Soaring to the top," Sulky added.

Andy rolled his eyes and wound his index finger around his temple. "Cuckoo!"

Jamie's famously good nature turned dark. "Well, you wouldn't fuckin' know a thing about being on top anymore, would you?" He spit.

"Hey." Will patted Jamie's chest as if that might depuff it. "Look, tonight's your night. We're here to have a good time and honor that."

"Honor my dick," Jamie said and gestured to jerk off the way only an expert could.

"Well, this is off to a good start," Andy said.

►►

All sorts of industry insiders and partygoers crowded inside. Rollins' house looked decorated as though it was bought "as is," filled with neglected repairs and unsold items from a fallen family's estate sale, then infiltrated by a tasteless audiophile. Red string lights hung around marble and oak mantels, chandeliers, and a battered grand stairwell. Fans topped giant speakers and a piano to circulate the fervor. Andy bobbed for a beer from what looked like a horse tub of slush atop a covered dining table that may have sat 20 dignitaries in a past life. Will felt a dull concern that Rollins' home might reflect the label's financial health.

Like every other house party since the beginning of time, there were a ton of people congregating in the kitchen. Sticking out among the throngs of runway models and almost-somethings was Rollins' partner, Mary. She looked too drunk to be operating a blender and too pregnant to be intoxicated.

"Holy fuck," exclaimed Andy. "Frida Jones is over there."

"Who?" Will said.

"Shut up, dude. You know, from that movie."

Will batted down Andy's finger in time to prevent him from pointing at the bombshell in a gold slip dress. She looked more searing and perilous than the sun. While the other gorgeous women appeared to be taunted by the trays of tacos on the kitchen island, Frida's pout looked sympathetic and fixated on Mary's antics.

"Let's go upstairs," Will suggested.

"No way. Are you fucking serious?" Andy said.

"Trust me, you'll have a better chance if you avoid them," said Will.

For once, Andy obeyed. The two of them backtracked to the main stairwell, which had become a loitering lane of traffic to use the first—or second-floor bathrooms. Andy and Will wove through them to get upstairs, which opened up to a large formal study with mahogany built-ins, shelving thousands of LPs that had replaced leather-bound books now stacked in piles on the floor.

Familiar faces emerged along the optically elusive wallpaper in the room. Bolero's Nat Dempsey and Greg Sullivan were seated on a pair of chesterfield armchairs, as if they were holding court in a banana republic. A serene, long-haired brunette looked familiar with her position on Nat's lap. Johnny Depp laid on the floor, tinkering with a banjo, while Kate Moss and Liv Tyler hung out the windowsill, twisted in velvet drapes trimmed with tassels. Rollins was mouthing off to the singer from Soul Coughing.

"Will Hawking!" Rollins called. She had one fist filled with obscure Can singles while the other swilled around an endangered crystal decanter. "You know this guy, Mike, what is it, Duff? Dufty?"

"No," Doughty said.

"Yeah, no. Doughty lives in my building," Will responded too quickly, revealing that he kept his apartment.

Andy scoffed. "Same boat," he said under his breath while walking off.

"What's that about?" Rollins said.

"He'll be fine," Will said.

"Look!" Greg shouted over at Will. "Look! It's the guy who doesn't believe *the hype!*"

Will approached his public enemies with a half grin. "Greg. Nat. Nice to see you."

"I doubt that," Greg said.

"Will. Didn't think you had it in you, taking those punches at us. Great to see you've got some fight," Nat said.

"We're in this together now," Will replied.

"Let's see how long that lasts. By the way, Karen, this is the guy who said, 'The only thing about Bolero that isn't average is how loud they are.'"

Will extended his hand to Karen. She had amber eyes and a sobering expression, as if she could commiserate with being the only other grounded person at the party.

Rollins began shouting downstairs to change the music and flick the lights. "Now, who's ready for some pinnacle shit?"

"Is it time to '*Light Up and Shine On*?'" Will asked, preparing another cigarette between his teeth.

Nat patted Karen to stand up. "I'll round up the rest of the knuckle-heads."

Will was surprised that Karen was nearly as tall as he was, and slightly taller than Nat.

When everyone headed downstairs, Will remained to peruse the discarded book collection. He could hear the preamble of excitable chatter below, the clinks and cracks of glasses toasting Bolero before their debut record would roar throughout the house. Will wandered a long, dark corridor. He passed an open door to an unfinished nursery when Jamie's voice dropped like a guillotine over the sound system. At the end of the hallway was Rollins and Mary's master suite, for lack of a better term. Will veered onto the back service stairs and sat on one of the narrow treads. He listened for flaws and mediocrity, but by Bolero's third keystone track, Will accepted that *Light Up & Shine On* was not even average. It was a bloody force.

Will flinched when his private party was interrupted by hushed flirting rounding up the stairs. The glistening legs and delicate heel clicks belonged to Frida Jones. Jamie's hands were spotting her waist. Will might've been invisible when they stepped past him. No eye contact was exchanged. Jamie looked bewitched. Seeing them shook Will from his isolation. He continued down to the first floor, which led to a butler's station, and then back into the kitchen, where a rowdiness was palpable.

Andy looked distressed, trying to manage Diana Campbell from Girl-crush on the far side of the island. When Will joined them, Diana slurred her greeting and leaned in to kiss him. Will turned his head to refuse.

"Rude!" Diana yelled and pushed Will out of the way. She then cornered Rollins. Diana began singing along to Bolero incoherently and pulling on Rollins' collar. Now it was Rollins' turn to look panicked. Will couldn't tell if Diana genuinely repelled Rollins or if Rollins was just playing it that way because everyone was watching them. Andy failed to extract Diana from the situation when Mary flung the french doors open from the back patio.

"What the fuck is this?" Mary said. Her face was redder than her hair.

Rollins stepped in front of Diana. "Nothing, Mare. Nothing! Everyone's just loving the record, baby!"

Diana weaseled out from behind Rollins. "Shut up, bitch!"

Mary stormed belly first over to them. She yanked Diana's bleached bun and heaved her into a pyramid of coupes. The shattering of all the glass was violent and left the room in a collective gasp. Diana lay there stiff as a board upon a bed of shards. Her face showed fright, as if she had been resuscitated through torture. Mary moved on and wielded her fist to beat on Rollins when suddenly the flush to Mary's face drained to white and her rage vanished. She whispered something Will couldn't hear. Then she screamed, "My water's broke!"

Everyone fled the scene in the kitchen with the force of water from a broken pipe. Will exited to the back patio. He hopped over a brick wall and reached the street in time to catch Jamie and Frida entering a discreet town car and pulling away into the night. Something like envy or bad lo mein rumbled his gut. He wanted to keel over, but there was a witness. A tall woman with long brown hair and knowing golden eyes. It was Nat Dempsey's girlfriend, Karen.

"Weird night," Will said and offered her a cigarette, which she declined.

"More often, they are," said Karen. "One of the reasons I try not to make an appearance."

"Does that explain why you weren't at Lochstock?"

"One of the reasons," she repeated. "So, you were at Lochstock?" She had a soothing, mature drawl for someone from Long Island.

"Yeah, we overlapped a few days with Bolero," Will said. "Our experiences were a bit different, though."

"What do you mean?" she asked.

"Ha. I don't know." Will ran his hand through his hair. "It wasn't my first rodeo. Different headspace. Anyway, it was nice to meet some new people."

"Oh. Like who?" she said.

"Let's see. Remy. He ended up mixing our record, so that was fortunate. And your friend, Ele?"

"Eleanor," Karen said.

"Yeah."

"You know she's in Germany for work?"

"Yeah. We're playing a festival in Berlin next month," Will said. "I was hoping she and I might get together."

"Don't you have a girlfriend?"

"I don't." Will felt Karen silently interrogate him, or perhaps whatever she was searching for had nothing to do with him.

"Give me your number," she said. "Nat's sending Eleanor a care package with the record and some other things this week. I'm sure I can put you in touch with her over there..."

5

JAMIE

THIRTY MINUTES AFTER BAILING on his own party, Jamie was at Club USA. Frida Jones had just fed him another pink pill he'd swiped from Rollins and Mary's stash. Her pearly fingertip was the first part of her that his mouth had touched, and Jamie was fiending for more. They were grooving at the center of a whirlpool with hundreds of raving misfits. Every song sounded the same, or maybe it was the same song that kept going back to the middle and around again. Frida was angelic except for the high hem of her dress. Her eyes were glacial lakes. Jamie wanted to dive into them. He wanted to dive into her—100% pure love.

No faux fog or high could hide that Frida moved like an expert. Each time she twisted into him was a seductive transmission. Jamie's nose pushed through her whipped light hair and slid across her elegant neck. Frida smelled expensive; it was nothing like drugstore shampoo on regular girls. The gold dress shifted around her body like a liquified sculpture, teasing him with near reveals. Lust leaked from Jamie's brain, amplified by whatever else these pills did. Anything seemed possible, though that attitude was his natural state. Last year Jamie couldn't hold a job as a cater waiter and he'd never been on a plane. Now his band's record was launching like a rocket and Jamie was already in outer space with a goddess. More success than sweat was soaking through his clothes. Everything was possible.

The DJ scratched into a new track. Jamie could feel that he and Frida were being entranced by the slower tempo and repetition, to get connected and to do it again, and again. His thigh became a saddle for Frida to gallop and grind. His hands held her butterfly hips, stretching his fingertips to rub her hot skin underneath the dress, hiking up from their motions. Frida's gaze was intense. She would see through his tender dreams and dirty tricks. It was love when he cracked her first laugh, after each of his hands groped her ass like two grapefruits from the grove of Eden. He would do her right. He would do anything she wanted if she relieved him of the tantric rage cartoonish enough to drown the entire dance floor with his cum bust.

It was precisely then that Jamie became a teddy bear clawed from a toy machine by a security guard.

"What the fuck?" Jamie yelped. He didn't even do anything!

The hulk had plucked Jamie's thumping heart away from Frida, cornering him with another bouncer. Jamie jumped to see over their shoulders that Frida was being escorted up to the mezzanine.

After a short, hostile detention, the second bouncer told Jamie, "You've got to leave now, son."

"What the fuck. Why? You've got to be joking!" But Jamie saw nothing comedic pulsing from the man's thick neck.

Jamie refused to go easily, which these pros predicted. The bouncers locked Jamie's arms and dragged him off the dance floor and down to the lobby. Jamie squirmed and skidded his Wallabee boots to grasp anything to fortify his resistance. Just as he risked being tossed into summer trash piles, Jamie hooked his leg on a railing and thrusted himself free.

Jamie looked back so his captors could see his triumphant grin, and then he took off, juking around brightly costumed bodies before scurrying like a hamster up the club's novelty tunnel slide. He climbed over a shrieking older lady in a sequin mini dress who was sliding down, but otherwise made it to the top of the slide without so much as a static shock and a thrill. Next, Jamie ran back into the strobing darkness of the main dance floor. He dropped to a crawl, taking his chances to be stomped out by neoprene soles. He was lucky this was a designer drug joint. The ground was covered with confetti and empty dime bags instead of broken bottles. He nearly reached the stage when his head butted two dicks bouncing in metallic speedos. Jamie recoiled until he stood up and was gifted a view of topless girls with flower-painted tits dancing in cages. They flanked the stage where a carnivalesque obstacle of drag queens hopped on neon dolphin pogo sticks. Behind them, Jamie saw a stage exit with unmanned steps that would get him upstairs. Jamie asked the silver-dong fruitcakes for a boost to climb one of the cages. The club was like his own tripped-out *Super Mario World*. Jamie beat the ground level by out-swimming the dolphins and advanced to the mezzanine in search of Frida.

The second level was less crowded, but possibly freakier than the first. Ball pits, swings, weirder ways to take drugs. Gender did not exist, just sex in every corner. But no Princess Toadstool, no Frida. Jamie gripped the guardrail and leaned over to look at the fleshy swarm below and above. There! He'd spotted Frida's golden silhouette. She was with some slick-back club king in a roped-off lounge on the third level. Frida was trying to walk away, but the guy grabbed her wrist, activating an unfamiliar anger in Jamie that carbonated his blood.

Jamie dried the sweat from his palms and took a risk better equipped but too stupid for a monkey. He held his breath and climbed over the rails to the third level. As if to pause the video game of his life safely, he momentarily tucked into a stairwell's shadow. Jamie could see Frida and the sleazy suit guy were no more than 10 feet away. He flapped air through his shirt to summon a composure rarely achieved in bedlam, and then unpaused to swagger forward and reunite with his princess. Jamie played it as if nothing had happened, like he'd just gone for a piss instead of ending up in an acid house remix of *The Fugitive*. He greeted Frida with a casual cheek kiss, ignoring her douchebag captor, with his gangster laugh going on about Ibiza or some shit.

"Well, I'll let you kids go then," the man said to Frida.

"Goodbye, Danny," she said.

The sleazebag signaled to call off his goons and then left behind a trail of his skunk cologne.

Jamie took his first relaxed breath in hours. "Are you okay?" he asked her.

"Dare I ask the same?" Frida said.

Jamie could barely understand her soft British accent as the words came out of her lips. He might've answered, but he could wait no longer to kiss her. He needed her mouth to need his, to want his, to suck the sweetness from her tongue and not stop. Under his clothes, he felt her manicured fingertips swirl and score into his back and for a moment he thought they might fuck, right then and there. But there was too much confusion. Why were people calling her name? Frida broke from their lip lock. Jamie turned towards the voices and was, for the first time, blinded by flash.

6

FRIDA

ALL FRIDA HAD REQUESTED were cobblestones when Danny's assistant coldly enquired about her preferences for where she'd like to live. The old world romance of cobblestones charmed Frida to the point she could ignore their precarious potential. Her charm for Danny had faded, but he was paying, and she remained committed to frugality, if not to him. It hardly mattered. New York wouldn't be her home much longer and she was rarely home, anyway.

For now, she'd adore the cobblestones outside her crisp wedding cake building and the flat's high ceilings. Colourful clothes filled her generous wardrobes, contrasting with the flat's warm white aesthetic. If she opened the window in the kitchen, she could smell sugar and hearth from the bakery on Prince Street. Comfort foods she needn't eat. The cobblestones were not only charming but significant. They were markers to keep focused on the someday dream she had set aside for herself. Someday she would leave the demanding gaze of this world and settle, sated and barefoot, in a quiet North London home.

Frida's road to this quaint someday with babies and bread required harsh opportunism. Despite her delicate feminine ideal, she could be as tough as a cutthroat. She'd endured horrible men and a thousand twisted ankles in dodgy heels. Frida's determined but detached nature was more than a sensual expression that picked up on film. She could look exhausted but explosive, and both were true. Returning late from a whirlwind shoot in Mallorca, she was especially exhausted. Instead of staying on to rendezvous with Danny in Ibiza, she came back to New York feeling intrigued and unresolved about what had happened the night before she'd left for Spain.

A scattering of envelopes greeted her on the white-painted wooden floors. She sorted them on the lucite console table in the entryway. Cheques for her. Bills to D GARIBALDI. Frida played back a bombardment of messages on the answerphone while she waited for the kettle to sing. Her sister. Her manager. Nikki Wilshire, the heiress-turned-model and Frida's dearest American friend. Invites to a slurry of events not worthy of entries in her datebook. Danny.

He'd said, "Jonesy, I'm staying off dry land the rest of summer. Listen, when you ditch that poor mop head from Club USA, I'll fly you back to the Med and you can make it up to me."

Frida's manager then left another detailed message with an offer to feature in a music video directed by Rick Russell. "The band is fresh. Like boyish, broody? Normally I'd say this is beneath you, but I know you've got that swinging sixties spirit at heart *and* they're willing to pay your rate. It's Q.E.C."

Quick Easy Cash, but Frida remained unconvinced. She was hesitant to act after her experience in last summer's blockbuster. They cast her as the easily seduced love interest discarded in the first act, the equivalent of "Bond Girl #1" without the prestige of that franchise. One critic had outright suggested that Frida "must've been more lively in the sack to land the part than to play the role." Cruelty wasn't particularly surprising to Frida. She had long believed that the world hated women and there would be no sympathy for the pretty ones.

The kettle then whistled over a less familiar voice. She rewound the curious message to assess the sincere, shy tone of the caller. Unlike all the other messages, his was as restorative as tea, and she would steep in its promise during her long sleep recovery.

►►

Frida strategised her callbacks the next morning whilst replenishing her body with Evian and two soft-boiled eggs. She seasoned them with the pinch of a spice kept in a decorative tagine from Marrakech. She made her transactional calls from the cordless in the kitchen, stood on one foot with the other rested on the inside of her knee, shrewdly consulting her diary and the ledger tucked under it. Frida took personal calls from an antique telephone in bed, with the pearl receiver relaxed between her neck and a goose down pillow. Today marked her first bed call to a boy. The novelty wore off when it wasn't Jamie who answered, but another boy who'd rather curtly placed her on hold.

When Jamie took the call, he sounded closer to the unabashed version she'd met the other night, not the sheepish suitor who'd left her the message. He was "stoked" to hear from her. His words and phrasing rolled playfully like Irish hills. "Can I see you at 8?" he asked.

"Depends." Frida twisted her cool blonde hair.

"Depends, eh? D'you know the Michelangelo?" Jamie sounded as though he was uncertain.

"No," Frida said, though she did.

"All right..." There was a delay for so long that she thought they might've lost connection. "Well, you're smart," he said. "Meet me there and don't wear any of those bonker stilettos."

Frida agreed and hung up, bemused. Then she slid a satin mask over her eyes and slept for the rest of the day.

▶▶

That night, Frida was properly late to meet Jamie at the Michelangelo, a hotel she'd known to be too Italian to be understated. It was unfashionably located, a planet north of downtown yet not upper-east or west of the Park. She wore bowtie, metallic ballet flats, and a baby doll dress Anna Sui had gifted *in lieu* of cash payment to walk for her a few years past.

Frida spotted Jamie from across the lobby. He was more handsome than she remembered. He looked misplaced, albeit comfortable, drinking something dark in a rocks glass and conversing with a neatly uniformed bartender. His laugh was like a cackle that bounced off the marble. Jamie wore a darker sports coat with looser dungarees and trainers. He was a fresh, casual distinction from the hotel's Renaissance and Rococo decor. She suspected Jamie was not from Manhattan, that he was one of the bridge-and-tunnel personas that made themselves known through their bravado. Frida did not mind in the slightest. She preferred extraordinary commoners to common lords.

Frida crossed the lobby bar as if on eggshells. When Jamie caught her presence, he hastily sauntered forward and embraced her with a hug and tender kiss to the cheek. He was pleasantly suffocating and caused her muscles to ease from their more practised homeostasis.

"I was just telling my man here about you," Jamie said of the old bartender behind the oak and brass.

"Really?" she said in a way that did not suggest she expected to know.

"It's so good to see you," Jamie gushed, his intentions without mystery.

"What, have you returned from war?" Frida said.

"What can we get you to drink?" Jamie asked.

Frida whispered her order into Jamie's ear. He smelled perfectly clean, and she did not miss the intensity of aftershave she more frequently encountered on older, wealthy men.

In moments, a flute with a twist was at her fingertips. "This is kind of a strange place, eh?" Jamie said. "Like an older crowd."

"It's lovely," she said politely.

"We're not gonna eat here though," he said.

"That's fine. Dinners can be dull."

"You Brits love your parks, right?"

"We do." Frida smiled mildly.

"I mean, I'm more used to getting chased through them rather than taking a stroll," he joked.

"I suppose I could've guessed that from the other night," she said.

Jamie's eyes lit up, showing that the memory excited him. "So, you know what's that way?" Jamie turned Frida to about face.

"I wouldn't dare guess, even if I knew."

"Aright. Well, I thought we'd catch a good buzz, then I can be your muscle for a walk through Central Park. You into that?"

His vow of chivalry amused her. "That sounds lovely," she said. Her response appeared to satisfy Jamie, leading Frida to conclude that they were both typically stingier to make an effort.

Jamie continued to graft as they drank. It felt as sincere as it did rushed. Or perhaps not considering the haste of their initial connection.

"That'll be us someday." He pointed to a mature couple, the husband learnedly placing a jumper around the curling shoulders of his wife.

"Are you a 'someday' person as well?" Frida asked.

Jamie's finger-thick brows bent. "A 'someday' person?"

"A dreamer, like," she restated.

"Oh yeah, livin' in the clouds?" Jamie leaned his side onto the bar to simulate sleep. "Daydreamer to the bone," he said. She followed his eyes as they wandered to the fresco of cherub skies on the ceiling. "I spent the whole of school staring at the window just zoning my way out. You know?"

"I do," she said, recalling the worst of her adolescence at boarding school the year her parents divorced.

"Before being in Bolero, the only thing I wanted to do was sleep, just be in bed. Like it's the only place trouble can't find me, and sometimes I really do wanna stay out of it."

It was too soon to tell, but Frida believed he wasn't putting her on, that this was just him. She wanted to reciprocate his forthcoming nature within the confines of her English sensibilities. "I don't suppose I owe you an apology for the other night... Dragging you into the papers and such," she said.

"Are you kidding? I had the time of my fucking life. First everyone hearing our record over at Rollins' and then getting twisted at that freak fest with you? You expect me to care what the papers say when there's sexy pictures of us in it?"

Jamie faced her and rested his hands on her shoulders before unexpectedly playing with the pan collar of her dress. His fingers warmed her neck as they fidgeted. She felt silly watching his innocent expression, batting lashes long enough to be false. It was almost childlike, had she not wanted to surrender to another public display of affection with him.

▶▶

Outside in the balmy liveliness of the streets, Jamie led her towards the park.

"What are you doing?" she asked after he'd stopped at the window counter of a pizzeria and ordered two regulars.

"I didn't say we weren't gonna eat." Jamie attempted to hand her one large slice that was folding like the first step to craft a greased paper aeroplane.

"Oh. No, that's okay. I'm fine," she said.

"Yeah? Trust me, you'll be more fine after a slice."

Frida took the plate without intending to eat the pizza until Jamie cinched his hand around hers and guided it towards her mouth. Frida bent backwards ever so slightly to resist.

"Open up," he said in a tone reminiscent of a parent feeding a fussy child, at which point she bit.

Her bottom teeth crunched, and her top teeth sank into the dripping cheese and balanced tang of tomato. When the cheese stretched from her bite, she noticed Jamie had cupped his other hand to protect oil from dripping onto her dress. It was heavenly, and Frida was hungry enough to chase the feeling to the crust.

The rest of their stroll through the park was tipsy and synchronous. Frida's walk was graceful, swinging toe forward along an invisible line. Jamie's was cocksure. She liked that he was confident to hold her hand and had not indulgently complimented her looks. The attention men and some women paid to her physical appearance was often gawking. They were crossing a bridge over the pond when Jamie scoffed and told her, "This place kinda reminds me of something growing up."

"You're not from the country?"

"No. But my dad took us all camping when we were kids, probably just to get lost and tire out in the wild, you know? One day we had to find the highest cliff or bridge to jump off into the lake. Whoever did the craziest jump could get a swig of beer or something. Nat almost died."

"Your brother?"

"Yeah."

"How so?" she said.

"We were up on this bridge, standing up on the ledge. We were looking down and I guess like, planning if we were gonna do a jackknife or cannonball or whatever. So Nat says he doesn't wanna jump, and then my dad fuckin' pushed him! That brown water smacked the wind out of him."

Frida wanted to say that was wretched. "What did you do?" she asked.

"A jackknife," said Jamie. "I mean, the whole thing gets you thinking that hesitating is bullshit. Sometimes you gotta just jump." Jamie placed himself between her slender legs and leaned her against the the bridge's cold stonewall. Frida let him scoop the back of her neck to pull her face towards his to kiss in the night's heat. His mouth was so giving, his tongue large and tender to encircle. An electric charge stayed with her after Jamie boyishly leapt away, kicking off the wall.

"So, are you gonna do it?" Jamie said.

"I'm not sure I know what you're talking about."

"You should've got a call. I talked to my bro. Everybody else is in." Jamie kissed her wrists. "You're fuckin' perfect."

"For what?"

"Our music video—for 'Muse Box.'"

7

NAT

NAT'S BAGS AND GEAR were stacked by the back door. KP would arrive within the hour to pick him up. Nat had clashing nerves. He was excited to film Bolero's first music video, but dreading the conversation he and Karen would finish after she put Julia down for bed.

While he waited, Nat tidied up. He cleared the kitchen table, washed dinner plates, and put crayons away. He stuck a drawing of Julia and Karen flying in flowers on the fridge with *Sesame Street* and *Yellow Submarine* magnets. Nat folded another drawing of him playing his blue Gibson into his back pocket. Julia intended to write "go bolero!" but was still learning her letters. Nat wiped down the teal laminate table with its tiny boomerang print and a crack from a dropped pot of stovetop popcorn that burned through oven mitts. Nat had scribbled many lyrics there, occasionally peering out of the tiny window above the sink that barely let the world seep in.

When Karen closed herself out of Julia's room, she sat down on the couch to fold laundry. Nat joined her, stood against the wall, and looked down at the boxes of Bolero's merch and the package for Eleanor crowding the coffee table.

Karen looked at him and smiled like it was predictable that she would say, "This isn't going to work anymore, Nat."

"How is this different than it's always been?" he said.

"Please, Nat. It's okay."

"But you are a part of this," he said.

"No. I'm part of something else." Karen stacked another one of Julia's small shirts. "I'll always care for you, but your life is out there now."

"Are you serious? You're like my *wife*, Karen!" Nat knew that was so wrong the second he'd said it aloud. It landed so discordantly that he felt ashamed.

"Keep your voice down. And don't pretend you can't see this." Karen spread her arms to showcase all his shit crowding her table top. "This is all too big to hide from and play house. Stop kidding yourself."

"Jesus, how am I kidding? I've always been honest with you."

"That's not it," she said. "I don't think you're being honest with yourself anymore and—"

"So it's all about me not being honest with myself? Not you having a change of heart? This is unbelievable."

Karen had finished folding and calmly put the basket on the carpet. "Fine." She sighed. "I'll own that. But I'd like the same from you... Admit the show is over."

"Choice analogy," he said.

"I love you, but—"

"But my tour continues on?" Nat tried not to scowl.

The van honked from the street. Even when KP wasn't behind a drum kit, his timing was impeccable.

"Nat. I know you've been in it with all this change, too, but this isn't out of nowhere. Since I met you, we both always knew my life was going to be here." Karen turned towards Julia's door and then back to meet Nat's eyes straight on. "And that someday yours wasn't."

Karen's eyes welled, and it chilled him. He had nothing left to say. He bent down to kiss her head and breathe her in. He tried to divorce his familiarity with her jasmine scent when he exhaled.

Nat over-committed one last time and grabbed everything on his way to the van. It was more than he wanted to carry in one trip, but he couldn't go back.

►►

Nat traded his domestic haven to ride shotgun in a van without a seat belt.

"Shit," KP said, sensing Nat's energy by the way he slammed the door. "Do you want to talk about it?"

"Fuck no."

"Thank God," KP replied.

After KP rounded up Sulky and Greg, they all sucked down a joint. Sulky spent most of the drive bitching about Jamie. He hadn't been home since Sulky showed everyone the stupid movie Frida went topless in with the guy from *Die Hard*.

"You've gotta admit, ever since Frida's been all over the news with Jamie... I mean, we are blowing up the charts," KP said.

"We would anyway," Nat insisted.

"I don't know, man. Never thought I'd appreciate Jamie's fuckin' mug so much," Greg said.

Nat didn't know what to make of Frida or if all the attention she brought would be worth the agony. It was too soon to know what kind of influence she'd have on Jamie, or the consequences of him ruining her.

Nat clamped onto the armbar as they headed deep into the trashy epicenter of Manhattan.

"Dude, how pumped are you about secure parking under the hotel for our gear?" Greg asked KP.

"Happier than I am to shit indoors."

Everyone split once they hit the lobby. The Sullivans left to meet up with Jamie and a bunch of Frida's model friends downtown. Nat noticed Lindsay waiting incognito in a trench coat and sunglasses. She clearly had a sexually charged roleplay planned for KP, and Nat was in no headspace to interfere.

The quick rise in the elevator made his ears pop. From his room on the 27th floor, the jagged skyscrapers competed with the light of the moon. Nat looked down and imagined all the dirt motels he'd shared four or more to a room during his roadie days. Even then, Nat preferred to make an early retreat. He'd hunker down in the bathroom with a guitar to take advantage of the acoustics and solitude.

Nat collapsed onto the enormous bed. The hotel sheets were white and pressed. His and Karen's were paisley and worn from years of his tossing and turning, searching, but lost. He drifted off, wondering if he could still count on Karen to send that package to Eleanor.

▶▶

"Rick Russell, video thriller for the radio star—this is Bolero's brainy brother, Nat Dempsey." After Rollins introduced Nat to the big, bearded director, she pushed him into the booth next to Bolero's manager. Joe Beck nodded with a mouthful of syrup-drenched pancakes. Rollins squeezed across the table next to Russell.

"Really feeling this dynamite song, 'Muse Box'," Russell said to Nat. "The whole *Light Up & Shine On* record. So, I wanna quickly go through the concept and assure this video's gonna reflect what you are."

"And what are we?" Nat asked.

"The way I see it, your vibe is nostalgic but forward. Totally unpretentious. Don't-give-a-fuck attitude, but you're not entirely apathetic," Russell said.

"Not entirely," Nat replied.

"Ball buster. I get it." Russell took a beat and then held out his arm like a shark fin. "You're also ambitious. You want to play stadiums a decibel above the fans singing along. And you love music. Being a fan comes across in your music."

"Is that a dig?" Nat said, distracted that the waitress had just topped off his coffee, disrupting Nat's careful ratio of sugar and cream.

"Nah," Russell said. "I'm not saying Bolero is derivative."

Rollins choked on her bacon.

Nat sat, not giving away that he was more curious than insulted.

"I'm saying you're fuckin' inspired by the holy canon," Russell said.

"The holy canon? For fuck's sake." Joe Beck broke his silence. "Can we cut the crap and get on with the logistics?" he whined.

"All right, all right." Russell lit a cigarette. "As you know, we're amplifying the concept since Frida Jones agreed to feature. Now, to me, 'Muse Box' is all about dreams. We collect these tangible scrambles of inspiration and try to contain them in a box. These make us who we are. Am I right?"

"Whatever you say," Nat said.

"Atta boy." Rollins chuckled. She'd trained Nat to shut up and let people connect to songs in their own ways.

"Right," Russell said. "So we're gonna shoot two storylines, showing the inverse of two relationships. The first is going to be Bolero's popularity growing, a crowd building while the band performs live."

"There'll be genuine fans in the crowd," Rollins interjected. "We had our street team hit the pavement and K-ROCK announced it on the radio."

Russell snapped. "That's good energy."

"That's fewer mouths to feed," Beck added while chewing.

"Anyway," Russell continued. "The other storyline is a relationship on the outs—the growing pains. Frida's gonna play the scorned girlfriend, y'know, pulling away, nagging, tearing down photos, throwing keepsakes and the boyfriend's shit away. These scenes of their decline will juxtapose with the band's rise, scenes of more and more fans joining the crowd and pinning up Bolero posters and paraphernalia and shit in their bedrooms."

Despite how closely this scenario hit home, Nat questioned Jamie's ability to take a joke. "You want Jamie to get dumped by his girlfriend in the video?"

"Oh, fuck no." Russell petted his gnarly beard. "That wouldn't be funny. Frida's going to dump your bassist, that Sulky kid. That'll give this an unmistakably comedic tone. Then, in the end scene, Frida will be freshly single, late night at the bodega for a pint of ice cream or some shit, and Jamie's gonna be the checkout boy. So they'll flirt, he'll ring himself up, hop over the conveyor belt, and she'll take him home."

"And we're just gonna wear what we wear?" Nat said.

"Absolutely. Look, this video is extra fucking important because it's the debut of your image to a seriously massive audience. And like you, this audience is fucking bored with glum, inauthentic, formulaic shit. Whiny white boys with holes in their jeans and tracks on their arms and millions of dollars in the bank."

"Amen," Rollins said.

"Right. So we got Frida and Jamie shooting the bodega scene offsite. Bolero's performance and all the other scenes are down at Irving Plaza."

"That's it?" Nat said.

"That and Aja might pull you for some shots," Rollins said. "You'll see her team floating around behind the scenes."

"Aja Green?" Nat said, quickly piecing together why he was familiar with that name.

▶▶

Nat was weaving his way around Irving, examining the surprising complexity of the operation and the number of people involved. Crews, set designers, caterers, and teamsters. The volunteers for the crowd hadn't even arrived yet. Would enough show? Was the big buzz around Bolero real, or did he delude himself to believe Rollins' hype?

"Sulky, what the fuck are you wearing?" Nat shouted up to the stage. "We're supposed to dress normal!"

"We've been trying to tell him, man," said KP.

"What're you talking about? I'm the star, ain't I?" Sulky patted his red smoking jacket. The material matched the curtains.

"You look like a bellhop in the *Ice Capades*," Nat said.

KP punctuated Nat's punchline on his drum kit. Then Sulky, KP, and Greg hopped down from the stage to join Nat at the back bar underneath the overhang from the balcony.

"Where the hell is Jamie?" Sulky said.

"I'm so fucking bored," Greg said. Nat watched him lean over the bar to case if there was anything easy to steal.

"At least everyone else is a professional, not looking pissed yet," KP said.

Rollins burst into the ballroom. She groaned while hurling herself under the previously unmanned bar, unscrewed a bottle of Jack, and took a Bluto swig. She then counted heads and poured a sloppy continuum of shots for the band standing around waiting.

"Here comes success," she toasted.

"You'll notice we're not making a video right now," Nat said, holding the glass up to her with mild contempt.

Rollins leaned over and said, "And here comes the zoo." She winked as Jamie and Frida entered with some film crew. A rumbling pack of fans trailed behind them.

Nat took his shot. The whiskey multiplied the sensation of relief down his throat.

Jamie shouted, "Check it out! We found the coolest fucking people in New York!"

Everyone cheered.

"Sonny, do you see what I see?" Rollins said to Nat.

Nat observed the crowd. Girls and teenagers were gunning towards the stage to stake their claims up front. Twentysomethings of every demographic noncompetitively spread the middle. Older heads gathered in the back to talk esoteric tunes and hit the bar.

"Do you see money?" Nat said.

"Pinnacle shit!" Rollins said and threw a dirty rag over her shoulder. She continued to tend bar, serving everyone beers. A grubby excitement elevated around them.

"C'mon, Bobbi. At least pull the cheapest tap," Joe Beck nagged. He was the only one who called Rollins Bobbi.

Rollins responded by throwing down her hat to collect tips.

Nat was the first to throw in a twenty. "Everyone, remember to tip your bartender. She's a new parent."

"The bottle service never ends!" Rollins quipped.

Nat realized a black-clad woman standing on the bar had caught his pure and slanted grin in a photograph. A camera and oversized glasses obscured the details of her face.

"Did somebody say they were looking for me?" Jamie barked down from the stage mic.

The pull of the crowd nearly lifted Nat from the ground towards Jamie, like a whirlpool down a tub drain after lifting the stopper.

►►

Nat contemplated his last jukebox selection when Aja Green's arm interfered by pressing W8-02. He'd been ignoring her throughout the day.

"Help yourself then," he said and returned to the darkest corner at the wrap party.

Minutes later, Aja dropped two brown cocktails on his table and said, "Welcome to New York."

"Welcome yourself. I live here," he replied. "I don't need to pick Velvet Underground on the fucking jukebox to prove it."

"I had to listen to you all day. You owe me. *Mea culpa*?" Aja said.

"Fair enough." Nat took a sip of the drink she offered. It was not his style. It was syrupy and might flush his face.

"You've been avoiding me," Aja said.

"Well, maybe I thought you were going to attack me. You were like a ninja out there."

"A ninja? Because I'm Asian?"

"You're Asian? I thought you were *Aja*," Nat said.

"Funny," she said.

"Not enough if you don't laugh. And no, because you were all stealthy in black, crouching around with that fucking camera like a weapon. I hope you caught Rollins' hat with the tip money being passed around like the collection at a fucking diabolical church."

"You swear a lot," she said.

"It's a sign of intelligence," Nat told her.

"A sign of intelligence. Says who?"

"Well, you just did." Nat noticed this response raised her eyebrow. "You know, you don't seem like the type to be photographing bands live. Seems like you'd rather be in control. Staging inanimate objects and shit. Photographing buildings or food."

"That's a primitive notion of control. What are you projecting?" Aja said.

"Projecting? Ha. I think I only know one other person who can call me out on that type of shit," said Nat.

"I can guess it's not your brother. Your girlfriend?"

"No. She wouldn't have called me on it, though she was perceptive enough."

"Was. Are you attached?" she asked.

"Only to this glass." Nat finished his drink. "And yeah, no. My friend, Eleanor, who happens to love you, by the way."

"Okay."

"I mean, I think she applied to work for you a while back," Nat said.

"It's possible I have her résumé filed," she replied.

"I'm gonna get us another round. What the fuck was this?"

"A Manhattan," Aja said.

Nat brought back two pints of Guinness. Aja crossed her arms.

"Oh, get over yourself," he said.

"Bottoms up," Aja said and chugged the beer with him.

"Another?" Nat asked.

"I need to leave and start working on these." Aja gestured to the canisters of film peeking out of her leather satchel. "My place is down the street. Come with me."

▶▶

Aja's apartment exemplified what Nat knew about her so far. Sharp style, but all business.

"This place is bigger than where we played our first gig," Nat said.

"Already feigning nostalgia, babe?" Aja pulled heavy blackout drapes to reveal a door that opened to the kitchen.

"Already calling me 'babe'?" Nat followed her into the kitchen, which was more like a laboratory. "Not much of a cook?"

Aja handed him a fancy beer from a fridge otherwise filled with film and said, "Don't spill this. So, Nat, have you been in a darkroom before?"

"Actually, yeah. In high school. Mostly to protect our friend from a handsy art teacher."

"Your friend. Eleanor." Aja started cutting the negatives, neatly slipping the strips into clear sheets. After she completed the first one, she instructed Nat to prepare the other rolls while she mixed different chemicals into three color-coded trays lined along the counter next to a rigged-up utility sink.

"She took that photo on our album cover."

"It's a good one. Either she has good instincts, or she knows you all very well."

"Both." Nat suddenly felt drunk. "She's gone, anyway. Filming a bunch of communists trying to find love and careers or some shit."

"Hmm," Aja seemed to eye the negatives approvingly. Then she tinkered with the lights until the room was the dimmest red. Aja positioned his body by what he'd learned was the enlarger. Nat listened to her parallel-talk through the process of preparing a test strip from one of the contact sheets.

"You know, success in our industries is similar," she said. "It's one thing to create a killer song or capture the right moment. The rest is about timing and exposure."

Aja let Nat take the lead to agitate the test strip from the developer, then the stopper, the fixer, the sink rinse. She kept her hands on his hips, guiding him onwards by her internal timekeeping. When moving the strip between trays, Nat ensured the distinct tongs didn't touch the different liquids. He couldn't recall a time when he had followed orders this carefully.

After the test strip, they went back to the enlarger to start on the full sheets. This time was more fluid, and Nat started getting into it. The revelation of rows and rows of images was mesmerizing. Like proof of his band evolving, looking cool, playing with tenacity. Seeing his and Jamie's instinctual dynamic and presence so frequently in print felt confrontational. No one else could touch them when they were in it together, and no one else could reason with them when they were at each other's throats. Well, maybe someone could.

Nat and Aja continued to work together in this trance until all the contact sheets were rinsed and hung up on the line. Finishing felt like resurfacing from an underwater dive.

"What next?" he asked.

"We wait," Aja said. "They'll be dry in the morning."

Nat felt set up to make a move he wasn't ready for. "Any chance you're looking for an assistant?" he said, rubbing tension from the back of his neck.

"Are you looking for a job or a favor?"

8

ELEANOR

E LEANOR TRUDGED UP EIGHT flights in the July heat. The bulky package added to the strain of carrying her messenger bag and groceries from the Aldi. After fumbling to enter the door, she dumped everything to catch a breath. She split her provisions between the bread drawer and the little fridge, taking out a beer to make everything fit. She'd never seen plastic beer bottles before being in Germany. Maternus tasted even better because the suds were practically free after she traded the bottles in.

She lived on a daily döner kebab, which was better than any halal cart back home. But nothing was better than pizza, and she sorely missed pizza. Money was tight. Sometimes she swiped toilet paper rolls from the flat where they were filming. The job itself wasn't that tough. Labor laws were strict, so she didn't have to pull the hours she did in the states. She took the language barrier and everything else in stride because she knew there was too much to be gained if she committed herself to being adaptive.

Eleanor carried the package, sealed with Bewilder Records packing tape, into her brown box of a room. The room had a completely foreign view of coniferous treetops, a curling river, and the distant peaks of some unpronounceable ancient war monument—no urban score. No people. Eleanor stripped down to cool off and placed her clothes on the back of her desk chair to extend their wear. The freedom to be naked with her imagination was often enough reason to skip out on Leipzig's limited nightlife. Then, Will Hawking started calling. She was flattered, but a little thrown to hear he got her number from Nat.

Will's calls must've cost a fortune. Their conversations felt secretive, even risqué. Part of her didn't want to tell anyone about them, not that the people who would even care were around to tell. Sometimes he sang to her this Creation song called "If I Stay Too Long." She could only bear this corniness by envisioning him there to tie her down with the telephone cord and stay just long enough between her thighs.

Calls were rarer now that Will hit the road for festival season, but The Reverie was playing at Berliner Rockzirkus next week, an easy train ride away. She'd already been to Berlin to cover the Allied Soldiers March. It was intense to witness the cast members express the consequences of unification. Berlin was not known for being seductive and neither was she, but she yearned to bring her walls down.

Eleanor stared over at the package, half-expecting it to grow eyes and glare back. She knew what was inside. Half a world away, Bolero's record release had come and gone. She took her key to the box and sliced the seams. The first thing she saw after flapping open the lids was a crisp business envelope with her name on it. Her throat rolled over what it might say. She felt weirdly deflated when a check from Bewilder Records for $2000 was inside with "Rate" in the memo. The envelope nestled above rolled up posters, stickers, t-shirts, some PROMOTIONAL COPY singles and cassettes lodged densely in packing peanuts. Eleanor dug her hands in until she felt the unmistakable thick jewel case, and a pang that typically preceded a cry from being overwhelmed. Eleanor held her breath and dredged up Bolero's debut album, *Light Up & Shine On*.

A yellow sticky note obstructed the cover, which read,

YOU'RE THANKED
YOU'RE WELCOME
YOU'RE MISSED.

Eleanor peeled off Nat's message.

"Are you fucking kidding me?" she exclaimed.

The cover design had used one of her photographs. She'd splurged on the fine-grain black and white Ilford film. One of John Lennon's solo albums inspired the shot. Eleanor staged the guys along the brick wall of the old Hobart building. Jamie leaned in a vacant doorway, staring at the camera with his signature gaze that seemed to proclaim that life was a joke, but also a joke he took too seriously. Then there was Nat. He sat on the stoop in front of Jamie, but his focus was on his guitar strings. Eleanor felt validated for not allowing Nat to wear sunglasses. His eyes were too important, even stripped of their colors and not focused on anyone in particular. She had KP and Greg flank the left. They were having a laugh over smokes. Sulky was on the right, aloof and toying with a lighter. Eleanor had taken the photograph a few days after Bolero got "discovered."

Even though she missed their show at The Hive, she still found out before anyone else when Nat urgently insisted she meet him at Sunrise Diner on St. Patrick's Day. The diner was where all critical sit-downs happened after hours. The waitress denied them celebratory drinks, not because it was 3 AM, but because they were already too drunk on elation.

Eleanor caught an edge under her thumbnail to strip the CD case of its cellophane wrapper. She cracked it open and immediately leafed through the booklet. All of Nat's secret lyrics were now exposed in small white text over her photos, collaged and recolored to bluescale. *Light Up & Shine On* was dedicated to "R-CREW & R-STUFF." Eleanor set the booklet down and put the CD in her Discman, even though it wasn't the right time to press play. She was having dinner with Adele and Robin before going dancing at Moritz Bastei. It'd have to be an early night because she volunteered to join a smaller production crew to film a castmate's home visit to Potsdam in the morning.

Eleanor redressed. She wore a black button-down dress that had thin straps. None of the buttons pulled anymore. She had become more toned from her routine of sit-ups while learning to count in *Deutsch*. She layered her dress over a white crew neck shirt that accentuated her skin, which had browned and freckled from lying out last weekend at Cospudener See.

She rode the banister like a kid down to Adele and Robin's flat. New friends that could pass for sisters, all three of them were from east coast families without the means to give them a leg up or a hand out. They were comrades, delightfully fated to hang together on the ladder's lowest rung to film random German twentysomethings during the melt of the Cold War.

Adele opened the door in her yellow bra and handed Eleanor a bottle of white, a ball of mozzarella, and a bunch of tomatoes, before returning to a pot of water boiling on the stove. Eleanor carried everything to the table to sit with Robin, who was scribbling with markers. Their flat was double the size of Eleanor's, with a big living room and a dining table, but it was contingent on sharing with a Sachsen roommate who feared Adele and Robin's wild off-brand of domesticity. The strewn corks suggested they were already buzzed. Billie Holiday (Adele's pick) or jam bands (Robin's pick) were always playing. Eleanor was grateful to listen to Phish, given the options.

"Dry Quality," Eleanor read fancifully from the wine label.

"Don't get too excited," Robin said. "It means it's quality when the bottle's dry."

"Oh my god, please make her stop saying that!" Adele exclaimed.

"*Prost?*" Eleanor said, then gulped from the heap she'd poured into a mug. "Mmm. *Apfel und... katze* piss?"

"You nailed all the prominent notes." Robin winked.

For dinner, they shared a humble bounty. A salad of tomatoes and mozzarella lightly dressed in olive oil, warm *brötchen*, hard-boiled eggs, and a head of roasted cauliflower with seasoned bread crumbs. Eleanor inhaled the food and their wisdom. Conversations cycloned around romantic histories and prospects. Robin would go off about sexuality being a spectrum. She was hung up on this girl from back home, but also wanted to cross the line with one of the male cast-mates from Stuttgart. The golden rule was to, "Never fuck anyone who isn't a feminist."

Adele had the longest rap sheet, but looked the most innocent. Eleanor coined Adele's pattern as "foster fucking." She oozed this ultra-nurturing maternal love that dropped one wounded warrior after another into her lap. Eventually, they grilled Eleanor. She'd made the mistake of telling them about Nat and Jamie, and how weird and unresolved she'd felt at Lochstock.

"Seriously, Ele. Who are you into?" Adele said.

"I bet I know," Robin said.

"Have you ever hooked up with either of them? Or both?" Adele asked.

"Or taboo—Same time?" said Robin.

"That's abominable."

"Fine. What about the other guy?" Robin asked.

"I don't know yet," Eleanor replied, not sharing that lately it was Will she'd think of with her eyes closed. His fleshy lips sucking her under the warm rush from the spigot.

"*Katze* piss!" Robin shouted, after accidentally spilling the white wine no one needed to drink onto Adele's lap. Adele tore off her pants and began to squeeze them over the sink.

"No way." Robin stared at Adele and gasped. Robin then pulled down her pants.

Everyone's mouths gaped, captivated by a discovery of epic coincidence. Robin and Adele had revealed the slot machine cherries tattooed below their bikini lines.

"Adele's are dripping!" Eleanor collapsed to the tile floor. Her face was sore from laughing. "Oh man. I feel left out," she eventually whimpered.

Robin held up her markers like wands. "I think it's time for her to join the coven."

"We can pretend we're at Ace of Spades off the boardwalk in Wildwood," Adele said.

Eleanor pulled her dress up to her neck.

"Remember, though," Adele said. "Just because you say yes to a tattoo doesn't mean you have to say yes to the townie in his Crown Vic, just because he bought you wine coolers and an airbrushed t-shirt."

"Holy fucking anecdote, Adele!" Robin tugged down Eleanor's undies to sketch out the placement.

Eleanor remained less inhibited than with most lovers or doctors.

"Wait!" Adele came over with the wine. "Ele, this could hurt." She poured the cheap Riesling into Eleanor's mouth.

Eleanor gargled a giggle and swallowed it down. Adele gripped Eleanor's hand while Robin simulated the sounds of a buzzing ink gun. Eleanor faked pain. Really, she was tickled by the marker and pained only by the delicacy of memory, the risk that she might ever forget a moment so completely happy and strange.

▶▶

On the tram, they caught up with the rest of the production team, including Max from the UK office. Max was polite and trilingual and had seen the Stone Roses at Spike Island. Therefore, Eleanor intentionally bounced into him when the tram stopped short at Johannisplatz.

"Have you already been up to no good?" he said in his quiet way.

"Ele got her first tattoo tonight," Adele announced.

"You have to hit the jackpot to see it, though," Robin joked.

"A tattoo. Did you really?" Max said. There was something familiar in the way Max's eyebrow arched when he asked her this.

Eleanor cupped his hand to share the straphanger. Instead of replying, she batted her curled lashes as if to admit that she liked the convenience of their equal heights and the proximity of his body to hers.

Max offered his hand to help Eleanor off the tramcar at the next stop, and she held it for most of the night. Between the cheap shots and unfashionable dancing, Eleanor got relentless to give herself up. Max felt safe, and she took him home. They wound around each of the eight flights while blathering nonsense, taking timeouts to wrestle and kiss against the communist concrete walls. Each kiss felt less fluent than the last, but she was stubborn to stay greenlit.

Finally, she led him through the door, tripping hard through the finish line. Her desperate laugh could not cover up that her knees had smacked and bloodied the beige floor.

►►

Eleanor woke up on her back and in her clothes. Bad signs. Rain clouds hung heavy outside the window, and a wet rag pruned over her knees. She could hear Jamie's voice singing through her headphones over Max's ears. Max was somehow asleep, seated unpleasantly in her desk chair with his arms crossed tightly and legs spread, reminiscent of the private school kids who slept through their subway stops. According to her watch, it was ten past two fucking hours too late for the train to Potsdam. She'd never been late for anything. They'd probably think she was dead. If this were New York, she *would* be dead. Eleanor scrambled to clean up her pitiful presentation. Max was awake and stretching when she returned to the room. He shooed away her peace offering of a glass of water.

"Max, I'm so sorry."

He laughed. "Yeah, you're rubbish, but this—" Max said, holding up *Light Up & Shine On*. "*This* is bloody fantastic."

"Do you want to stay?" she said, totally unsure of herself.

Max looked amused by her question and said absolutely not. He rubbed her on the shoulders awkwardly, told her to rest up, and then took a copy of Bolero's album as an apparent parting gift.

After Max left, the sky surrendered to the inevitable storm. Rain smacked the window. Eleanor released a scream into her pillow until it curved into a wheezing, pitiful laughter. On any other day, she might listen to Warren Zevon, The Smiths, or The Cure to suit her shit situation. But on this day of reckoning, there was only one thing left to listen to. Eleanor fixed the headphones over her ears and pressed play. That first riff she'd heard a million times sounded different now, like she hadn't really heard it right before. Eleanor's battered knees pulsed to the beat. The production made Bolero's songs sound more powerful, realized, and deliberate. She tucked her teeth over her lip to stop it from trembling. By "Muse Box," she'd forgotten everything that happened and felt energized by the promise that anything might.

►►

A few days later, she could sense exactly when he'd call.

"Well, what do you think?" Nat said without a salutation. They hadn't spoken since she left Lochstock, but hearing his voice crashed their continental divide back to Pangea.

"I don't even know what to say," she said. "I mean, it's hard to believe how good it is."

"Hard to believe?" he said.

"You know what I mean! It's just, it's better than I ever, ever could've imagined, but I should've because it's exactly what it should be."

"So you're saying I'm a genius, right?"

"Shut up," she said.

"Well, I'm just glad it got to you," said Nat. "I've been waiting this one out, to give you a chance for a fair listen first."

"I'm so glad you did," Eleanor said, twirling the cord, unsure of what else to say now.

"How are you doing somewhere out there, kid?"

Kid? Nat's tone sounded like a big brother more than a friend, and certainly less than something more than a friend. It was off-putting.

"I'm alone, but not lonely," she said.

"I bet you love that," he said.

"You know me."

"I do."

"How is Bolero world?" she asked.

"Not crashing yet." Nat then rattled off a dizzying schedule of gigs. Publicity on late night TV and radio shows. Venues getting changed to hold bigger crowds. Namedrops. "It's kind of crazy," he admitted. "If you're not talking about O.J., you're talking about us."

"How's Karen handling everything?"

Nat sighed. "Couldn't expect to pull one over you. We've been done since, well, what's the postmark date on your package?"

Karen gone made Bolero's rise feel way more real. "That's kind of fucked up."

"Before you think about accusing me of being cliché, she was the one to break things off. If you can believe it!"

"Well. She's smarter than you," Eleanor said.

Nat cackled. "Oh, fuck can I ever count on you to level me... Well, Miss Huston, you are missed," he said.

"That's nice," she replied, which it was, but it lacked the sincerity and ownership of an '*I* miss you.'

"That's nice? So, what'd you think about the cover art?"

Eleanor hadn't been able to place all of her feelings about it. Yes, she had permitted the use of her photographs, but hadn't prepared to be forever linked to his record. "I want to thank you and hit you at the same time."

"What's to stop you from doing both?" he asked.

"This ocean between us," she said.

"Always something, isn't it?"

9

WILL

D ASUKI PUSHED WILL IN a wheelchair off stage after their encore. The crowd at Berliner Rockzirkus went wild for the gimmick. The entire festival circuit had been a whirlwind, riding out 30-minute sets across Europe. Each country had the same tasting McDonald's french fries and different tasting cigarettes. There'd been some rebuilding along the road, but that meant turning a blind eye to a creeping of bad habits. Dave had been briefly hospitalized in Spain for exhaustion.

Now that The Reverie's performance was clocked, Will ditched his lanyard backstage, grabbed his bug-out bag, and navigated the marshy herds to his car service. The rest of The Reverie was up for a dangerously aimless weekend in Amsterdam before their Sunday slot, but not Will. Will told them he planned to stay in Berlin for Damien Hirst's solo exhibition, an event no one would question or be tempted to join.

Will's actual agenda involved discovering what a luxury hotel suite meant by German standards and undressing Ele in it. Will kept this plan to himself to avoid tension until it was worth it. The secrecy had turned up the heat on their slow burn of getting to know each other over phone calls. Ele was magnetic and friendly and asked good questions. She really turned him on after sending a photo of herself pointing to The Reverie's logo on a public posting advertising the Berliner Rockzirkus. Her expression was lively and suggestive, not the conflicted, sleepy gaze that he encountered at Lochstock. And as modest as a t-shirt can be, hers was snug enough to shape every curve and pointed detail underneath. On the back of the photo, she'd written "SHOULD I COME?" in a slanty uppercase. Yes, you should, he thought while rubbing himself on casket ride nights in the tour bus crossing country lines.

▶▶

"*Mitte.*" Will's driver confirmed as they entered the city limits. "Middle of everything."

Near the Brandenburg Gate, the driver pointed and mentioned Clinton had just given some big unity speech there. Zipping through the city was a shellshock of eras, cranes, and closures. Despite his extensive travels, Will had never been to Germany and wasn't particularly interested in exploring its layers. It was aesthetically neither Zen nor Baroque enough for his tastes.

The hotel was on a mellow, tree-lined street across from a canal. Through the doors, Will walked down an unexpected gallery-like hallway, sparsely displaying banal modern art. He found Ele at the lobby bar. She had just been served something in a cup and saucer.

Will fluffed his hair and snuck beside her. "Another one of those, *bitte.*"

"Hey! I know that voice," she said, nestling into him for a side hug.

"What did I just order?" he asked her.

"*Kaffe mit schlag,*" she said.

Will's discovery that she was drinking caffeine instead of alcohol aroused him. He, too, was in no rush to dull any senses.

"I wish I could've gotten here early to make your set, but I'm kind of on thin ice right now. How did it go?" she asked.

He'd almost shared it was for the better, but said, "All good. Went well." Will exhaled a deep breath and spread his hand across his chest. "Relieved to be here now."

"I can't believe we're doing this," Ele said.

"I can," Will replied. He put his hands on her shoulders. "You're tense."

"I know. I need you to help loosen me up."

Will would've sworn her eyes were blue, but right now they looked racy green.

▶▶

In the morning, Will woke to a canvas of Ele's freckled shoulders backlit by clouds and orange rippling roofs. She pulled his arm around her tightly, inviting him to slip his hand between her thighs. Her purrs implored him to squeeze himself as deeply as she could wriggle him inside. Even after releasing last night's round, this would be no marathon. The sensation was so much that he lasted long after his burst, wincing and waiting until he felt her body's unmistakable clench and liberation.

Will wanted the weekend to slip away like this, in and out of each other. But Ele was not the type. She proposed an ambitious list of activities. They'd have to go beyond the walls of the room.

"Weren't you just here?" he asked.

"Yeah, but it was for work, and it wasn't with you."

▶▶

Will was outside a *bäckerei*, unclear on which pastry among the display might be Ele's favorite, when some fans recognized him. The one with the best English explained he had been at yesterday's festival.

"Now I know you own shoes," the kid said, commenting on Will's barefoot performances.

Will noticed that Ele had shied away from the interaction. Will asked the kid to take a photo "of me and my girlfriend," to conclude their chat. Ele protested before handing over her point-and-shoot camera.

Will pulled Ele in by belt loops and they faced each other like a prom pose, though she said she hadn't attended hers. Afterwards, they went into the bakery and ate *pfannkuchen,* which Will contested was an unremarkable doughnut.

"Is the doughnut proof you're missing America?" he said.

"Maybe. I may not scream New Yorker, but I feel like I scream American here."

"I don't know. You may have that the wrong way around," Will said. "You're pretty New York."

She looked at him like she was suspicious of how to take his comment. "Was that weird for you to be noticed before?" she asked, one cheek squirreled away with dough.

"Not really. I guess it is when you're caught off guard. You know, when you're in the middle of being anonymously yourself."

"Yeah. I feel like I'd have to be on all the time. Not that track had a ton of spectators or anyone gave a shit, but when I was competing, I hated that feeling of being acutely observed. I'd rather go unnoticed."

"I noticed." Will gave her some footsie under the table. "But I'm afraid to report that you're noticeable."

"Eh."

"What, you don't think you're beautiful?"

"Ew. I don't know. Who cares?" She stuck her hair behind her ears. "So, have you ever cheated on anyone?"

"Wow. Can you promise me the pleasure of these *non sequiturs* every time I compliment your looks?" he said.

Ele laughed. "I mean, you didn't technically call me beautiful, but as someone you called your girlfriend to strangers, I feel like I should know these things, right?"

"Okay then. I don't know how to answer this one."

"Shit. That's a weird start," she said.

"Well. I'd say my last relationship was the only serious one, and even that was different in terms of commitment. We weren't always exclusive. There were times Cath initiated us to be with someone else, usually other women. Some of those times I was on one thing or another, which you know I don't even drink anymore."

"Hmm... I think we need to do something later," she said.

"Is it a threesome?" Will joked.

"Too soon," she replied.

But Will suspected it wasn't a matter of timing; it was more that Ele would never be that kind of girl. For now, that was what he wanted.

After breakfast, Will was subject to Ele's aggressively paced tour of Berlin's gray, grim, and brightly graffitied walls. "Think of the east like Joy Division and the west like New Order," she said.

"That's one way of putting it," he said.

Berlin was both godless and spiritual. Ele was revealing her contradictions as well. Sometimes she was assertive, other times her shoulders curved inward, and she'd lose inches from her tall stature. She'd switch functionally to German with a practiced accent, which was impressive but silly. Some of her tirades compelled Will to quiet her by diverting her mouth to press against his.

"Do you ever get those eerie feelings, like when you swim into one of those hotter pockets in the ocean?" she asked.

"Sure. In the ocean," he said. Ele shoved him, and he was taken aback.

To break up all the walking, Will convinced her to pop into a gem shop overwhelmed by incense, global trinkets, and narrow aisles of categorized crystals. Ele pointed out the cards describing the properties of the stones. She didn't know that Will knew this world. His mother, Cherise, had been into her chakras and crystal healing his whole life.

"Let's pick something out for each other—something we each think the other needs," Ele suggested.

"As long as you don't think we *need* rocks."

"In your line of work? You never know when you might need to rock."

"Then as long as you cool it with the rock puns," he said.

"I malfunction when I try to flirt with you. Okay, let's make like a stone and roll," she said, shuddering at herself.

Will knew immediately what to get Ele, though there was no basis for its alleged spiritual properties. In a driftwood dish, Will found the moonstone section along with a poor translation of its characteristics, which read:

<u>**MOONSTONE - GODDESS STONE**</u>
NEW BEGINNING OF STRONG INSIDE GROWTH.
GIVE TO LOVER UNDERMOON TO HAVE PASSION.
AMULET TO PROTECT SENSITIVE NATURE
OR REUNITE LOVERS.

Will selected the least gaudy necklace, which wasn't saying much. After discreetly paying, he returned to the more aromatically neutral atmosphere, where Ele was already waiting smugly.

"How did you beat me?"

"You really don't know me," she replied.

They walked another ten minutes before sprawling onto the grass beneath a green-domed cathedral at Lustgarten. Ele handed him the small paper bag from the shop.

"Impatient much? I can't give you mine until tonight," he said.

"Open mine anyway," she insisted, then nestled alongside him.

The stone was green, rectangular, and raw. "It's a calcite," she said. Will caught Ele's excitement to watch him examine it. She eagerly pressed her thumb above his to guide it through a ridge. Without referencing the card, she recited, "It's supposed to bring you renewed vitality, prosperity, and release you of whatever is holding you back."

"Ha. This is more apt than you know. But it'll probably just make me think of the color of your eyes today." Will tucked the stone into his pocket.

"Well, whatever makes you think of me," said Ele.

"I wouldn't be here if I didn't think of you."

"I guess," she said.

"What is your face?" Will said.

"I don't know. I'm an optimist unless it comes to stuff like this." Ele plucked on longer strands of grass.

"You remember the first time we talked, but I said I'd seen you before, at the Zoo? That girl looked so assured and untouchable."

"Great. And now what?"

Will smirked. "You're very touchable."

Ele ran her hand through his hair until her fingers caught a snag, and he flinched. "I'm a spaz. Thinking about our first chat at Lochstock."

"You are a strange kind of charming," he said. Will withheld that he was drawn to the mystique of her relationship to the Dempseys. What kept his interest was more sincere. Like an iceberg, Ele seemed deep and to be navigating through oceans on her own.

"I was sort of charmed by you," she said.

"I'd have thought you would have ruled out guys in bands, knowing some of the psychopathic friends you keep," he said.

Ele sat up and retied her loose shoelace. "Psycho is a little much."

"Whatever you say," Will said. "So, why were you into me?"

"I don't know. I remember just really wanting to sit next to you."

"I was on that couch for a long time waiting to see if you were gonna take a break from your gangly dancing and come over to me," he said.

"Oh yeah? Well, you probably could've expected I'd come over. But to me, you were unexpected." Ele said.

"Why? Because of what you think of me in the band or something?"

"No. I hate the pretense of thinking you know someone before you know them, but maybe? I don't think you're the same person you are on stage. I think it's just somewhere you have to go to tell that part of your story," said Ele.

"How wise, Miss Huston," he said.

"Ah! Please don't call me that," she said. "Kind of reserved..."

"Noted... Would you say the same thing about me and Jamie?" he asked.

"Not at all," Ele replied. "Jamie's not a storyteller. Jamie's a character. He's the same person off stage, or at least he'd like to be because he's definitely at his best on stage and part of who he is on stage is Nat coming through."

"I'll agree that Jamie's best on stage, a safe distance from me."

On the way back to the hotel, Ele ordered them street food for lunch, not knowing Will didn't eat meat. The taste of whatever was shredded to fill that pita was so good, he was glad he hadn't told her. When they returned to the hotel, Will devoured Ele to her quick and indisputable finish. Afterwards, Will confessed that he'd broken his vegetarianism, attributing his carnal drive to the protein. Ele proposed they get steaks for dinner.

▶▶

It was their last night together. Ele had done herself up by wearing some noticeable makeup. The mascara darkened her long, light lashes. It was the first time he'd seen her wear a dress. The flimsy fabric hardly touched her body, but would reveal her shape with the slightest movements. It was sexy in the only way he felt she knew how to be, not that it wasn't effective.

Euphorically groggy from his midday sex nap, Will lit a cigarette and shared it with her. "Do we have to go?" he said.

"Definitely!" Ele walked away to open the window. "We could never be here again."

"We could've never been here at all," he said.

They were both right.

Ele took them to the city's oldest *biergarten* before going to Berlin's newest nightclub, some multi-story debauched disco that wouldn't open until midnight.

"If you weren't in The Reverie, what do you think you'd be doing?" she asked.

"I'd be an eternal philosophy student," he said, somewhat concerned that she'd probably consumed her weight in pilsner and pretzels by this point.

"Really? I hate philosophy!"

"Who hates philosophy?" he asked.

"Carve it on my tombstone! It's just too *shut-up* already, theoretical. That's my philosophy, anyway," Ele said.

"Okay, okay," Will said to calm her. "My new philosophy is to dip more food in mustard."

"Good, because mustard is like the baseline for civilization," she said.

Will laughed and leaned over to invite her greedy, vinegary tongue into his mouth. He'd missed the taste of everything she was experiencing, from the bitter beer to the silly freeness of mind.

"Oh, I have something to give you," he said. Will handed her a velvet pouch from the gem shop.

"No way, is this—"

"Moonstone," he confirmed.

Ele cackled for the first time in his presence, then handed the stone on its silver chain back to him, scooping her hair for him to put it on her. She thanked him with a tingling strand of kisses across his long neck.

When Ele went to the restroom, Will finished her beer and popped an Altoid. When she returned, he suggested they ditch the disco and go back to the hotel.

Ele agreed as long as they had a robe party.

▶▶

Will had ordered waffles and a pair of scissors.

"Scissors?" Ele repeated back.

"Excuse my language, but I think it was Jamie who told Kurt Loder that I was 'two tits and a spoken-word set from being mistaken for Patti Smith.'"

"Hmm... That sounds too clever for Jamie, but Nat wouldn't use the word 'tits.' Anyway, everyone loves Patti Smith," she said.

"I want you to cut my hair," Will told her.

"Seriously? You have no idea how qualified I am to do this!" Ele said.

"What if I told you this is the true nature of this rendezvous?"

"I'd believe you," said Ele.

"I actually don't think I've ever had a professional haircut," Will said.

"What? That's crazy! Because no offense, you're rich." Ele said this with what he sensed was offense.

"None taken?" he said.

"My dad keeps a military cut," Ele said. "I'd have to go with him to Tony's constantly. I mean, not really all the time, but how time in childhood memories seems absolute, you know? Tony is an old school barber. My dad and him live by the same creed."

"What's that?" Will asked.

"You keep a close shave and your mouth shut," Ele said.

"Do Nat and Jamie know your dad?"

"Oh yeah. To this day, my dad will threaten them with a high-and-tight, especially if they call him 'Mick' instead of Mr. Huston, which is a huge no-no."

Will made another note to address Ele's dad formally if they ever had to meet. After their room service order arrived, Will handed Ele the scissors and went into the bathroom.

Ele removed his shirt and used his shoulders to step herself up onto the ledge of the soaker tub. She turned him so they both faced the mirror above the sink. Through the reflection, Will observed Ele roll the terry cloth sleeves to her elbows and carefully assess her assignment before beginning.

"Now, honey," she asked in an even thicker New York accent than normal, "What are we thinkin'?"

"Short but shaggy," he said.

Ele held his hair in her hand, and before he could inhale to hold his breath, she chopped off every strand long enough to tie up. "Wow, you're not messing around," Will said.

"Now let's frame you out, handsome," she said.

Will watched her dampen and comb through his hair, then deftly pull up sections of his locks between her fingers and trim from them in a way that seemed artful and systematic. "I can't believe Ele Huston's secret talents."

"I really do love a haircut," she said. "But it doesn't have much to do with actually getting a haircut—Turn to me."

He now faced the moonstone resting upon her chest. "I'm intrigued. Why's that?"

"It's not that interesting. It's just that hairdressers are always so chatty and maternal. You see them only a few times a year, but whenever you do, it feels like you can tell them anything. They pretty much blindly support you—Head down—And it's like they have all the time in the world just to listen and feel sorry or proud about whatever stupid thing you have going on—Keep still—Anyway, I don't know what it would be like to have my mom around, but I feel like the closest thing is when I'm getting a haircut."

"I very strongly want to kiss you right now," Will said, but Ele ignored him, stepping back to examine her work with her hands on her hips.

"I think we're done," she said. "Take a look."

Will turned back towards the mirror and gasped. "Wow." He shook his head and pushed his hair back with his fingertips. It felt good. He felt good.

"I'm kind of scared how good you look," she said.

Will thought the same of her standing above him. He pulled apart her robe and dropped to his knees to taste her. She was like burnt sugar spun off the sea.

Ele whispered yes, but then sank. "Wait, stop," she said.

Will's head spun. He sat with her on the bathroom floor, scattered with hair. "What's going on up there?" he asked.

Ele closed her eyes like she was trying to fight off a cry. "This is just a lot for me."

"What is?"

"I don't know. What you know about me now." Ele tried to laugh. "Having to be okay if this is it."

"What is *this*?"

"I don't know," she said and hung her head.

"Ele." Will took her hands and squeezed them. "Look at me," he told her, but when she did, he didn't know what to say. She seemed to want him, and he liked that. But she also seemed to want something else, and he wasn't sure what that was about.

10

NAT

N AT'S GUT WAS GRUMBLING. To say that the California diet of Mexican food and spliffs did not agree with him would be an understatement. He was with Jamie, being led from another not green green room through a windowless maze at W-ROX, LA's most popular radio station. They were here to promote Bolero's back-to-back sponsored (i.e., free) concerts at the Santa Monica Pier Fest. Most media plugs called for Nat and Jamie, not the whole band. The rest of Bolero were ambivalent, if not relieved, to be excluded. Nat was left to control the messaging and Jamie. Jamie was unpredictable. He could be grumpy, tired, belligerent, or like an eager kid on Halloween ready to trick-or-treat for the press. Nat had to strategize to cope, to play the press like a game he didn't give a shit about winning, even if that wasn't always true. Nat found he could be painfully honest as long as he sounded disingenuous, and reserve a deadpan tone for absurdities. Sometimes in interviews, he'd take a firm position, then flip his opinion quicker than the sound of all the slow walkers and their floppy sandals out west.

Rollins encouraged Nat's gamified fuck-all approach. "Spin heads," she'd said.

▶▶

Nat and Jamie were cold in the hot seats across from W-ROX's airwave personalities, Big Mouth Bob and Kitty "Not Cat" Stevens. It became clear to Nat that Jamie had gotten too high on the ride over to the station. Once they were on air, Jamie started blathering about how he used to harass one of the college rock disc jockeys out on Long Island. "He was a Sting apologist!" Jamie exclaimed, then imitated police sirens.

Bob was too busy exercising his big mouth on a breakfast burrito to reel in the directionless banter. Did they eat anything else out here but fucking burritos? Nat's stomach rolled over again. Kitty seemed desensitized to Bob's general disgustingness. Her look was foreign to Nat. If video killed the radio star, Kitty would survive. She wore a teal bikini top and khaki shorts despite the studio's refrigerative climate. Nat could not determine if she was aware of her suggestive disposition, asking her questions in a half speed while sucking on a bulbous lollipop. Jamie's cartoonish tongue was not unreasonably wagging at the display.

Nat might have failed to convince listeners how excited Bolero was for today's show. The whole band had hated playing these scorching soul suckers up and down the golden state. The heat was as bad as the crowds, except for when the crowds were worse.

"And are you loving LA?" Kitty asked.

"Absolutely." Nat yawned. "It's a thrill to play for audiences as big as Jamie's ego."

"We're livin' for the peaks and valleys," Jamie said, miming lewd shapes.

"Los Angeles is pretty much Long Island with palm trees and smog," Nat said.

"Is that where you guys are from?" said Kitty, maybe a couple licks from the center of the Tootsie Pop.

"Word, no. We're from the future," Jamie said. "Where's your sound effect guy? Don't ya got a rocket sound? Or something taking off?"

"I think he's taken off." Kitty rolled her eyes.

"Oh, he's taken off years ago," Nat told her.

"That's right. I took off and I can tell you—aliens totally exist, dudes and dudettes!" Jamie said mockingly with a surfer's affectation. It was spot on Spicoli. "Seriously though, what kind of radio station doesn't have a laser beam?"

"How about we do even better?" Big Mouth intervened. "After all, we're ahead of the times here at W-ROX! Now, here comes our top track for the third week in a row, Bolero's 'That's Not My Name,' the second single off their smashing debut record, *Light Up & Shine On*."

Off the air, Jamie was briefly agreeable again, in a way that only hearing himself or laser beams could enable. As their song played, Nat challenged Big Mouth to a staring contest while Jamie lightly bantered with the valley cat. Kitty was dishing it back well. She must've needed all the sugar in that sucker to get her going this morning.

"... And that was Bolero's 'That's Not My Name.' This is Big Mouth Bob and Kitty 'Not Cat' Stevens here, live in the studio with Nat and Jamie Dempsey of Bolero. Now, which one of you wrote that song?"

"I did," Nat said.

"I like it," said Kitty. "It's hella fierce but also kind of like, has a jingly hopeless Kinks vibe. What's it about?"

Nat was kind of impressed with her evaluation, but agitated by her question. Jamie put his hand over the mic like he was ready to spill his interpretation to her off the air. Nat punched Jamie's thigh.

"Next question," Nat replied firmly.

"So, you're one of two sets of brothers in the band? Is that right?" asked Big Mouth.

"That must be fun," said Kitty.

"You know, fun is not exactly the word I would use," said Nat. "But it is more fun than dysentery."

"Haha! More fun than dysentery. Name of our second album," said Jamie, and then went off on Greg and Sulky, saying that they were next door, signing up at the weird mall-like mega church.

"Listen, you're lucky the Sullivan brothers aren't here," Nat said. "Their personalities are as mediocre as their musical contributions."

Jamie howled. "Burn!"

"Is that so?" said Big Mouth.

"Yeah. They landed on third base growing up in our town and hanging around long enough to fill out my band," Nat said.

Jamie's posture altered from a vagrant's slouch to a paratrooper about to deplane. "*Your* band?"

"*My* band." Nat knew he had shown too much frustration in his reply. But it pissed Nat off that he pissed Jamie off. That was the genesis of most of their spats.

"Ho ho, sounds like fighting words," said the Mouth nervously.

"You'd be singing in the shower if it weren't for me," Nat claimed.

"Oh yeah? You'd be babysitting and selling fuckin' gear at Guitar Center without me," Jamie said.

Nat was still babysitting, but he'd traded in Karen's six-year-old daughter for four morons in their twenties.

Big Mouth seemed aggravated by how sideways and sweary the interview was getting. "That cuss is gonna cost you, fellas," he said, trying to play it cool with his boisterous on-air voice.

"Oh shit, my bad," Jamie said.

"Double whammy!" said Bob.

Nat put his arm around Jamie's shoulder and laughed aloud to deescalate the bickering. He felt Jamie take a regulating breath.

"Well, whatever, we have loads of money now," Jamie said. Nat was pretty sure Jamie had no idea how much money they had, but he was right.

"Oh yeah? You guys are living large?" Kitty pointed her question at Nat. She had been fairly preoccupied with her cuticles until now.

"Me? I'm just living my life in 12 bars," Nat said.

"Yeah, and I just need the one bar," said Jamie.

"Amply supplied," Nat specified.

"Very ample," Jamie said.

"Give it a rest, man!" Nat said, now thinking Kitty wouldn't cut it on TV. Her face was finally expressive in its appall. "Sorry to all the people tuning in over the airwaves. This is the first time Jamie's heard the word 'ample' used not to describe breasts."

"Bullshit," Jamie said. "*Everyone* uses the word ample to describe breasts."

"Should we open the lines to callers?" said Nat.

Kitty's reaction was to bite her lip like she was in a Whitesnake video.

Later, when they were leaving the station, she dropped her number in Nat's shirt pocket.

▶▶

Muted on the TV, Crocodile Dundee had just gotten to his hotel in New York. Dundee's peach suite wasn't much different from the one Nat was sulking in over 2,000 miles away. Nat's head was bruised, his voice strained, and his skin burned. He felt like more types of shit than how many he'd succumbed to take that day. Day One at the Santa Monica Pier

Fest had been a disaster. It was like the devil had caught up with Bolero in the city of angels. Jamie surrendered by the third song. He abandoned the stage, holding his throat with one hand and flicking off the audience with the other.

A shoe struck Nat, leaving him both baffled and pissed. Like, who throws a shoe? Was it premeditated? Did the dickhead bring a spare? Or was that individual so sick that they preferred the feel of crushed glass and pavement melting their barefoot over not assaulting him? How does one even take seriously the critique of an apparel-heaving nut job? The irony of Nat's head swelling from the incident was not lost on him. This shit kept happening. Shoes, bottles. Why was that a thing? Rollins was not sympathetic. She endured the first wave of punk when people spit on each other to genuflect.

Rollins had interrupted Nat to check in on him and was doing nothing to hold back her strange pleasure at having witnessed Bolero's flop.

"No substitute." Rollins chuckled.

"For what?" Nat kicked his shoes off to lie atop his bed like a hostile patient.

"A bust!" Rollins said. "You're just an unteachable baby balloon before that first bust. I'm telling you, there's no substitute for a bad gig!"

"A bad gig? I had to step in for our alleged voice-shot singer who just walked off stage after I took a fucking sneaker to the face." Where was one of those ubiquitous flip flops when he was being assailed?

"At least the abuse came before your crooning," Rollins said. "And no shit, you sounded good! Don't get any ideas about that, though. You've got heart, sonny. But you need your frontman. You're still number one and three on the charts! And we're up for five Apex Music Awards in a few days. Five!"

"The only time they weren't in full revolt was during 'Muse Box,'" Nat lamented.

"See? They knew all the fuckin' words. I'm telling you, it's not that bad," Rollins insisted.

Nat stewed on his new goal to be so popular that crowds would sing along loud enough to make anyone's vocal efforts less consequential.

"Ain't no substitute," Rollins said again with her loaded chortle, and then answered the drawling knocks at the door.

After letting in Old Betty, Bolero's new tour manager, Rollins left to launch into another phone call that sounded like the continuation of some manic deal. Old Betty looked like Florence Nightingale in biker drag with a pack of ice for Nat's face. She and her husband Fern had joined the Bolero crew as a test run for the big tours coming up. God knows how Rollins knew these aged, honkytonk hall monitors. Actually, Betty looked rather like Mick Dundee with her dried sandy hair, leathered skin and vest. Maybe Nat'd get her a bowie knife for Christmas. By the looks of it, she probably already had one.

"Baby will be fine, Bunny," she said to him. Betty gave everyone endearments, and Nat doubted if she knew anyone's actual names. "I told Birdy to make him a toddy. Baby's under lockdown for the night."

Jamie was Baby. Obviously.

Jamie's girlfriend, Frida, was Birdy.

Nat was Bunny. Hell, he'd been called a lot worse in the last 12 hours.

"You'll be fine too, Bunny," she said, rattling around in the suite's kitchenette. "I'll get outta yer hair after I fix you some things to calm whatever's making you look like the dog that ate his own shit."

If Nat were in a better mood, he would've appreciated Betty's crass indulgence of his pain. But it grated on him to feel taken for granted by the rest of the band, even Rollins now. Nat hated that the band voted to chase the money and play this block of corporate bullshit stateside when their counterparts like The Reverie were off touring Europe or doing Lollapalooza. Between that and Jamie's walking off the stage earlier that day, Bolero's era of democracy needed to end fast.

Rollins reentered the room and slapped her hands together like she had to rouse the attention of a distracted gym class. "I forget. Do you like the good news or bad news first?" she asked, removing her hat to swipe some of the sweat from her forehead.

Betty intervened and said, "Bad news first for Bunny." She then dropped a sad buffet of food for Nat and left.

"That's right, right." Rollins snapped her fingers. "Jamie gets good news only."

"There's no point in telling Jamie anything other than his fucking horoscope," Nat said.

"Right, alright. So the bad news is you're still on the hook for tomorrow's show."

Nat took his punishment silently, like he did when he was a kid, and this was nothing by comparison. But Nat wasn't a kid anymore, and in his mind, he'd already resolved that there was no way he was showing up tomorrow to be held captive to philistines for a repeat of today. Nat kept this decision to himself because Rollins was addicted to negotiating as much as she was to everything else.

"What's the good news, then?" Nat said.

Rollins took a deep breath, held it, and then said, "*Blame the Youth*," as if she were exhaling a bong rip.

Nat perked slightly. *Blame the Youth* magazine was a last line of defense against advertisements disguised as music journalism. *BTY* was honest and incorruptible, like Nat saw himself. "The cover?"

"You bet your ass. Fine fucking way to amp up our road to that world tour," Rollins said. "Linda Kaminski is the journo taking the lead on this. She'll hook up with you when we get to Vegas and cover you through the Apex Music Awards."

"If she can stand it," Nat said.

"She's a pro," Rollins said.

"Whatever." Nat answered his ringing room phone. It was Greg airing grievances about the radio show that morning. Nat pretended the call was important to get Rollins out of his suite. Then he hung up on Greg.

Nat poked around at the spread Betty had prepared for him. The oatmeal and banana slices took him back to breakfast when visiting his grandparents. A train and a bus and switchback stairs to the fifth floor of their tenement apartment. Nat was scarred by the step that split his chin open. His pops ripped off his undershirt to stop the bleeding. He sat Nat on the counter over the kitchen sink and tried to distract him with stories about the time he'd gone AWOL during the war. How he'd have ridden the rails to death if he hadn't fallen for Nat's gram instead.

By now, it was after midnight on the east coast. Nat called Aja at home. She'd be awake and working. Aja had already scooped Nat's good news of the *BTY* magazine feature and upcoming tour. When Nat looked for sympathy after sharing his bad news, about the festival and Nat's takeover when Jamie abandoned them, she had none to spare.

"You did what? You sang? I shouldn't have to be the one to tell you that wasn't the best solution," Aja said.

"You know, they're my fucking songs. I can carry them," Nat said to defend himself, trying to mask his frustration that he didn't carry them well, or as easily as he'd have liked.

"Don't confuse your image," she said.

"Our image? Excuse me for being concerned about the audience and salvaging some type of finish instead of preserving our image."

"Is that what you think you were doing? Whatever. I am sorry your experiment to front the band you're creatively responsible for failed. That doesn't have to be a bad thing," she said.

"Oh yeah?"

"Now you know you need Jamie, and you can put the notion of going it alone out of your head."

"You're saying I had that notion?" said Nat.

"You didn't?"

"Whatever. Great." Nat yawned. "Have a nice night," he said and hung up.

Aja had dragged him further down. It wasn't that he didn't regard her opinion, it was that she didn't give a shit about him. Nat thought about calling Eleanor, but it'd been too long and he couldn't compute their time zones. Instead, he shamelessly comforted himself with his memory of her mouth, her top heavy lip. Her front teeth that gave the illusion of elongating when she smiled hard. Then the teeth would slip over to nib into her bottom lip. Thinking about her made Nat feel less sick and ashamed. He grew longer, imagining her lips in forbidden ways he'd never known, and finally relieved the only thing he hadn't left behind of himself on the thankless stage earlier that day.

▶▶

The pressures had subsided enough by morning to improve Nat's mood. He was ready to take one out of Pops' playbook. Ideally, Nat's going AWOL would change the dynamic in Bolero, relieving him of all the responsibility without granting him sovereignty. Maybe it'd all go to hell. Maybe he'd just go swimming.

Nat's accomplice had said to be ready in 20 minutes. Two hours later, he was riding shotgun as Kitty's cliché convertible purred in the freeway gridlock. They were leaving LA, headed southbound to somewhere she called "the Del." He felt liberated to be anywhere other than where he was supposed to be.

"I can't believe you don't drive," she said.

"Look, I have a license and all. But do you know how long it took me to master playing guitar? The idea that I or anyone else should get behind the wheel of a car after a 5-hour driving course seems fucking insane to me, actually."

"Geez, I'm surprised you even get on the road."

"You gotta live, Kitty," he said and fiddled with the radio dial. R&B didn't suit the mood, and Kitty refused to listen to her own station, so they settled on classic rock. Just as Jackson Browne was reminding Nat to take it easy, the radio edit cut into another goddamned Eagles song.

"Fucking criminal," Nat said. "The outro is the best part of that song. You're in radio. Can't you do something about that?"

Kitty laughed and turned the volume up, which did nothing to drown out the orchestral effect of her gum snapping. Nat found Kitty's off-air personality more muted than he expected; like she got paid per spoken word. But he appreciated her role in quieting his overactive commentary and gifting him the opportunity to be a passenger, to stare into other people's cars and think about other worlds across the eight lanes instead of his own. Eventually, the roadways narrowed, and Kitty's car caught speed over the last stretch. They crossed a low, long bridge curving over water to a detached oasis with a massive white castle capped with red roofs that resembled the hats of garden gnomes.

Nat put the label's plastic card down to check him and Kitty into an Ocean Suite at the Hotel del Coronado. They changed into their suits and met out on the balcony, which overlooked the sea. A few triangles of crochet cleverly covered Kitty. She'd twisted her black and bronze curls up into two garlic knots. They shot some tequila and then hit the beach. By now, Nat had spent weeks being taunted by the Pacific and its arid chill. He'd yet to be immersed in its wild barrels. Nat thought about the last time he was at the beach. Bolero's first drummer had driven them to the Rockaways in his van. That guy probably lived in that van now.

Down by the waterline, Nat asked if Kitty expected him to call her.

Her answer was "Duh."

"Why's that?" he asked.

"Because you're smart and you'd be stupid not to," she said. "But I didn't expect to be your getaway driver. What's my cut?"

"I'm not sure yet. What do you want?" The cool liquid salt cloaked his feet, pulling them under wet sand. By now, Nat felt more at ease with Kitty's attention. He was closed off to indiscriminate affection and wary of being interchangeable, or someone's second pick to Jamie. The notion that the same woman could want Jamie and Nat was unfathomable. When Jamie was in the mood to be monogamous, the runoff was Greg's territory to clean up because KP was a prince to Lindsay, and Sulky hated women more than he hated himself.

"How about some actual answers instead of that fluff you gave me on our show?" she said.

"I'll give you one," Nat said before dodging her to chase the next wave out.

Even in peak summer, the Pacific was wholly cold and didn't offer a simple transition from the shallow to the deep. Nat swam out hard to hasten his blood flow. He powered through the breaking waves and foamy builds until he was suspended below sea level with no ground to touch. Nat looked back at Kitty. She splashed her body with the ocean and then strutted back to the dry sand to lie out. Under the cloudless sky, he felt brightly struck by what he'd accomplished with Bolero so far, and that it'd reduce more rapidly than rocks to sand if he stayed too long away from the mess he'd abandoned in Los Angeles.

Nat let the next wave carry him back to land.

Kitty tossed him a towel to dry off. "'That's Not My Name.' What's it about?"

"Really? That's your one?"

She nodded.

Nat paused. He'd accidentally wiped sand into his lips with the back of his hand and spit. "When I was real young, they called me Nathan. My dad's name is Nathan, Nathaniel. But he... he fucked up too many times." Nat twisted the towel around his neck. "And I'm not him. Simple as that." It felt good for Nat to say it, even though it didn't feel good to have lived it.

He saw Kitty looked pleased that he'd answered her. She suggested they go back to the room.

▶▶

Out on the balcony, they smoked a joint in their bathing suits. The setting sun made Kitty's body glow. It was still slick with beads of oil and water. Nat let the slightest breeze knock him into a seat.

"I'd like to see those off," he said about her white cat-eye sunglasses.

She obeyed and then dared to hang them from the string between her breasts. They dangled when she dipped over to remove his sunglasses, saying, "Show you mine, show me yours." Kitty hovered above him and touched his cheek. "What are you thinking, always hiding behind those shades?"

"Said by the woman on the radio instead of in front of a camera."

"I'm in front of you," she said, peacocking her hips at his eyeline. Intimacy was like staring at the sun. They both made Nat reel. "You might even have prettier eyes than your brother."

Nat pawed at the bows that tied her bikini bottom. "What can I say? I'm rarer than that bit of heterochromia."

"Huh? What does that mean?"

"Nah. You had your one," he said, feeling brine drip down his fingers as he pinched Kitty's strings.

She guided his hands to pull the bows apart. It'd been a while since Nat had a cat in his bed. He'd left one behind in a house he no longer lived in.

▶▶

Nat fidgeted in the morning because doing nothing did not jive with his work ethic. He was relieved when he heard the excitable tenacity of pounds at the door. Nat could guess it wasn't Old Betty. He pulled on his boxers and lit a cigarette before confirming it was Rollins through the peephole and opened the door. There stood Bewilder's chief executive outlaw. She appeared forlorn, and mostly—if not entirely—sober.

"You look like shit," Nat said to her. Then he watched Rollins' demeanor relax after catching Kitty in her glory, rising to shut the bedroom door.

Rollin smirked and scanned Nat from head to toe. "Well, you look chipper," she said.

"So Dragnet, how'd you find me?" Nat asked and snapped his fingers. "Credit card trace?"

"Heh. Let's talk," she said.

Nat brought Rollins out to the balcony. She took off her hat to salute the sea. "Look. Between this and that—" she said, nodding to the ocean and pointing to the exterior wall of the bedroom, "I can see why you left." Rollins cleared her throat. "You coming back?"

"I don't know, am I?" Nat said.

"Well, your brother's fine," Rollins reported.

"Fucking, obviously," Nat said with a twinge of relief.

"We canceled the second show at Santa Monica," she said.

"Oh? I'm glad the ingrates had a day off, too." Nat stubbed his cigarette out.

"They couldn't do it without you, sonny. I'm gonna be real right now, not to be tough, but to be honest. They should've been able to. Full disclosure. I called in a favor to replace you. But there you have it. It all falls apart without you."

"Okay."

"So, what do you want?" Rollins said.

"Let's start with what you think you can give me," he replied.

Rollins threw out a number and some conditions.

Much like the rest of Nat's 24-hour AWOL, it ended up being better than he expected, and more than he ever would've asked for.

▶▶

After Rollins left, Nat found Kitty back in the bedroom with his Stone Roses T-shirt over nothing else. The shirt was a gift from Eleanor intended for his birthday, but was lost in transatlantic mail until Christmas.

"What happened?" Kitty asked.

"You take off that shirt right fucking now and I'll tell you," he said.

She obeyed and threw it at his face, an experience considerably more enjoyable than getting socked by an old Reebok. "Geez. Are you always so bossy?"

Nat put his hands on her knees and she peeled open her tanned legs. "No," Nat said. "But I think all that's about to change."

REACHING THE APEX WITH BOLERO: NO JACKETS REQUIRED

Linda Kaminski | *Blame the Youth* Magazine

August 20, 1994

Soda fountains pump under hieroglyphics inside the black pyramid while I wait for Bolero. They're late. Maybe they're stuck on the sluggish inclinators that have replaced elevators and climb the walls at an angle. Or perhaps they've taken the Nile River cruise that cuts through the lobby's hypnotic carpet. Las Vegas is riddled with stuttering wheels of fortune, inauthentic counterfeits, sad bastards, and overpriced relics. This place is precisely symbolic of

the guitar music scene from which Bolero
emerged unexpectedly to demolish.

Two years ago, the Luxor Hotel & Casino
was a trailer park, and Bolero was just
an unsigned band rehearsing in a storage
facility on Manhattan's ugly sister island. Now the resort is a haven for high
rollers, and high rollers are exactly what
Bolero has become since the release of
their thrashing debut album, *Light Up &
Shine On.* The band is a day away from the
26th annual Apex Music Awards. The occasion
will not be inside this monstrous apex, but
up the blazing strip at the MGM Grand. This
is the band's first award show invitation.
It's the first time anyone's been invited
to the Apex Awards with five nominations.

Bolero's bassist, John Sullivan—or "Sulky,"
as he is known for his demeanor—rolls his
eyes. Sulky is the first to arrive at the
Tut Hut, a food court where people mostly
drink and stay overstimulated on the casino
floor. He is annoyed that no one else is
here. He had to give up his place in line

for a virtual reality ride, and now pouts at his purple Crown Royal bag full of quarters.

Rhythm guitarist Greg Sullivan and drummer Keith "KP" Parker turn up next, carrying trays of chips. KP takes off his bucket hat to cover his impressive double-decker stacks of mostly black and orange chips. He attributes his tardiness to a "hot hand." Greg's fate was on the flip side, but he winks and insists he's "just in it for the cocktails and cocktail waitresses." Unlike the Dempsey brothers, there's no semblance between the Sullivan brothers. Greg is a hockey enforcer, whereas Sulky looks like my barista's mop.

Across the frenetic room, Jamie Dempsey is a magnet that attracts the eye. He staggers like a bonny prince with zero responsibility to rule. Bolero's frontman is talking to everyone, not just the few who approach him. He wears well a collarless button-down shirt and workman's pants, somewhere natural between a skater and a mod. Sulky jogs over to Jamie and herds him to the Tut Hut.

While Sulky is into the games centered
on virtual reality, the other assembled
bandmates seem quite satisfied with the
pleasures of their new reality, which is
centered on them. None more so than Jamie.
He's an ecstatic puppy looking for praise
and a bone. But like the puppy, he sometimes
nips at the hands that feed him.

Two days ago, Jamie walked off stage during
their concert in Santa Monica. The band then
canceled yesterday's show. Everyone samples
different excuses while wearing smirks.

"Technical difficulties."
"Scheduling conflict."
"Weather."
"Bad burritos."

It is by this point strange that Jamie's older brother, Nat Dempsey, Bolero's songwriter
and lead guitarist, is not present. They
don't seem to think he is going to make it.
They laugh and resample the same excuses.

"Technical difficulties."

"Scheduling conflict."

"Weather."

"Definitely burritos."

Conversations dwindle to juvenile ballbusting, disappointment that there are no showgirls around, and clashing critiques of the "Winds of the God" spectacle performed daily at the Luxor's Pharaoh theater.

"Sorry I'm late. What are we fighting about?" Nat Dempsey interrupts gingerly in denim with a serving tray of booze for the boys. He's escorted by Bolero's sturdy tour marm, who calls Nat "Bunny," and an enormous, bearded man who looks like he buried a few Pagan bikers before reforming to play Santa Claus at the mall.

There's a reaction of *en garde* with Nat's arrival. It's like the principal came into the classroom, though what principal drops a tray of Jack Daniel's served in Egyptology guest shop shooters? Nat tucks his sunglass-

es into his jean jacket pocket before
pulling up a chair to straddle. He's got
thick, dark eyebrows that seem to weigh
down his lids and fix a high in the sky,
eagle-sharp expression. When asked about
Santa Monica, Nat puts a stare on Jamie,
whom he sits across from at the now crowded
round table.

Nat asks Jamie pointedly, "Do you know what
happened?"

Jamie answers, "So long ago. I don't
remember."

Nat yawns and says, "Yeah, me neither."

Greg's posture relaxes at this exchange,
which I can only gather, shows that the
Dempseys have come to some coded resolution.
Then it's back to banter. With Bolero,
everything is a joke unless someone doesn't
find it funny, at this point, the joke is
subject to a dialectical debate Socrates
never would have imagined. Unless the odd

man out is Sulky, which, as an odd young
man, he usually is.

I discover that the boys in Bolero are an
intersection of beliefs and brothers. It
requires a level head and patience just to
be in the presence of their menacing doses
of camaraderie and bickering. Musically,
they see themselves as an intersection
of generations. Greg claims, "We got the
melodies of the sixties, the attitude of
the seventies, the excess of the eighties,
and the youth of fuckin' today."

The result is a debut record with vicious,
chromatic harmony that gets its cosmic
power from the natural laws of sound. It
all kicks off with the first track, "Rise
and Fine," a declaration that burns like
a deftly crafted cigar. You think the best
part is the start until you experience the
end. Scale that to 12 songs, and it clicks
why *Light Up & Shine On* is paced to be
one of the fastest-selling debut albums in
American history.

Nat pretends convincingly that he's not that impressed. "Not much honor taking the title from who, Guns'n'Roses?"

Bolero shares a similar appetite for destruction. They pathologically pick fights with all of their contemporaries, even bands like The Reverie who live under the same label. "No one's safe," Greg says and laughs. I can attest to this, as our evening may have involved manually recycling beer bottles and trouncing lifelike talking camels that were, quite frankly, asking for it.

Even with its softer brushes, *Light Up* should be branded with a warning label about its side effects to evoke a personal rebellion and a nihilistic *laissez-faire* attitude towards everything else.

It all started with hype. Bolero kicked off with a paid-in-spades strategy to launch the music video for their first single "Muse Box," taunting the airwaves to catch up. The concept was clever, and the execution was better. Under Rick Russell's direction, the video came across as silly and atmospheric without being gimmicky or the type of slick everyone is tired of.

"I was a bagger at a grocery store, so it was just like a trippy shift back at Waldbaums," says Jamie, who bags Frida Jones instead of her groceries in the video. It cannot go without saying that Frida Jones was brilliantly cast. She was unexpected as she has international recognition, and captivates as the epitome of Rolling Stones muse with her British roots and Bardot hair. Even I am not jaded enough to ignore that her chemistry with Jamie is electric.

Talking about the music video only interests Jamie, much like talking about the music only interests Nat. Soon, the bottle of Jack is empty. The band leaves the Tut Hut to dine at the casino's most upscale restaurant, ISIS. Initially, they are turned away because of the jacket requirement dress code. There is a joke to be made.

"What about a bolero?" Nat protests.

Now, the music industry is ripe with applying "cool" but meaningless monikers, but what *about* the name Bolero? Like the rest of the band's inventions, that information is kept close to Nat's chest. Disambiguated, the name Bolero curiously fits the band based on two hypotheses.

First, a bolero is commonly associated with a short jacket inspired by a matador's *chaquetilla*. In a bullfight, the matador must demonstrate control over the bull while risking his life to get close to it. Is Nat the matador? Is the bull fame, or is Jamie the bull? After all, it is historically complex to be brothers in a band.

The second hypothesis considers bolero as the genre of Latin music and movement. There is evidence of castanets, common in Spanish Bolero dances, subtly layered into the percussive outro of *Light Up*'s quieter spellbinder, "How She Found Me." The song's slower rhythmic structure is in ¾ meter, also common to bolero styling, which is both

romantic and punctuated with drama. In a
way, these two characteristics conceptual-
ize each of the Dempsey brothers' contributions to Bolero's music. In the least
obvious way, Nat is the romantic. Then,
in the most obvious way, Jamie brings the
drama.

When I tell them critics have described
Bolero's music as having a lot of hubris,
I get the reaction of sitting on a Whoopee
Cushion.

"You're gonna have to use simpler words,"
Nat says. "These guys weren't in school
that long." When asked about his own schooling, Nat seems offended by the assumption
that he is under- or over educated.

Greg begins to sing "We don't need no
education" like cement scraping to set
bricks in the wall. There are reasons the
vocals on Light Up are limited to the
Dempsey bloodline.

I can appreciate Nat's sparing and effective
backup vocals. He says this is on princi-
ple, because he doesn't want to imagine a
world with more than one Jamie. Therefore,
he won't stand for "overdubbing multiple
fucking Jamies to back himself."

But there's no contest about who the lead
singer is in this band. Prince Jamie will
never be king, but his voice rules. We hear
throughout the record that Jamie's voice's
ultimate strength is not its range but its
versatility. It takes exciting leaps from
snarling to soft, and close to fucking
far-out limbs. The best example of this is on
the third track, which they've released as
their second single, "That's Not My Name."
It's an exceptional, intriguing example of
talkback between lead vocalist and lead
guitar that layers well onto the alternating
tension of Jamie's singing, which emotes
between anger and acceptance. If Bolero's
first single, "Muse Box," wasn't still at
number one, "That's Not My Name" would've
claimed it. What a tasty predicament for
Bewilder Record's golden-or should we say
platinum-boys.

I doubted Bobbi Rollins earlier this year when she told me, "I just saw a band shoot the head off a snake." Many of us thought Bewilder Records had been relying on its street cred to bumble their way through the nineties before signing Bolero out of obscurity and investing in this debut that is both ripping and unignorable. The production and mixing were in the proficient hands and mad scientist mind of Remy Welsh. He gave *Light Up* exactly the power wash it needed to avoid clinical reproduction, flirt with commerciality, and demolish as much division between band and audience as possible for the immersive effect of experiencing sound. The band recorded in just weeks at Lochstock's infamous Balmaha Studio.

"Remy's a fucking menace just like us," says Jamie. "That's why we could trust him when he'd say to be disciplined, go with the mo. Get in and get out."

"I didn't want recording to end," Nat admitted. "I'd still be there now tinkering."

"You don't even want your *songs* to end," Greg jabs.

Nat laughs. "What can I say? I'm a sucker for an outro."

"Most of the time [the songs] just have to fade out while we're all still wailing," Sulky says.

"You're always wailing," Greg says.

"Brothers," says KP, the only man in the band without a brother. He has been busy playing No Limit with the casino's wine cellar. For someone who bashes things for a living, he's got a delicate nose that gravitates towards pinot noirs of peaking vintages. More common of drummers, there's a mercenary quality about KP. He's a little older, newly engaged to a psychoanalyst, and isn't part of the original Bolero lineup that formed in Hillside, New York (allegedly on

a dare by Diana Campbell, the lead singer
of the pop art group Girlcrush).

KP is from Bay Ridge, NY, and met Nat when
they were employed by a hairier band to
tour as techs for their respective weapons.
"Nat'd rip into how shitty that band was.
I could tell it was because he thought he
was better than them. So, I was interested
to see if that was true when I got a call
from him last year asking to try out. 'Try
out…' That little shit."

KP fills his mouth with an '83 Oregonian
Pinot and says, "This will still be good
in 25 years." What about Bolero's music? I
ask. "Oh, hell yeah."

No doubt, *Light Up* has sparks of imagination
and derives its inspiration from the good
grapes. The musical composition, though, is
sometimes more memorable and direct than
Nat's lyrical tendencies to be impression-
istic, evasive, or occasionally leaning on
cliches. He counters with a mixture of

defensiveness and humor when presented with examples, like sunshine and rain.

"Well, I'm a thinker, but people respond more to feelings. We can all feel the weather, right? If you wanna listen to lyrically pretentious bands junking up choruses with a philosophy or vocabulary lesson, listen to The Reverie."

Then, there's the reemerging imagery of dancing. "Well, I don't think Neil Young is much of a dancer either, but I saw him play live once, and that song about when you dance? I felt that."

Nitpicks aside, Nat's songwriting efforts are effective. Sometimes they really grip, no more so than in their first single "Muse Box," which is like the Energizer Bunny, effortlessly holding the top of the charts. The anthem rather universally evokes what dreams we carry with us as the blueprint to actualizing. There's a philosopher somewhere under Nat Dempsey's armor of sarcasm and streetwear.

The album closes strong with "Maybe Tomorrow." Jamie's voice sketches like an angel with a devil on his shoulder above completely overloaded acoustic guitars and synthesized strings played by Remy. Unlike the rest of the album, this song is the only one that stretched Balmaha Studio's arsenal. It's not perfect, but it's good and ambitious. "Maybe Tomorrow" is symphonic, all about the momentum of sound that builds over a puttering drum march. There's no chorus, but one is not missing, and the song fades out to this great refrain: "Maybe I won't miss yesterday if you'll have me tomorrow."

No one knows what Nat Dempsey and Bolero will do tomorrow, but maybe it wouldn't be reckless to bet a stack of KP's chips that they'll be walking away with at least a few statues.

That's hardly what they're after, though it's hard to say what they're after. Besides Nat's chase for something greater than he has yet to vocalize, they don't seem to be

driven by much more than a belief observed by
Jamie. "The universe had us all around with
nothing better to do and nothing we could do
better. It was fucking destiny, man."

Nat looks at me with his two-tone eyes like,
"See what I mean (to have a brother like
Jamie)?" and to an extent, I now do. There's
a moment of solidarity held in silence among
the otherwise mouthy bunch—an exceptional
feat for how much brown they've downed.
It's as if they're just coming to grasp the
sanctity, that this is their moment.

Come Sunday night's award show, the world
will be watching…

11

FRIDA

I T WAS NOT QUITE the morning of the Apex Music Awards when Frida woke to Jamie's laughter from the corridor. She could overhear him poorly attempting to whisper a slurry of thanks to an employee of the Luxor who'd led him back to their hotel suite. Frida lay still, listening to Jamie wobble about their room with the lights off. She heard his gargling of mouthwash before plopping atop the covers in his clothes. Frida continued to play sleep when he pulled her in softly for a cuddle and mumbled a "Missed you, babe" before sensing his body and breath shift to sleep. Frida cradled his hand wrapped around her, a reversal of how she'd clung to her fluffy cat, Starman, as a lonely in-betweener.

Frida sometimes shuddered at her past, when she'd subjected herself to violation and woken in beds to the loveless touch of men. Before Jamie, no man had offered her an instinctual feeling of safety in her body, that she was not betraying herself by giving it to someone else. All Jamie's other flaws seemed ancillary or endearing. For example, the absurd hour of his reentry into their bed after returning from an interview did not stir alarm or prevent her from joining in his peaceful slumber.

Several hours later, it was Frida's turn to move about whilst avoiding to wake Jamie. She had as many commitments as he did leading up to the night's big event, which began with a visit to see her friend, Nikki Wilshire. Nikki's parents were also parents of the studio network that produced the Apex Music Awards Show. The Wilshires would be among those hosting the pre-party in the ballroom of the MGM Grand before the evening's televised event. All the Vegas strip was crawling with musical contenders and their financiers, including Jamie's band and their label, Bewilder Records. Even the Wilshires were intrigued by Bolero and the record number of nominations they had received. She hoped Jamie wouldn't disappoint.

►►

Nikki shooed away the bellhop who'd escorted Frida along with her valet. The bellhop was at least the ninth employee who had implored Frida to "Have a *grand* day" from the time she had entered the MGM. Nikki's red hair was wrapped in jumbo curlers, and her body wrapped in a luxe lavender kimono. Concealer already covered the freckles on her nose, and who knows what had already gone up her nostrils.

"They're so annoying," Nikki said. "Have a grand day, have a *grand* day!" Smoke swirled from her ciggy, which dangled manically from its holder. She put it out dramatically into a half-eaten yoghurt and then sprawled herself on the chaise. "Like, smile, serve, shush, and buh-bye, people!"

Frida ignored Nikki's tirade and tended to her pyramid-shaped stack of black luggage.

"Excuse me. Did you bring the Luxor with you? What on earth are you doing with those body bags?"

Frida looked over at Nikki's arsenal of monogrammed Louis Vuitton trunks. "I don't know how you risk travelling with anything recognisable. I've had too many things nicked."

Inside Frida's discreet duffels were designer garment bags and boxes with free or loaned pieces she'd begun to air to weigh her options for today's events. Frida noticed Nikki eyeing the black Chanel cropped jacket with leather woven trim around its lapel and edges, with three pearl buttons on each cuff.

"Was that this spring's?" Nikki asked.

"It was a gift."

"Ugh, whatever. Karl and everyone at Chanel hates me because of Donna Martin." Nikki had named her pug after the *90210* character she most detested and related to in real life.

"I don't understand," Frida said.

"Donna Martin ate his cat's food when we were on the boat in Saint-Tropez, and getting more was this whole ordeal. Like, we're on a boat, people. Fish for it? Anyway, he hates me because of that. That and I don't speak French."

Of course, Karl's first language was German, and he also spoke English. But it was fruitless to suggest that it wasn't Nikki's monolingualism that did not translate in certain houses of fashion.

Frida presented the only item she'd hand picked, and held it against her shape. "What do you make of it?"

"A bolero? You clever bitch! I love it. Over what?"

Frida narrowed her finalists. More Chanel, the matching pale blue tweed bustier and high-waisted mini skirt, or a vintage cream-coloured satin and lace slip dress.

"Ugh, not the Stevie Nicks nightgown. So not you, babe."

"Oh? I quite like it. Just trying different things..."

"Is that how we explain Jamie?"

Frida frowned. "Don't be crass. This is his night. I'm absolutely chuffed to shy away."

"Um, hello. I'm not hearing that you're 'chuffed' for me," Nikki said. "Can you believe I'm presenting 'Best Music Video' with Naomi after that debacle last year? People still think we hate each other. I mean, I hate her as a person, but I love her as a friend. Anyway, if Bolero wins, it's totally because of your pussy power."

"That's a bit much," Frida replied.

"What's Jamie up to, anyway?"

"I haven't a clue. I left him to sleep." Frida withheld her concerns that Jamie hadn't been himself since Nat left the band and Bolero cancelled their shows in Los Angeles. As of this morning, Frida had left Jamie without knowing how the rest of the band would handle attending the awards without Nat.

"My parents are like, fetish excited to meet Bolero," Nikki said, flagrantly admiring the arch of her brows in a compact mirror. "They're like vampires."

"Strange, really."

"What's Nat like? I'm bored of Marcus," Nikki said.

"What about Adnan?" Frida asked.

"Ugh. He was way too rich to be so poorly groomed. I think he's in Brunei, anyway. Is Nat anything like Jamie?"

"A bit of the same humour. Nat's quite witty. Much more wry, though." The truth was, Frida knew little about Nat. She sensed distance and time would be the best ways to warm him towards her. It seemed unlikely that Nikki and Nat would hit it off, but Frida believed love could make anyone a melt.

"143?" Nikki had intercepted Frida's buzzing pager. "Ew!"

Frida excused herself to phone Jamie back, tucking herself between the drapes and away from Nikki's bewitched ogle.

"I didn't want to wake you before I left. How did it go with the journalist last night?" Frida asked.

"Oh, Kaminski? We buried her," Jamie said.

"Pardon?"

"I don't even know." Jamie laughed. "Last I knew, she was running through the hallways thumping on doors, yelling for Rollins. That was after she got stuck on one of those giant llamas and spit on the security guards."

In the background, Frida heard someone say it must've been the belly ring.

"What must've been the belly ring?" she whispered to him.

"Oh yeah, she kept saying she swallowed one."

"Jamie, how does one—"

"She and Greg were doing body shots off this dancer," Jamie said.

"That's revolting," Frida said.

"I didn't do it!"

"Is she okay?" Frida asked.

"The dancer's fine."

"No, the journalist," said Frida.

"Kaminski? Oh yeah. Probably. Amazing fucking night."

"And, is Nat—"

"Yeah. Big bro showed up last night. All good."

"Did you see my gift?" she asked.

"Damn, stop beating me to the punch. I'm gonna thank you. Now I can count down 'til I see you later."

▶▶

It was near showtime. Frida was staring at her peeptoes and Nikki's pumps planted in the vast jungle of the MGM's hideous but soft-underfoot carpeted ballroom. Nikki was babbling among their model brigade, energised by sneaky spoonfuls of powder. Frida had abstained. As it was, the scene—the crowd's gestures and posturing, the clash of formal and funny attire—overwhelmed her. Jamie was flicking like a pinball between her and everyone else. He was so natural and buoyant in this environment. The Wilshires had fawned and drooled with haughty laughter over Jamie's shiny status and class mannerisms. Who would believe these were the same monsters she'd witnessed hold a grudge over an untucked shirt?

Frida was glaring about when she found herself in Nat's path. He looked handsome but a bit cagey, offering her a terse partial embrace.

"You look nice," he said. "Smart jacket."

"Congratulations," Frida said, too shy to add that she was relieved to see him.

"Nah. None of that unless we actually win, right?"

Nikki interrupted. "You must be Nat."

"You must be trouble," Nat said. Nikki had been wedging her hand between her recently augmented breasts to better secure a pendant of cocaine.

"This is my dear friend, Nikki Wilshire," Frida said.

"Oh, the Wilshires. Your parents must be thrilled you're in charge of the party favors," Nat said, then turned back to Frida to say, "Hey, I saw Jamie's watch. I hate to break this to you, but Jamie can't tell time."

Frida blushed.

"That's funny," Nikki said.

"Not funny enough to laugh, though?" Nat said.

"I like that," Nikki said and began huddling them together for one of the event photographers.

"Yeah? Well, I like whatever this dress is," Nat said to Nikki as the camera flashed.

"That's the idea," Nikki said.

"Very, um, regal interpretation of punk. Are these fucking gold safety pins?"

Nikki shimmied her hands down the body-con cut dress. "It's Versace."

"Ah, I hate the French," Nat said.

Frida masked her chortle as a gentle cough.

"Versace is Italian," Nikki said.

"I was joking," he said.

Nikki laughed.

"See?" Nat said. "Isn't laughing better than saying something is fucking funny?"

"You're good," Nikki said to him.

"You wouldn't still be talking to me otherwise." Nat then excused himself to talk to a petite, tanned beauty with darker wild curls. She looked a bit like a mermaid.

Frida and Nikki expertly repositioned themselves to eavesdrop on their conversation.

"I was looking for you," she said to him.

"Is that a bikini top?" Nat asked her.

"I got it on the strip."

"The strip club?"

When the woman did not reply, Nat said, "I'm sorry. I'm in a mood."

"You've had a lot of those since we left Cali."

"They're not all bad, are they?" Nat rubbed his chin.

"Look, I'm gonna sit with Howard and the New York team. See you around," she said and left.

"Was that your date?" Nikki asked Nat in a way that communicated judgement and jealousy.

"No, that was my chauffeur," Nat replied. He smoothed two fingers over his right brow and then excused himself once more.

"Well, I'm outtie too," Nikki announced as Jamie returned with two glasses of champagne.

Frida loosely held the tilted flutes while Jamie dizzied her with a snog. His palms thawed the skin of her hips.

"Is it time already?" Jamie said.

"You tell me," Frida said and tapped her finger on the face of his 60s-era Smiths W10 wristwatch. She bought it because it had reminded her of the military-style jacket Jamie wore when he first visited her in London.

"I told you, you gotta help me set it." Then Jamie was summoned by a wave from Bobbi Rollins' pork-pie hat. "Be back in a minute."

There was a brief flickering of lights, the first silent stage direction for everyone to find their places within the theatre for the show's start. Alone, Frida dropped her head to examine her ankles. She spotted a slight chip of lacquer on her pedicured toe. Would it remain unseen by others? Her toe folded, ashamed. What if she were invited up on stage if Bolero won for Best Video? That wasn't typical, and she wouldn't dare join them, but would the offer be nice? Frida pulled her arms across her body, and her fingerprints traced the textured trim along the waist of her bolero.

Then, a longer flickering of lights. When Frida lifted her head from her daze, she had lost sight of Jamie. Some moved about, though Frida stayed put. She had established herself as the type to wait to be collected. As she was searching for Jamie, she spotted Nat. He'd reentered one of the exit-only doors, which blended with the wall. He gulped and jerked the neck of his white collar and then walked in his determined style that projected a desire to remain unbothered. Even with very famous people, he politely avoided shaking hands.

Frida continued to watch Nat navigate the room, almost assuming his movements. For instance, she'd lost her breath when, abruptly, Nat came to full stop. His eyes had gone from evasive to fixed on what might have been a ghost but for the bliss that looked to bloom in him. First, in the thin happy creasing of skin below his stare, and then with the brimming show of his teeth typically stored with emotions in a sealed mouth. Nat's shoulders and head relaxed back, like a step into the sun.

Frida traced Nat's vision line to the source of his transformation. It was a girl Frida had never seen before, more likely to be a dear friend than an estranged lover. She was far away from Nat, swirling a straw in her drink, and stood alone at the long white bar. Frida looked back at Nat. He was on the move again, now like a train towards the girl who still had not seen him. Frida's heart raced with Nat's pace, her curiosity burning away like cooking wine into a reduction of hope.

And then Frida's heart sank. Nat had halted again. His face formed a pale grimace, as if he'd bitten the inner flesh of his cheek. He surveyed his surroundings as though pleading not to have been seen. That's when Nat realised Frida had witnessed it all, which startled her to the onset of tears. The fit girl with tousled honeyed hair was no longer alone by the bar. She was being held between the arms of another.

Then came the third, forceful flickering of lights and halt of music.

It was showtime.

12

JAMIE

AFTER THE LIGHT STROBING kicked into high gear, Jamie shot like a hammered salmon upstream. He loved the adrenaline and an excuse to shove around the ushers and assistants herding all the celebrity cattle from the pre-party into the theater. Jamie was supercharged from his day-long drunk and ready to bring on the night as soon as he had his girl by his side.

Luckily, Rollins' PA helped reunite Jamie with Frida. Jamie didn't understand why Frida looked so melty, like she'd just seen a mangled bunny. It couldn't have had anything to do with Jamie, which made him eager to twist her out of the bad mood. Frida often responded to his efforts, which gave Jamie a deep satisfaction that he was doing something right in a way he didn't seem to get right for anyone else other than his mom.

Jamie took Frida's hands and rubbed them like he was trying to start a fire. "What happened?"

"It's nothing," she said.

Jamie was obsessed with her face and how fast her expressions could change. He tucked her into him, and they marched behind the PA's long ponytail that whipped around like a lasso and wrangled most of the Bolero and Bewilder Records crew. This included Jamie, Frida, Rollins, KP, and his fiancée, Lindsay.

Rollins shoved her elbow into Jamie's billowy street jacket. "These video game biceps ready to curl up them statues tonight, kid?"

Jamie flexed.

After breaching the entrance into the theater, they were guided by the hypnotic floor to two reserved tables near the raised stage. The stage was uplit with purples and showcased a giant 3D build-out of block letters for the Apex Music Awards. Awards were a joke, but if he was up for one, what was the point in losing?

"We're gonna sweep this thing, right?" Jamie said.

"See how close you are to that stage? Telltale you'll be getting up there to collect," Rollins said to him.

"Dude, KP's already swept this trip in fuckin' coin and casino comps," Greg said.

"That true? How much did you score?" Rollins inquired.

"That's between me and whatever I lowball to Uncle Sam," said KP.

"Keith!" Lindsay nudged KP. She looked cool but crazy in her black mesh long sleeves.

"I'm just kidding," KP reassured her, twisting the black hairs that fell to the sides of Lindsay's angular face. "It's all gonna be for that Italian wedding, *belladonna*."

"When is the wedding?" Frida asked.

"Early October," Lindsay replied. "The schedule slows down before their rehearsals start, so we'll squeeze it in. Getaway to a Tuscan villa or something."

"That's fabulous," Frida said.

Jamie kissed Frida's hand. He'd had regular impulses to marry Frida since the night they met, but he was young, and who was he kidding?

Jamie realized he had way too much energy to sit at this table set for dinners no one was gonna eat. What a waste. Actually, KP and Greg would always eat. They were the hungriest mother fuckers in Bolero. Sulky was too much of a headcase for food, like the bony girl you'd see in an after school special on TV, staring in the mirror imagining fat. Nat was fussy, too. Their mom, Joanie, always said that Jamie was the better eater. If Joanie were there, she'd probably wear her pearls unless their old man pawned them. Jamie decided to have Frida pick out an expensive strand to buy for his mom tomorrow.

"What are you thinking about, love?" Frida asked him.

"Shopping." Jamie laughed, amused at his own truth. "Nah, just kidding. I kinda wish Joanie was here."

"She'll be watching from home, no?" Frida said.

"Yeah, yeah. We got her hooked up with the whole entertainment system earlier this week for it and all... You know she doesn't give a fuck about all this, though." Jamie said this with pride in his posture.

"And you don't care either?" Frida asked.

"Fuck no."

Frida leaned forward with her cigarette, inviting him to light it. This always turned him on. "Are you taking a piss?" she asked.

"Not a drop," he said, emphatically making the 'p' sound pop. Frida rubbed her face into his neck, giving it a soft nibble.

Jamie called over one of the servers circling. The kid was probably Jamie's age, but he reminded Jamie of himself a few years ago when he wore the same itchy, cheap suit as a cater waiter. Jamie gave the kid a couple hundred to drop extra Champagne and a few bottles of Jack on their table.

"Serving's a way better gig than washing dishes," Jamie whispered to Frida.

"Better than this gig?" she said and dropped her arms back, which cued him to take off her jacket and place it on the back of her chair.

Underneath the coat, her stomach was bare between the two pieces of blue couchy material she was wearing.

"Nah. This gig would be perfect if I could keep taking things off," he said. "Where'd KP and Lindsay go? And where the fuck is Nat?"

"KP and Lindsay are over there talking to some—"

"No fucking way!" Jamie exclaimed. He locked his slippery hand into Frida's before dragging her to The Reverie's table, where Will Hawking and their girl Ele were hovering.

"Ele!" Jamie howled, disrupting her reunion with Lindsay and KP. Jamie lifted her for a rough twirling hug. When he let her down, he said in disbelief, "Are you for real? What the fuck is up?"

"I know, this is insane," Ele said, blinking makeup out of her eye.

"You seen Nat yet?" he asked.

Ele scrunched up her hair like she did. "No. Kind of a story there."

Frida and Will had now flanked their reunion.

Jamie pulled Frida close to introduce her. "This is my fuckin' top class, knockout girlfriend, Frida."

"Oh dear. We'll have to workshop that," Frida said.

"Your girlfriend? No way!" Ele hugged Frida, nearly picking her up and swinging her around like he'd just done to Ele. "I'm so happy to meet you!" she said in her animated way by gripping people's hands and gleaming into their eyes. It was different from the chill nuzzling affection Frida showed in public.

Ele tried to introduce Will to Frida, but Jamie interrupted. He bumped Will's shoulder with some friendly bravado. "This guy is old news, man," Jamie said.

Will ignored Jamie and went in on Frida for one of those British double kisses. "I'm glad we're meeting. It looks like we'll be doing this campaign—"

"So how d'ya like that?" Jamie interrupted Will again. "Being up for the same category? Best singer?"

Will acted all tired and fake modest, like. "Yep. Something must've been in the water at Lochstock."

"I don't even remember drinking water at Lochstock. Anyway, Ele, you look different," Jamie said to her. "Barely recognized you."

"Bullshit. Is that good?" she asked, smoothing out the bottom of her black dress.

Jamie'd seen plenty of Ele's skin over the years at the Hillside Pool. But she'd even skipped prom to avoid a dress, and now was looking like a legit babe with whatever bra was pushing her goods out of this one.

"Besides the company you're keeping? Definitely." Jamie laughed.

"Fuck off, Jamie." Ele shoved him.

The lights completely dimmed, but for the floor, and ceremonious music began to play.

"Oh, no! Do you think I'll see you guys later?" Ele asked. "I still wanted to—"

"I'm sure that'll depend," Will said, motioning Ele back to their seats with his hand on her back.

"Depend on what?" Jamie said. "If the better man wins?"

Will huffed. "Whatever you say, Jamie."

"Nice meeting you all," Frida said, all hunched over like Princess Diana, obeying the escorts back to the table for the start of the show.

"That was an awfully long hug," Frida whispered to him.

Jamie scoffed. "Nah. Ele is fuckin' family."

By the time they'd returned, Nat was at the table facing the stage. Jamie shouted to Nat across the tall pillar candles. "Never believe it, man. Ele is over there. Sittin' pretty with The Reverie and shit!"

Nat just nodded. All deadpan like that wasn't crazy, which was crazy.

Some theme music started, cuing Rosie O'Donnell and Adam Sandler to enter the stage in drag versions of each other. Sandler came out in one of those red-and-white softball uniforms from *A League of Their Own*, and O'Donnell was dressed like the *SNL* character, "Opera Man."

"Ele is your family?" Frida tried to question Nat over the sounds of the opening skit.

"Eleanor. Yeah, no. She is *like* family," Nat replied while taking the sunglasses out of his shirt pocket to put on. Why didn't Jamie think of bringing his shades?

"Oh. Ele is Eleanor. I thought she was quite nice," Frida said.

"Ele is the best," Lindsay said, and KP agreed while ferociously eating his Caesar salad.

"Am I the only one who thinks it's fucked up that she's over there and didn't even tell you?" Sulky said. "She wouldn't even be here without us."

"Huh. Never thought of it like that," Jamie said, scratching his chin, already stubbled since the afternoon's shave. As relentless as Jamie's facial hair was, he liked that it added an edge to the boyish appeal he had in spades.

Lindsay crossed her covered arms defensively. "How do you figure that?"

"Cause she wouldn't have met The Reverie or Will if she wasn't already at Lochstock with us," said Sulky.

"Quit stirring shit." KP tossed his half-eaten dinner roll at him.

"Can everyone just shut up?" Nat blew out one of the pillar candles in front of him, splattering wax onto Sulky.

Sulky shrieked. His reaction gained him no sympathy but attention from some surrounding tables, including the skinny, melting rock stars with dyed black hair, adorned in lots of frills and rings, next to them.

"Damn, those guys look so fucking old," Jamie said. That could never be him, not in millions of years or dollars.

"They look like they're made of the same wax in these candles, man." KP poked his finger in the drippings. "Trippy."

As the show continued, it became harder to talk, except during the commercial breaks. This made everyone get more wasted because they had to be quiet. The best way for Jamie to be quiet was to be drinking. But the sure way for Jamie not to be quiet was to be drunk.

Early in the night, the drummer from Nirvana got up to introduce a tribute to Cobain, who killed himself the same week Bolero went to number one. People teared up, even Frida. They had some string orchestra do a medley of some of their biggest songs, all the while this video played of him through the years. How did people not wanna live? This guy even had a kid. What a buzzkill.

Afterwards, Rosie came back out to cut the somber mood. "Now I'd like to welcome two catwalking clothes hangers who probably hate each other as much as they hate food. They can't even *stomach* a last name. Heyo! See what I did there? Anyway, here's supermodels Nikki and Naomi to present the category of 'Best Music Video.'"

Jamie watched Frida Wimbledon clap for her friends as they walked dramatically to the podium. Nikki read Bolero's "Muse Box" among the nominees. Jamie's senses blurred. The girls then announced "Muse Box" in unison, and a vibration of applause summoned Bolero's table to rise.

"Here we go, boys," KP said, putting pressure on Jamie's chair to pull it out.

Jamie and the rest of the band clustered together, floating on heartbeats and snickers, with Nat at the helm. Once they arrived, Jamie laughed at Nikki for popping the collar on Nat's shirt. On stage, everyone was bigger. Jamie turned his back on the audience to point and stare at their music video on the big screen.

"Well, this isn't even about the music, so it doesn't mean that much to us," Nat said, standing too far away from the mic. "But thanks to our people for hooking us up with director Rick Russell so my brother Jamie could relive his old job back at the grocery store and earn us this... very uniquely shaped award."

Applause and music anticlimactically signaled Bolero's stage exit. Nat handed the award to Greg.

"It's like a sword for your anus," Greg said and then passed it along to KP.

"A crystal butt plug," KP said.

"Let me see." Sulky took it from KP.

KP suggested, "Maybe we can gamble with it later."

Backstage, Nikki called Jamie a dumbass for not thanking Frida for starring in the video. Naomi agreed and pawed his face with her clawlike fingernails. But Jamie was impenetrable at the moment. He was batting a thousand.

When they got back to their table, Frida gave Jamie a congratulatory kiss, then turned to continue her bridal conversation with Lindsay. In less than another bottle of Jack, Bolero went back to back to accept awards for 'Breakout Artist' and the hat-trick, 'Song of the Year.'

Jamie brought his drink and his mouth to the podium for that one, telling the world to "Get ready. This ain't the apex, it's just the summit."

"This is what it's about—the music," Nat echoed.

Jamie got the guys in a huddle on stage before breaking to snatch the statue from Nat. Jamie motioned to Greg to go long and then gave it a QB toss. Greg dove to catch it, skidding under the base of the stage curtain. After they made it down the stairs, Jamie hopped onto Greg's back and covered his eyes to test his blind navigation to get back to their table.

When they returned, Jamie played musical chairs and sat next to Nat. "We're taking on the world, brother!"

"For better or worse," Nat said.

"Grim shit, man." Jamie pinched the creases of his mouth with disappointment. "Already forgetting we all stepped up for you and acted nice for that music journalist and shit."

"Acting nice? She got thrown out of the hotel. What should I be thanking you for?" Nat said.

"Why the fuck can't you enjoy this shit?" Jamie said.

"I am," Nat argued. But Jamie knew his brother. Nat was heated underneath his cold front.

Next, Sammy Hagar came out to present 'Best Male Singer.' When Jamie's name was announced among the nominees, he pointed to himself and nodded, tongue wagging at one of the camera operators wheeling around.

"I'd sell out Bolero so fuckin' quick to be in Van Halen," Greg said.

Nat joked, "If you were good enough to be in Van Halen, I'd fucking fight to keep you around!"

Jamie was revved up like a muscle car, squeezing Frida's femur under the table, waiting to hear—

"The winner is Will Hawking from The Reverie."

Jamie's grip on Frida's thigh went limp. Frida pouted blankly. Lindsay ripped a bitchy cackle. Nat hand signaled, "Check, please."

"Boring phony. I sing like that on my day off," Jamie said. He was further annoyed that no one praised him for controlling his juvenile desire to trip Will when he passed Bolero's table to collect up on stage.

The next production break seemed to drag on forever. Jamie's trusty server brought over more booze, but the whole edge of the awards show had gotten dull for him. The spectator sit-still thing had Jamie's mind and legs bouncing like they were keeping a millisecond beat.

"Can we just fuckin' leave already?" Jamie asked.

"You're out of your mind," Nat said.

"I wish I were out of my mind... I'm bored out of my mind," Jamie declared.

"It's almost the end of the show," Sulky said. "We're still up for 'Album of the Year.'"

KP's eyes bulged as he pointed to the stage. "Oh no fucking way," he said.

A wiry pop king in a toy soldier costume walked out to present the last award. The audience offered him a mixture of awkward and forced applause due to recent allegations. A quick video cut through clips of the nominees. His mousey voice announced Bolero as the winner. Everyone shot up in an ovation. "Muse Box" began to blare over the PA, and confetti dropped. Frida's lips slipped right off the corner of Jamie's mouth before she backed away from him and the incoming chaos of Rollins, and the rest of their Bewilder family now crowded around the table to clank glasses.

KP was the first to say, "Yo, I'm not fuckin' going up there."

"Dissidence, eh?" said Nat.

"Yeah, fuck that." Greg pounded his open palm into a fist.

Even Sulky spit enough hot air to put out the remaining candles on the table.

Nat turned to Rollins. "What's the fallout if we bail?"

The clock was rapidly ticking down on their 30-second timeout.

Rollins shut her eyes and swirled her fingers around her temples for a psychic reading. "Corporate loss, then rebound. Critic split. Media blitz. Hype? Sales? Cred? I'd guess we win twenty-fuckin'-fold."

"Those are my kind of odds," KP said and slapped Rollins five.

Nat turned to Jamie, asking for his younger brother's advice for possibly the first time in his life, to which Jamie pulled Nat by the back of his head until their foreheads merged.

"At the end of the day, I don't give a shit," Jamie said.

Nat guffawed. "At the start of the day you didn't give a shit!"

"Alright, let's fuckin' bounce!" Jamie declared, and they broke like a basketball team planning to shoot a blooper reel.

The crowd's ovations derailed to a smattering of confusion and surprise over Bolero's mutiny. "Muse Box" had now abruptly mixed into some weird elevator music signaling the show's emergency production break.

"Pinnacle shit!" Rollins said while forcefully bumping the release bar of the nearest exit.

13

ELEANOR

E LEANOR DIDN'T EXPECT THAT she'd return to New York from Las Vegas with an invitation to interview with Aja Green, an incredible photographer she had applied to work for over a year ago. Her excitement nearly eclipsed suspicion. So far, the experience was weird.

"Light," Aja said, dryly scanning Eleanor's work.

"Well, I actually wanted the exposure to be like—" Eleanor protested as delicately as possible to this icon.

"No no," Aja corrected her. "As in, there is not much here."

"Oh, right. Sorry," Eleanor replied, then added, "Well, most of my experience is in film production. I'm still waiting for the last campaign I worked on to come into print and—"

"I like that you worked in Europe," Aja interrupted. "And not like 'family vacation' or 'study abroad' Europe. I mean, who goes to Dresden?"

It was Leipzig, but Eleanor did not attempt to correct Aja again. "Well, it was a good experience… I learned to trust my instincts, especially because of the language barri—"

"Chill," Aja said, halting Eleanor's remarks with her hand and dead-end expression. "This isn't a real interview."

"Okay." Eleanor relaxed the rigidity of her spine, but was no less intimidated by Aja's claim that this was somehow not intense.

"Look, I need someone who follows orders, wears black, never sleeps, and never sleeps with anyone we work with. Got it?"

"I sometimes sleep," Eleanor shared as a truth with the delivery of a nervous joke.

"Fine." Aja agreed, like that was a negotiated term.

"Fine?" Eleanor repeated.

"Yeah, fine," Aja said. "Trial starts next week. You'll be in touch." Aja motioned Eleanor to the door. She had already diverted her attention to neatly arranged contact sheets and contracts.

"Really? Okay, great. Thank you." Eleanor shot up and gathered her things to leave. "If you want, I can still send over that—"

"Bye," Aja issued, containing Eleanor from her post-hire jabber.

Outside Aja's studio, the dirt of the city's floor rustled to part ways. Eleanor's return to New York had arrived along with the teasing gusts of autumn, which tempered the hot trash steeped in summer. The city didn't feel like home as much as the street grid was part of her footprint. Eleanor wanted to scream with relief before swallowing her anticipation for the night to come. Last week she patched things up with Nat, but only superficially at McSorley's when everyone was around. Tonight would be just the two of them, something that hadn't happened since before *Light Up & Shine On* was even recorded.

When Eleanor was in Germany, she and Nat barely spoke. There were many explanations she reasoned contributed to that, but it sometimes kept her up at night to know if there was a main reason. What Eleanor knew was that she missed Nat unequivocally. And he did not know because she had not told him, nor had she told him about what happened in Santa Monica, or how it hurt her to watch him act like they were strangers in Vegas.

Eleanor hit the streets to get back to her new apartment. She grabbed a Snapple at a newsstand and was astounded by the quilted display of magazines, from respectable periodicals to rags, almost all with Bolero on their covers. The noise from the Apex Awards still hadn't died down. Eleanor picked up a *Blame the Youth* magazine to browse, drawn in by the photos that had almost caricature shots of Bolero in former jobs they'd had before their skyrocket rise. At one point, everyone but KP worked at the same strip mall. Sulky was at the pet store. Greg tore tickets at the movie theater. Jamie was the self-proclaimed hottest grocery bagger the world had ever seen. Nat lasted a single shift at Guitar Center to purchase a haul of gear before he was fired, forever altering their employee discount policy.

The guy at the newsstand heckled her for browsing. "You read, you buy," he said.

▶▶

It was seven o'clock. Eleanor imagined Nat standing outside her door as long as she'd been standing inside, waiting for the time to be just right.

One knock, followed by two faint taps.

She thumbed the deadbolts and chain lock, then opened the door to her new place. It was a 5,000 square foot upper deck of a building in Hell's Kitchen that everyone called the Roller Rink, or the Rink. It was like a boarding house for young women freelancing in volatile or exotic industries. B-models, artists, party promoters, fire dancers, musicians, street cred-seeking trust funders, and Eleanor.

Nat looked better than ever, but she sensed a nervous current when she hugged him and felt his kiss slip to where her jaw met her neck.

"Happy Birthday," she said.

"You know, I almost got caught in that elevator," Nat said.

"Oh shit. I've heard that happens. I always do the walk up," she explained.

"That's like five flights?"

"I got used to eight in Leipzig."

"No kidding," he said in a way that seemed to withhold a compliment.

Eleanor walked Nat past all the storage lockers and into the belly of the Rink with its beaten planks and high ceilings. Lingerie and dresses were line drying in front of a wall of industrial windows.

"Jesus, what is this place, a brothel?" Nat said. "Don't let Greg or Jamie here. It'd be like foxes in a henhouse."

"Diana got me a room here."

"Diana Diana? Campbell? So it is a brothel," Nat said.

Eleanor rolled her eyes. "Diana and Lara from Girlcrush both live here."

"You know that's gonna be a problem, right?"

"You think so?"

"Consider me an oracle," Nat replied. "Anyway, I can't talk too much shit on your place. Before they forced me into The Gibson, I was crashing at Bewilder's HQ."

"Only you would be forced out of squatting in alphabet city to live in a classy hotel." Eleanor walked them through saloon doors into a kitchenette that was almost impossibly small to function. "So you haven't been with Karen for a while, then?"

"Yeah, no. I told you. That ended even before we shot 'Muse Box.'"

"I guess I forgot," she said.

"Well, I don't know what that's supposed to mean. But I get it. I mean, Karen was right that all this—I mean, we were just over."

"Well, Karen was always smarter than you," Eleanor said.

"A quality I continue to strive for in all my relationships," he said.

"With that criterion, you'll become more promiscuous than Jamie."

"There she is."

"Do you think I could go see Karen next time I'm in Hillside?"

Nat hesitated. "Can you do me a favor and let that one breathe a little?"

"Yeah. Course. Drinks?"

"Immediately," he said.

Eleanor bumped Nat's head on a cabinet door she'd opened to get glasses, then continued to clumsily make gin and tonics. It was the first time she'd bought ice or limes.

"Which room is yours?" he asked, preempting their journey to her thin-walled bedroom down the hall.

"Yikes," he said. It was a fair reaction. It wasn't nice. It was temporary. She had a bed without a frame, a scarf-covered lamp for the occasion, and a citrine velveteen armchair she'd inherited from the previous lodger. Everything messy was kicked into a shallow closet and everything valuable was locked in her steamer trunk. "I'm only relieved that you can't open the windows to jump out and kill yourself."

"Fuck off, rich boy."

Nat grinned. He took off his Levi's jacket and reclined onto her bed, keeping his feet politely off the edge. He picked up the *Blame the Youth* magazine she had been reading earlier without commentary. It was a moment she wished she could keep. His face buried in a magazine with his face, his hip bones defining an appealing trail above the loose waist of his jeans.

"Those photos are so amazing," Eleanor admitted. "I actually have big news…"

"Yeah?"

"Aja Green hired me this morning to be her assistant."

"Aja? That doesn't surprise me," Nat said without looking up from the spread.

"Really? I was fucking surprised." Eleanor took a sip of her drink. The cool quinine refreshed her throat like a pool dip on a day the heat won't break.

"You've got a great eye," he said. "I mean, both of them are good," he mumbled into his glass.

The gin hit Eleanor with a flush to the face. "Is that just a way to compliment yourself?"

"What, cause I picked your shots to use for the cover of *Light Up*? No way. That wasn't a favor to you." Nat closed the magazine and tossed it at her. "I wouldn't just give away the cover of my album. I want those on the shelves forever."

"Okay, I believe you. What was it like being interviewed by Linda Kaminski?"

"Ha! Kaminski was fucking fantastic. You know she got so tuned up she didn't make it to the Apex Awards? Can you believe that? She actually did not show up to cover us at the show."

"What happened?"

"I don't know. I called it quits before her. The last I saw, she was getting escorted out of the Luxor for climbing up these talking camels. It was a fiasco. What was your take on the article?"

"I loved it. You know, now that I think about it, I actually love that it doesn't cover the awards. It's all about the like, anticipation and the backstory."

"The music," Nat said.

"Yeah, that's why it's good. It wasn't some melodramatic Bolero explosion distracting me. No offense. It felt more important," Eleanor said, moving onto the bed and leaning against the brick wall. "And I love that she called you out—like your lyrics about the weather and the dancing. You do not dance!"

"I dance," Nat said.

"Beyond your singular move? Staring at your feet and waving one hand up? Let alone the idea of you dancing with anyone else... please."

"It's a song! It's fucking feeling. Do you give this much shit to Will for their lyrics about, about magic carpet time travel in space and shit?"

"Okay, okay."

Eleanor got up to change the subject and refill their drinks. On her return, she felt ready to air select grievances.

"You know, that was really a prick move ignoring me in Vegas," she said.

"Oh yeah?" Nat fluffed her pillow behind his head, almost like he was excited, getting cozy for the confrontation. "I was a prick? I don't think anyone deserved a fucking award for the way they acted that day."

"Yet you got four. Seriously though, what was that about?" she probed.

"Look, it wasn't about you. But to be fair, I hadn't seen you in months—heard from you in weeks—come to think of it, I've never, in our decades of knowing each other, even seen you outside the Tri-State area. So fuck me for being taken aback to see you all glammed up on this big, stupid night with our fuckin' rivals, no less."

"Rivals?"

"Whatever, you know what I mean," he said.

"Well, you looked pretty happily preoccupied," she said.

"Yeah right," he said, dipping his brows to frown.

"You know. It wasn't supposed to play out like that. I came to see you," she told him.

"Came to see me where?"

"Santa Monica," she said.

"What are you talking about?"

"When I knew I was going to come to the Apex Awards, I didn't want that to be the first time—I wanted to surprise you beforehand at your show at that Pier Fest... Second night."

"Fuck," Nat said.

"Yeah. I made this big deal to rush and get there and showed up to find you canceled? I looked like a fucking idiot vouching for you guys and dragging Will through the desert twice in two days."

"When you put it like that—" Nat paused. He slouched his shoulders, which she took to show some sorrow for his part in the disconnect.

"When you put it like that, you're an asshole," Eleanor said.

"Fair enough. But from my perspective, were you not a little bit of an asshole, too?"

"Not even!" she said, but in a way he would know that she agreed.

"Fine. Sorry. So, how was your time in California?"

"You know it sucked," she admitted.

Nat laughed. "Well, I guess ruining your time with Will is reason enough for me to apologize for being an asshole."

"What happened to you in California?"

"Haven't you read up in the magazines?" he said.

"Fuck off." Eleanor threw her issue of *BTY* back at him.

"Where to begin," Nat said. "I've certainly told the story a few different ways... but I don't really know. I'm pretty certain I didn't want to break up the band or anything. But I think I needed to know how it would feel to walk away. It was an important lesson—for me to know that I want this, but I could take it or leave it if it doesn't go the right way."

"You could take it or leave it like that? I don't believe you," she said.

"Well, maybe you'll be around the next time I'm tested to see for yourself." Nat finished his drink. "These are really delicious." He crackled on an ice cube. "This is what Frida orders when she's not sustaining on cigarettes and a saltine."

"Wow! How have we not talked about Jamie's girlfriend? I mean, Frida Jones."

"Girlfriend? Is that what he said?" Nat asked. "You know, I wouldn't have a bad thing to say about her if it wasn't for the fact that she's dating Jamie. That's just mental. Anyway, I think California all comes down to thinking I'd teach Jamie and everyone else a lesson in leaving."

"Did it work?"

"For the most part. I feel like a million bucks. Maybe closer to two, if you know what I mean." Nat winked at her and put his hands behind his head.

"Okay, Billy Joel, don't get too relaxed. We have dinner plans."

"Oh bummer. Really? I was hoping we were just gonna drink here, maybe order a pizza," Nat said.

"I should've known you'd still want the same things," she said.

"I'm a simple man," he replied.

Eleanor sprung up and lifted the lid on a container of brownies she'd been stashing. "Well, I didn't get you a cake for your birthday, but Lara baked us something if you want dessert first..."

"You know? I thought it smelled like drug butter and chocolate when I got in here," he said.

"It always smells like that."

▶▶

"I gotta tell you, I do not know what Belgian food means," Nat said. "I just picture a big medieval cathedral of waffles."

"They have the best ketchup," Eleanor said, eager to unravel the cloth napkin to cover her lap.

Nat's face was red, not in a blotchy way, but warm. He was radiating a silly smile and licking his teeth with his mouth closed. "I hope that's not why we're here," he said.

Eleanor's eyes leaked with tears over the idea that someone would go somewhere for the ketchup. The waiter came over. Before he could get a word out, Nat said, "She'll have the ketchup."

"Oh my god, I missed you!" she blurted out to him in the middle of the waiter's spiel of the specials. Then Eleanor ordered them each *moules en frites*. She and Nat cried, taking turns enunciating *moules* as 'mules.'

"I've gotta say, you've been missed, too," Nat said in a caught breath.

"Stop it." Eleanor felt the tabletop absorb prints of her fingers after she'd slapped it. "I'm tired of that. You've been missed?" She continued to gesticulate like a righteous conductor. "What the fuck does that mean?"

"Okay, okay." Nat wiped the corners of his barely visible eyeballs. "Miss Huston, I missed you. Sorely."

Eleanor exhaled relief similar to when exiting the teacups ride at a carnival. The waiter brought over large steins of beer and tried to walk away. "Are they gonna take our order or what?" she asked Nat. Or had they ordered?

"Hey—hey man," Nat said. "We'll have two of the mules, please."

"But sir—"

"Yeah, I know. Sorry. I don't care how you say it. It's cool," he said. Eleanor tapped Nat's hand, but he insisted, "I know what I'm doing," as though he was pleading with the cops to allow him to continue a drunken joy ride.

It wasn't long before two bussers served their belligerent quadruple order covering the table real estate with four giant bowls, the contents at first opaque from all the aromatic steam, accompanied by four plates of fries, and four silver gravy boats with the alleged best ketchup and mayonnaise.

"What the fuck is all this!" Nat asked aghast, leaning straight backed against the pew like booth.

"What? They're mussels!" Eleanor cried.

"I mean, I didn't think it was actually going to be mules, but..." Nat stood up and surveyed outside their booth. "I feel highly visible right now."

"I just feel...high." Eleanor laughed and broke a sweat from all the *herbs de Provence* and the briny and buttery bounty, adjusting her eyes to the accidental gluttony. Her stomach contracted from hunger and all the laughs spent in their gleeful, baked reunion.

Nat took all the sturdy leather-bound bifold menus and built a privacy fort around them. If anything, the other patrons probably wanted to be further from their booth.

"Look, these menus are practically thicker than the walls of that skank warehouse you're living in." Nat then acknowledged their feast with some trepidation. "Eleanor, I love you—"

"But?" she asked.

"These look like a bunch of witch cauldrons filled with genitalia."

"Nat, I love you, but I can't let you be a rich person who only eats oatmeal and McDonald's."

"Fine, but I'm telling you right now, I'm taking you to McDonald's on your birthday," he said.

Eleanor took the lead, letting Nat watch her dirty, savory tutorial. Eating with only hands and mouths, scooping juices with shells, and dipping fries to make red and white Starlight swirls of mayo and ketchup. Eleanor then observed Nat. He morphed from perfunctory to perfection through his repetitions.

"I've never seen you like this," she finally said after catching him lick his finger.

"The ketchup really is good," he said.

"It has truffles," she told him.

Nat leaned back in the booth when he was full. "Damn. Who am I?"

"You're Nat fuckin' Dempsey. You're 25 years old. The world is your oyster, or mussel, or mule," she said. "So, where am I taking you next?"

Nat contemplated for a moment, pleasure rubbing his hands across his belly. "Back to the Rink. More G&Ts."

Eleanor knocked down their house of menus. "After all that shit talk about my place?"

"Come on. You know I don't want to be with anyone else."

▶▶

It was still night when Eleanor woke up, panicked by the climatic sounds of moaning and thrusts. They were coming through the makeshift divisions, the weak walls of separation between her sexually active roommates in the Rink. She looked over to find Nat. He was asleep on the floor. His arms and legs were crossed, with only his head leaning on her mattress as a pillow.

Eleanor lay still and stared at him. She reached out her arm across the negative space in her bed and soothed her fingers through Nat's dark hair, which felt thicker than a paintbrush. Her soft strokes woke him. He tilted his head back and their eyes found each other like nocturnal animals used to hunting alone, not threatened by their own kind. She closed her eyes to whisper, "You can come up here," though she was scared that he might.

She opened her eyes again to find Nat had hid his face in the mattress. Eleanor watched as his hand inched towards her bare leg until his blind touch found her. He began to trace what felt like a letter she was desperate to read above and below the bend of her knee. When he retracted, she reached out to stop him, to interlace their fingers. He squeezed her hand as if to say wait.

She couldn't accept why it felt so much like relief and torture when he withdrew.

In the morning, he'd left behind his jacket. Eleanor put it on immediately and rubbed the cuffs between her fingertips. In the pocket was an All Access badge with her name and a sticky note that read:

ALWAYS A PLACE FOR YOU...

14

WILL

MEANWHILE, IN PHILLY, THE Reverie was one last leg from New York, ending three weeks on the road after the Apex Awards. They should have been celebrating over one of those super-sized diner breakfasts that happen when normal people are eating lunch, but the mood was dire. Dasuki had met a girl after their show last night. When he returned to the hotel in the morning, he discovered Dave was missing.

Will and the rest of the band had just reconvened by their bus parked at the Electric Factory to learn their searches for Dave had come up empty.

Dasuki zipped up his track jacket to bite on its collar. "What are we going to do?"

"We're gonna get a new fucking bassist," Andy said.

Will kneaded the pressure points on his temples to resist groaning. "Come on, it's not like Dave's trying to hurt anyone."

"Bullshit, Will." Andy retied his hair back as if he were preparing to fight. "He's fucking up himself, isn't he?"

Dasuki threw his long arms up. He could almost reach the marquee sign that still displayed 'The Reverie SOLD OUT' from last night. Dasuki's exasperation seemed to middle between Andy and Will's positions of harsh intolerance and detaching concern, respectively. Besides Dasuki, the rest of The Reverie were yo-yos. Even when they were on the up, it was just a matter of time before they got tangled in the string. Dave would get sick. Andy would get sick of Dave. And Will would be reminded of how sick of it all he was.

Besides Dave's unknown whereabouts and welfare, Will had another problem that was time sensitive. About a month ago, Will had agreed to be featured in a Levi's campaign. In the past, he'd refused to take part in anything corporate. It was against The Reverie's ethos. The photo shoot for the campaign was in about four hours.

"I hate to bring this up," Will said. "But I think I'm going to have to catch a train or something to make this thing..."

"Seriously?" Andy said. "So fuckin' sellout, man!"

Dasuki sighed. "Here we go again."

Will argued that the proceeds were going towards something ethical, a stretch. Was it not ethical to get his bandmates out of the red?

"Don't even act like this isn't your ego," Andy said.

"My ego?"

"You took this job to fuck with Jamie," Andy said. "You signed up the second you found out Frida Jones was the other face of the fucking campaign."

"Yo. Enough," Dasuki said. "Will, can you call Cath? See if Dave checked in with his sis."

Will groaned.

"Don't be a pussy," Andy said.

Reluctantly, Will hopped onto their bus to rummage through Dave's stuff. Looking at Dave's handwriting in his address book made Will feel eerie, like he was already a ghost. Dave occupied space like a white noise, a gentle muffling rhythm that was slipping like fingers off strings. Most of Dave's phone numbers were dealers, identifiable by city under the letter H. Will found Cath's number and then entered the dead air of the nearest telephone booth to make the call.

Fran answered, an unpalatable reminder of who Cath was living with now. Cath hadn't heard from Dave. She sounded like a pilled-up housewife, becalmed as her cigarette burned the house down. There was no alarm in Cath's low, monotonal voice. She promised to get the word out when Dave turned up. Not if, but when.

Will returned to Andy and Dasuki stewing on the curb with the rest of The Reverie's touring crew. "Let's go." Will waved them aboard the bus. No one argued. They were all aching for comfort, for omelets, for Jersey's turnpike gates.

The ride home was silent. Will sat up front, as if the gods would honor his sitting shotgun as valor worthy of clearing congestion. Will thought about how easy his life was before meeting Cath, before she introduced him to her brother Dave. Back then, Will's major inconvenience was the recurring 2 AM fire drill in his dorm. He'd throw on his shearling-lined corduroy jacket over his bare chest, grab his vintage Gibson SJ200 Sunburst, and strum on one of the benches until everyone was cleared to reenter. Being that Will attended an art school so predominantly female it was barely coed, his shtick was beyond the effort necessary to attract suitors.

Cath wasn't one of those girls who'd walk over to Will and suggestively whirl their toes or hair in circles. He'd only seen Cath around campus sketching, appearing amused but never smiling. She looked like a ballerina. A real one, rigid but fluid. Her caricature back-burned slowly over the Christmas break when Will was alone back in Rye. Will's older sister was newly married and out of the house, and his parents were on some aboriginal retreat in Australia. Will had nothing but time to smoke grass, think about this mystery girl, and listen to *Goats Head Soup* and *Let's Get It On*. They were the perfect records to stay warm but still feel the cut of winter. They were also the perfect records for Will to find his voice.

Back on campus in spring, Will introduced himself. She spoke in a soft mumble, but it was pleasing in the way words came out of her puckered mouth. When she revealed her name, Will smirked. It was the first and least of many ways in which she did not live up to what Will had invented. Cath looked at him like he was crazy when he asked her out, which Will found beguiling because everyone else took him so seriously. She rejected him initially, but suggested he meet her brother, Dave.

"Why?" Will asked.

"He's a songwriter," she muttered. "But he needs someone like you."

As the tour bus inched back to New York, Will questioned if anyone still took him seriously. Cath had left him for a woman who shared the same DNA as Rollins, and his band was in such a hole that he was selling himself out to modeling gigs.

▶▶

There were so many mirrors on set. By avoiding his own reflection, Will's gaze landed on Frida. She was maneuvering her breasts with technical assistance to tape them, to secure some optimal level of cleavage in her denim top. Frida stared back at Will vacuously. He took this for her either not thinking he was being voyeuristic or not caring if he was. Will returned the focus to his own reflection.

"I look like one of *The Outsiders*," he said, uncertainly outfitted in a medium wash blue denim vest and jeans. The vest hung tight and nice on his torso, but that didn't change the fact that it was a vest.

"That will not work for the shot," the smaller photographer yelled at him, still snapping candids of Will, despite whatever wasn't working.

"What do you mean?" Will asked.

"Lose the underwear," he told Will.

"Are you kidding me?" Will mouthed as the little man pushed him behind a room divider the size of a napkin. Will took both the jeans and his briefs off, then put the jeans back on. He'd begun to button them when he was interrupted again.

"No, no, leave that one unbuttoned," the photographer commanded. "*Unzipped* is the entire campaign. No zippers," he said, and dropped to his knees.

"Then why are these buttons?" Will asked before suppressing his humiliation as the man invasively shot his bulge for illogical and artless consumption.

Next, Frida was placed next to Will for a his'n'her series with the larger photographer who barked orders in German that were then translated by the small one.

"Face forward. Relax your hips. Play with your belt loops. Will, play with her belt loop. One hand. Right hand in your pocket. Out. Out. Cross one arm and hold it. Will, right hip forward. Face Frida. Frida, stay facing forward."

"Is this pretty weird?" Will said to her.

"I don't think about it," Frida said, barely opening her mouth to speak.

"Frida, turn away. Arms above your head like you're under arrest. No, no! Bent on the back of your head. Turn your back on the camera. Hands in your back pockets. Will, right hand in her back right pocket. Frida, left hand in his back left pocket. Further. Thumb out. Good. Good," the small one said, while two cameras machine-gunned and several assistants stayed out of the frame to move some of the lighting and equipment on set. "Closer. Closer. Turn towards each other. Bend back at the chest. Back in. Closer. Okay. Good. Good. Will, wrap just your left arm around her waist, more, more all the way back, as far back as you can."

"Jesus." Will was so close to Frida's mouth that he could detect her brand of cigarette.

"No talking. Breath!" the big photographer snapped.

Will rolled his eyes. Frida's full mouth flattened slightly from its pout to a partial grin.

The small photographer continued his directions. "Now both turn to me. Frida. Good, good eyes. Will, stare like, like someone's taking her away. Fierce. Good. Good. Now tell him a secret Frida, but eyes on me. Right, right. Will, you do the same. Eyes almost closed. Mean. No, sleepier. Half smile. Surprised. Both of you. Who wants it? You want it. Both of you. Now just Will."

Will felt like he might be experiencing an acid flashback, thrusted in jeans with weird jazz, the juxtaposition of harsh and soft commands, and the camera snaps all bouncing off the warehouse. Eventually, the pressure broke Will to sweat, and he detached from his forced grasp onto Frida.

"Can I get a cigarette?"

The larger photographer flicked his hand as a response.

Will top-buttoned his jeans, conscientious not to expose too much bush or dick, and stepped outside to smoke on the fire escape.

Despite the autumn air, the wrought iron was sunbaked and hot on his feet and forearms pressed against the guardrail. Will drew alternating breaths of burning tobacco and the breeze he could see capping up the East River. It wasn't the modeling gig that was too intense, he told himself. This was a capitalistic exercise to sell sex to sell apparel. It was that everything else had become too intense.

Will came back inside to find his departure had inspired everyone to break. Frida was sitting with her unrelenting posture on a sunken, white armchair, wearing a bib to sip her tea. Will took the opportunity to apologize for arriving late and for why he was out of it, without giving too much away about Dave.

"It's fine," Frida said. "I'm sorry to hear about your troubles."

"I guess you know all about how it is with this kind of band drama," said Will.

"Pardon?" She recrossed her legs.

"Sorry, I didn't mean to overstep."

"It's fine. You know how the press exaggerates. Everything is going very well, as I'm sure you know from Eleanor."

"Right," Will said. "We should get together sometime."

"Of course. I'm sure it would be nice to get to know each other better before the wedding in Italy."

What wedding?

▶▶

With the shoot and most of his errands in the rearview, Will had reached the last step of his post-tour routine: to get into bed with someone. Ele tried to cancel. She said she wasn't feeling well and didn't want him to see her new place. He insisted and brought her soup and swag from the Levi's shoot. Ele wore a gray Champion t-shirt covering less of her legs than her tall wool socks. It wasn't her best look, but she embraced him for long enough to ease some of the tension from his body.

"Could've used you at that photoshoot today."

"Why's that?" she said.

"The head photographer was German."

"Man, that already feels like another lifetime." Ele thanked him for the clothes and declined the soup. "I have my own ways." She was cradling a glass bottle of yellow sport's drink she explained was mixed with cough syrup.

"Oh yeah? Are you a doctor?"

"Psh, no. I'm an athlete," she said.

Ele led him into her bedroom and invited him under the covers. She zipped herself into a sleeping bag underneath her comforter and shivered. Will could barely feel her through the puffy, bundled layers that shrouded her. It was a terribly drafty place she was living in, even compared to his band's charity rental.

"You sure you want to stay here? You know I have that place in the West Village."

"I'll live," Ele replied. Her words reminded Will that it was still unknown if Dave would.

Will prepared to unload. "It's been a long day..."

"I know. I'm surprised you agreed for us to do that art stuff with Cath tomorrow."

Will sat upright. "What are you talking about?"

"Yeah, she called here looking for you a few hours ago. She said Dave showed up at her place, that he lost his wallet or something."

"Ha! Oh man, that's great," Will said.

"Great that he lost his wallet?"

"Better than the alternative," he said.

"You want to elaborate?"

"Not really."

"Well, Cath said we should meet at Glasgow Gallery tomorrow before Cafe Tabac."

"It's *Galsgow*..." Will corrected. "Like, where *gals* go? It's Fran Rollins' place."

"You want to go?" Ele questioned.

"If you said we'd go."

"I only said we would because she made it sound like you had already agreed."

"We'll just go then," he said. "Do you think you'll be feeling better?"

"This stuff has never failed me."

Soon after, she said goodnight and rolled over. Will was left to think about the last time he'd been with Ele in Vegas, when their sex had turned to fucking so hard they would've collapsed had he not bent her over a counter to brace them. While she slept, Will wondered if that was another lifetime too, and if she had become someone else entirely.

▶▶

The next day, Will resented his amenable curiosity to meet up with Cath and Fran by the time they got to Cafe Tabac. They'd just climbed the stairs to the upper lounge when Fran wiped the corners of her twisted her pompadour to a point. "Listen, Rico Suave," she told Tabac's model/manager Roy, "If Madonna's here, I swear. Either she's out or we're out."

Unfortunately, Madonna was not there, so Roy seated them in a red-tufted booth. It was as uncomfortable as the conversation. Fran started commending Will in this patronizing way on Cath's behalf. "Generous guy, you are. Really supported Cath coming into her own as an artist, am I right?"

"He is very generous," Cath affirmed.

"Endowments you want everywhere except up the ass. Am I right, sweety?" Fran said to Ele.

Ele coughed up some of the cocktail she was chugging.

"Will used to have a new girlfriend every September, like a newly assigned teacher," Cath said.

"Until you," Ele replied kindly, which bothered Will more than if she'd been territorial.

"Oh, Will would be as likely to do that to prove me wrong for pointing out his pattern," said Cath. "Has he taken you to Rye yet?"

Ele shook her head.

"So she hasn't met Cherise?" Cath said to Will.

"Too soon," Will replied. "Cherise is smothering, like sandalwood."

"I can't believe you call your parents by their first names," Ele said.

Will rolled his shoulders.

"When I first visited Rye, Cherise showed me all of Will's memory lane albums, pointing out his girlfriends in each class photo. What a 'little prince' you were." Cath reached over the booth and touched Will's hand.

"So, how did you and Fran meet? Through Rollins?" Ele asked Cath, then said to him, "I'm sorry, is that awkward?" as if he could answer honestly.

"I was working on this silkscreen series of 1950s housewives," Cath explained.

Fran interrupted and said, "Cath came to a book release on Hollywood lesbians at The Strand."

"So you were doing some R&D before going gay?" Will felt Ele reactively kick him under the tabletop.

"Whoa, boy. You may look like you're from the seventies, but this is the nineties, and it's damn near antiquated to believe someone *becomes* gay," Fran said, schooling Will like he was some kind of neanderthal.

"Didn't mean to offend you," Will said.

"Luckily, I'm only offended by politicians and hotel art," Fran said.

Will sucked an inhale from a cigarette so deeply, as if he were willing it to kill him immediately. "Ele is a photographer."

"Not really. I don't want to talk about it." Ele borrowed his cigarette.

"You do anything important? With anyone we might know?" Fran asked.

"Important? No. I just moved back to New York and started working for Aja Green."

"Oh, that cunt! Better watch your back, Ele," Fran said.

"Well shit," Ele said. She looked so uncorrupted.

"Well shit? Ha. You're a crack up," Fran said.

"Thanks," Ele said. "Hey Cath, I loved the album art you designed for The Reverie. You're ridiculously talented."

"I spend too much time with drawing fluid and screen filler," Cath replied modestly.

"You know Ele has a cover in her portfolio, too," Will said.

"It's not the same," Ele said. "I just contributed photographs."

"Would I know the album?" Cath asked.

"Yeah, unless you live under a rock. Bolero's *Light Up and Shine On,*" Will answered.

"Shut up!" said Fran. "I love those guys! Loved when they stuck it to Jacko! My sis really caught a marlin with Bolero. We've partied a few times. And of course, I've known Frida for years."

"That's who I had to shoot with yesterday," Will shared.

"Frida? Anyway, that Jamie is a cut up!" Fran said.

"I'd say you have no idea, but if you meet Jamie even once, you get the idea," Ele said.

"Haha. I gotta tell ya," Fran said, leaning over to whisper to Ele. "This one time—"

"Hate to interrupt you, Fran. But it's getting late," Will said. "Look, Cath, are we gonna talk about Dave?"

"What do you mean?" Ele asked.

"Is this the right place for all that?" Fran's attention diverted to a new group of girls who were granted entry upstairs, including Diana and Lara from Girlcrush, two of Ele's many roommates.

"I didn't choose the place," Will said. When Ele got up to greet them, it occurred to Will that she wasn't wearing one of the new Levi's jackets he'd brought her from the shoot, but an older one he didn't recognize.

"Come by tomorrow," Cath mumbled to him. "You can see Dave and Fran will be out."

Ele returned and sat next to Will. Lara and Diana followed her and hovered by their booth. They'd been partying hard, judging by their heavy steps and the volume of their voices.

"Oh, my god. I don't even know who I love most. I think it's you," Diana said, pointing to Will.

"Why's that?" Will asked, thinking there's no way Diana was sober enough to remember Bolero's party at Rollins' house, when he denied her a kiss before she was thrown into a tower of champagne.

Diana brushed Will off and moved on to Fran. "No, it's you."

"You've got the wrong sister, toots."

"Hey, screw you guys for keeping me up the other night," Lara said to Will and Ele. She made some exaggerated moans and pounded on their table for effect.

Will sat back and tried to look intrigued.

"Nuh uh. Wasn't Nat over? For his birthday?" Diana asked both questions in a patently rhetorical way.

"Uh oh, big boy," Fran said to Will.

Will the Buddhist had never wanted to punch anyone until this moment.

"Yeah, no," Ele said, itching her throat. "It was, but he didn't stay over. I mean, he did, but not 'with me' like that. I swear!"

"Yeah, yeah. We all know you're a *good* girl," Diana said.

"Yeah, Di. You should try it," Lara said. "When you're good girls like me and Ele, you get to be bridesmaids." She mimed a curtsey in her acid-wash jeans and Birkenstocks.

"Tell you what, sweety. You can be our bridesmaid, okay?" Fran said to Diana and petted Cath's hand.

"Hey," Ele whispered to Will. He felt her hand and attention hold on to him for what seemed like the first time since he'd returned to New York. "KP and Lindsay are getting married in Italy. Any interest in fucking a bridesmaid?"

"Which one?"

"The one who's trying to be a really good girl," she said.

Will showed how much he was interested by gliding her hand further up his tightening pants.

15

NAT

"**I** DON'T HAVE IT," Jamie said almost inaudibly over the flight announcements and travelers shuffling about JFK.

"What'd you think you're big enough to travel internationally without a passport?" Nat said.

"I forgot it, alright?" Jamie replied.

"Jesus Christ. You're lucky this isn't disrupting band business," Nat said before leading the pack away from Jamie to fend for himself at the gate check.

Rather than annoyed, Nat was relieved Jamie would probably miss a chunk of KP and Lindsay's Italian wedding festivities. There was plenty of runway for the label to figure out Jamie's blunder before Bolero's bustling schedule resumed in London.

"Did you mastermind this?" Nat joked quietly to Lindsay, who, even for an overnight flight, was dressed in one of her costumes, something like a sixties Pan-Am stewardess.

"No, I thought this was your wedding gift to us."

"Hey, miss. Can I get a warm towel?" KP asked Lindsay.

"Hey! Ow!" Lindsay replied after flinching. KP had pinched her butt as they approached the jetway. KP was red wine drunk from the lounge, on top of the world, before they'd even lifted off.

Nat stepped back to wedge between Will and Eleanor. He looked over her shoulder and peeked at her ticket. It was a petty win: they'd be seated a few rows behind him. Nat hadn't prepared for Eleanor to invite Will to Italy, not after the way things went on Nat's birthday. Then again, maybe Nat's reservations about going further with her that night had cost him. That thought was brutal.

"So, no Jamie. Will Frida still be joining us?" Will asked while they inched slowly to board.

"Frida's already in Milan for some fashion thing," Lindsay said. "She and Nikki are meeting us at the villa tomorrow afternoon."

"Shit. Nikki Wilshire's coming?" Greg said. "Is she a gift for the groomsmen?"

"Don't say things like that," Lindsay said.

"Did she bully you for an invitation?" Will said, like he wasn't the least important guest on the list.

"I wouldn't say that. I'd say she strongly suggested attending," Lindsay said.

"You are such a diplomatic bride," said Ele.

"Yeah, well, Nikki made diplomacy easy," KP said. She was hooking them up with a honeymoon at her family's villa, somewhere on the Amalfi coast, a destination Nat never knew existed until yesterday.

"Guys, seriously though. What is Jamie going to even do?" Sulky asked, practically swaddling himself with detachment anxiety.

"Yeah, Jamie doesn't even know his phone number," said Greg.

Sulky scoffed. "How would his own number even help him? Idiot."

Nat was suppressing his dread about what Jamie might be capable of getting up to solo, but the upside of his absence was worthwhile for the redeye alone. Nat hated flying. It combined his fears of being trapped and out of control. Dying next to Jamie's incessant talking was up there with castration by sharks. By himself, Nat could work on his speech. KP had asked Nat to be his Best Man. KP's two teenage brothers would be his other groomsmen. They looked just like KP with their long arms, flatter Roman faces, and idiosyncratic facial hair that naturally grew in the shape of a goatee. Nat had questioned KP's choice. Why not his brothers?

"They don't know dick," KP replied. "Their balls haven't even dropped yet. You? You *know* me, man."

Nat was honored. He'd only ever expected to be the default Best Man at Jamie's weddings, for however many of them Nat could stand.

Lindsay's sister, Tina, who looked nothing like Lindsay, would be her maiden of honor. Tina brought her silent husband and noisy toddler in tow. They were fish-out-of-water normal. Lindsay had asked Eleanor and Lara to be her other bridesmaids. Luckily, Diana and the rest of Girlcrush were not invited. Even though Lindsay and Diana had never been close, excluding her would probably cause strife. That's just the way things were now. Anything about any of the extended Bolero family—true, or otherwise—could be weaponized and leaked to a thirsty outlet. As an official band policy, tabloid tales weren't to be taken to heart but as fodder for ballbusting. Some stories were downright funny. Like Sulky and Jamie being secret lovers or Frida being a paid hag. Sulky might've leaked those himself.

When the plane took off, Nat waited until he heard the ding signal cruising altitude to open his eyes. He tried to appreciate the view of the gray glow above the night clouds storming below his window seat, then pulled a pen and small-ringed notebook from his pocket. All he had written so far were two radical equations.

Eleanor jumped into Jamie's empty aisle seat. "Do you still hate to fly?" She sucked on the thin red straw from her drink and examined him.

"Even in first class."

"Just think about the alternative," she said.

"Economy?" Nat dropped his pen to fidget with his thumbs.

"No. You're such a brat. Of not going anywhere." Eleanor paused, seeming to sit with that alternate reality before she continued. "But really. Imagine the past, having to take those epic, relic passages across seas... and then on foot or horseback... eating stale bread and catching biblical influenza..." She rattled on, practically glimmering at her descriptions, romanticizing these grim adventures.

"You're mental," Nat said, though he would catalog Eleanor's expressions to humor him on future flights.

"But—?"

"But what? I didn't say but... You've been doing that a lot."

"Doing what?"

"Butting me." Nat nudged her elbow that had encroached onto his armrest. "Like you expect me to have something else to say."

"Like you *don't* have something else to say," Eleanor said.

Nat looked down at the open book on the tray table in front of him. He watched her look at it, too.

$$KP - LINDSAY = PONYTAIL$$
$$KP + LINDSAY = NO\ PONYTAIL$$

"I remember that ponytail!" Eleanor said. "Didn't you guys hide it in Sulky's Nintendo after he cut it?"

"I had no part in that, but I swear that might've kickstarted Sulky's rapid degradation."

"The Nintendo or the prank?" Eleanor said.

"Good one," Nat said.

"Wow. That was before you guys were really even a band. So... that's your speech so far?"

"Yep." Nat tapped the pen insecurely. "I am Best Man material."

"I'd say not to let that go to your head, but it'd be too late."

The softer prodding of Eleanor's breath near his ear when she spoke made Nat's head tilt towards her. He jerked it back when she got up to leave him alone at the top of the aisle.

▶▶

"No offense, but don't you have to do your makeup or something?" Nat said to Lindsay.

It was the day of her wedding. She had her black hair up in curlers and had been lecturing him on mind reader delusion and other psychobabble since breakfast. At least it was pleasant to zone in and out of the epic views from their flaxen and rust villa somewhere far up the end of a dusted, winding road outside Florence. It was early October, but no one told Italy. The countryside was still baked in sun. The weather felt straight up voluptuous.

"Look." Lindsay snapped her finger to regain his attention. "We aren't all knowing," she said.

"Not even us?" Nat said jokingly, with an awareness that he and Lindsay had a reputation for slinging the most unsolicited advice.

"Not funny. I'm just saying that guessing what someone else is thinking is not knowing. The same goes for you expecting anyone else to know what you haven't owned up and said."

"Are you trying to say something, Lindsay?"

"You know what I'm trying to say."

"So you *are* expecting me to mind read."

Lindsay minimized her otherwise massive brown eyes to slits. "Look, Nat. At some point, you'll have to grow out of all these suggestive riddles and gestures if you want anything to come of them."

"Is that so?"

"It's not enough," Lindsay said.

"Oh, I don't know about that. For Nikki, it might even be too much," Nat said.

"Nikki? Tell me you're kidding," Lindsay said.

"Yes, I am kidding, but I shouldn't have to. I'm not the one here with someone else." Nat raked his calloused fingers along his scalp.

"So?" she said. "Hasn't it occurred to you there's always the possibility she'll be with someone else unless she's with you?"

"Chill out. I'm still getting my feet wet," said Nat.

"You are old enough to swim in the deep end," Lindsay said.

"Okay, doc. Can I steal your line and say our time is up?"

Lindsay pinched his cheek, which reminded him he needed a shave, then she got up to walk over and welcome the latest arrivals.

"Lindsay—" Nat waited for her to turn around before giving her a telepathic expression of gratitude.

"Wiseass," Lindsay remarked before turning back to greet Nikki and Frida.

Frida looked like a classic movie star with her hair pinned neatly under a scarf. Nikki looked like a sex worker on a cruise ship being trailed by a bleach-blonde male assistant. The assistant was carrying Nikki's fat little dog and dragging a massive trunk on wheels twice his size, which kept getting caught on the pebbled walkway.

Nat turned away to avoid having a conversation about his brother's whereabouts, but sat out until the staff who ran the villa began setting the surrounding tables.

▶▶

Nat stood with his thumbs in his pant pockets between KP and his kid brothers. The four of them were obstructing the postcard view of terraced hillsides for the onlooking guests. According to the string trio, the ceremony was about to begin.

Nat had pictured marrying, desiring to have someone to give and be all of himself. Parts of his relationship with Karen felt marital, but when they fell in love, he was so young; he was copping for something else that was still ahead of him. Nat was older now. He knew more of himself. He knew how to wait and was close to move, to embrace what he wanted, even though it felt like an ill-communicated trust fall.

When he saw Eleanor appear at the edge of the green grass aisle before him, Nat hard swallowed. He couldn't have expected she'd be wearing white, nor had he seen fabric like that. The slip moved like water down her body to the Florentine floor. Imagining Eleanor in a white dress differed from actually seeing it, like there were limits to imagining things that needed to be experienced. She held sunflowers and wheat and leaves between her hands, and swayed forward quickly, like she only could, before taking her position with metered space across from him. Her face was stunning and sincere as she stood facing the Tuscan glow of the sun, which was like citrus flesh. Nat allowed himself to be exposed and admire her until KP stepped forward for his bride.

The trio began to play Elvis' "Can't Help Falling In Love" while Lindsay made her teasingly slow march forward in a retro yellow dress with flowy sleeves in the shape of church bells. Her hairstyle completed the look, a big Priscilla beehive thing with white flowers decorating it like a cake.

The ceremony began in Italian, but KP and Lindsay read vows they had written to each other in English. Nat felt the love in their voices, the nervous vibrations, and the weight of their sentiments that shared vulnerability and strength. Two 'I do's', one dipping kiss, applause. Nat took Eleanor's arm, and they giddily trailed the newlyweds away from the sacramental ground as a hunk of "Burnin' Love" played.

►►

Following the ceremony, the wedding party took pictures in the gardens and groves on the far side of the main villa. Nat returned to cocktail hour with the bridesmaids. They stopped to find Frida and Will entertaining Tina's daughter. The little hellion didn't give a squat when her mother returned. Nor did Tina's husband, who appeared to be busy fiddling with his wind-up watch.

"Aww, aren't you two good with her?" Tina said to Will and Frida. "Do any of you want kids someday?"

Lara laughed and walked away.

Nat noticed Eleanor didn't need to respond verbally. Her body recoiled as though someone had dropped an ice cube down her back.

Will had also noticed. "Really?" he said, handing the little girl he had scooped up back to Tina.

"You don't want to get married either?" Tina asked Eleanor.

Eleanor scrunched her hair the way she did and said, "I don't know. I mean, that I think I can—"

"I should've expected Lindsay's friends to be so alternative," Tina said, apparently not as interested as Nat in Eleanor's cliffhanger about her views on matrimony. To be fair to both Eleanor's position on children and Tina's impatience to get a response, Tina was juggling a crying child who'd been yanking at her Vanna White updo.

"Well, I'd quite like to have children," Frida said, tenderly touching the little girl's stumpy leg to calm her. Nat exercised restraint, not making a dig about Jamie being her first.

"You can do that with your lifestyle?" Tina asked Frida.

"Is that a fair question?" Will said.

"Well, I do plan to leave, which is to say I would not want to do both. Raise a family with the burden of all this," Frida said. Nat hadn't heard Frida be so definitive before.

"The burden of being rich and famous?" Tina chortled. "I'm sorry, I can't take this seriously," she said and walked off with her kid and husband trailing.

"Was Lindsay adopted?" Nat said. Only Eleanor laughed.

"I suppose my use of burden was insensitive." Frida had wrapped herself tightly in a pale blue pashmina that matched her dress and shoes and bag and eyeliner and eyes.

"She set you up to be criticized either way," Will said. "And there are burdens that override any of this being worth it."

"Really?" Eleanor spoke with a riling tone Nat knew she got when people disagreed with something she was passionate about, down to the superiority of a corner slice of Sicilian pizza from Gino's. "I feel like I'm just getting started," she said. "I mean, some of us grew up stuck between two airports, never having been on a plane."

"Relax. This doesn't need to be a whole class thing," Will said.

Eleanor said nothing but began pulling out some pins holding her styled hair back. Nat could see the frustration further flushing the make-up on her cheeks when, in broken English, the DJ invited everyone to be seated at the long rustic table for dinner.

▶▶

Nat was two fork stabs into his salad when he was called up to make his speech. He climbed out of his seat, narrowly sandwiched between Nikki and Eleanor, and walked to the head of the table where KP and Lindsay sat. The sun was slowly setting. Nat rubbed the pages of his drafted speech in his pants pocket. But he'd decided now not to read from them. Nat waited for KP's gesture to begin. It was the same chin up he used to signal Bolero's drum-led sets on stage.

"I'll try to keep this quick," Nat said to the simmering table of guests. "Not because I don't have a bunch of brilliant things to say, but because I feel the same way about speeches as I do about drum solos—I fucking loathe them." Nat heard only a scowl from Tina, who had been trying to stick a barrette back on her daughter's hay-like hair. Nat gulped.

"Right, well. I wanna thank these two spectacular people, KP and Lindsay Valanni, now Parker—the newly pressed LP, if you will.

"So, when I met Keith Parker, he had this long ponytail. I guess you could say it was more like a mule's tail because he looked like an ass. Wow! Mules have been coming up in my life a lot lately." Nat caught Eleanor hiding a smirk. "Anyway, we were roadies for this band, entirely suspect, and one day, not long after our girl Eleanor introduced him to Lindsay, KP showed up at rehearsals walking tall... his hair sharp short... and he quit! Like that. Only a good woman, I mean, love, makes you transform like that, right? I was so fucking vicariously inspired that I quit, too.

"That night I was at our local, Down the Hatch, and I gave some mental rousing speech that was definitely better than this one, and convinced Jamie to start a band.

"A year or so later, KP joined Bolero. Lindsay was going through a Priscilla Presley phase, which, judging by today, I guess never really ended.

"One thing I love about KP is that he keeps his composure, but he's still a nutcase. Lindsay should count counseling all of us towards her clinical hours. Even this morning, she took time to... well, luckily this is not about me." Nat realized he'd taken a *faux pas* gulp of his toasting wine.

"Sorry. It's like Jamie's not here and now there's too much pressure not to be the biggest dick in the room. I can say that 'cause he's not here."

"Don't act like you wouldn't say that if he was," Lindsay responded.

"True. Anyway, I admire Lindsay and KP because they are always true to themselves. They bring out the best in each other and are patient when they're not their bests... They're connected even when they're apart.

"Some might say it's crazy to get married now. But KP is actually an expert in timing. I envy that." Nat raised his glass that his grip had warmed.

"May we all be as lucky to have the love you guys have forever. Cheers to K and LP."

▶▶

Nat started drinking more liberally now that he'd given his speech. Wine wasn't his usual sauce. That was KP's thing, and his purple-mouthed benders were laced with too many grape and geography lessons. But the hard stuff was at the bottom of a steep dirt hill, and Peronis weren't gonna get Nat anywhere fast enough tonight. Nat went with the red, which smelled like a dug-up tin of tobacco. His first taste was so dry, it scraped against his tongue before absorbing quicker than a drizzle on the desert floor. Each glug coated more of his mouth, activating more of his senses. He'd glugged at least a bottle by KP and Lindsay's first dance.

Nikki pulled Nat to join the circle around the newlyweds' steppy sway to Bob Marley's "Waiting in Vain." He made it a few verses before rerouting Nikki to KP's brothers. Nat stepped away to sit near the brick oven they'd used to make pizzas the night before. The sun was finally receding into the rolling hills. The vista was *bella,* but needed to be sacrificed for darkness. A party could never be brought to its full potential in daylight. Mischief and confidence needed moonlight to bloom.

Frida approached Nat and sat down. He lit her cigarette.

"Why thank you, roomie," she said awkwardly, as she only was when appropriating American slang. They were sharing a bungalow on the property with two adjoining suites. Nat offered Frida wine, which she declined.

"You seem to be having a good time without Jamie," Nat said. Frida showed a guilty pout. "Not that there's nothing wrong with that. I, for one, am having the best time without Jamie around." Nat lifted his glass.

"Italy suits you," she said.

He shrugged, even though he agreed.

"I do miss Jamie," she said. "And, well, it's lovely to dance at a wedding, isn't it?"

"Oh, fuck no. Dancing is like sex."

"Pardon?"

"I mean, it's not. But it's pretty fucking intimate and you do it in front of everyone?" Frida looked deferential and uncomfortable. "Oh, fuck it. I know I'm wrong! I'm going to get more wine."

Nat returned to the help-yourself bar offerings on a cluster of wrought-iron tables painted white. They reminded Nat of the patio furniture that was at his grandparents. KP's younger brothers were making something diabolical with cola, red wine, and a dusted bottle with an artichoke on it that looked like poison.

"*Torta!*" someone shouted.

Nat huddled unavoidably near Will and Eleanor next to a small table with a giant layered cake as tilted as the tower in Pisa.

"I didn't know cake cutting was an Italian tradition," Will said, looking like he was pissed by the taste of his own cigarette.

"Hundred bucks says Lindsay smashes it in KP's face," Nat whispered to Eleanor.

"Your bets are too rich for my blood," she replied.

"You just don't want to lose," Nat said.

Lindsay flicked the frosting from the knife onto KP's face.

"Told you," Nat said.

Eleanor huffed. "Just because you called it first doesn't mean I didn't agree!"

The villa's *strega nonna* doled out thick slices of the canary and cream cake on crystal plates. There was no point in refusing the cake woman. Nat had tried but was scolded, praised, and then hit before accepting. A Roberta Flack song started crackling through the DJ's speakers. It sounded so cool. Nat wished he were wearing a sharp tux instead of his assigned brown suit that wore him. He'd wear a tux to his wedding, he decided.

Candles and speckled lights shimmered over the slate, where partygoers started to double down on the bacchanal offerings and dance. Greg and Sulky had a race opening bottles. Nat was the real winner, swiping the first to be decorked and taking it with his cake away from the action. Nat followed a subtle trail of slabs in the grass about fifty yards until he reached the pool behind hedges and was out of sight. The pool was less neon and more noble than it'd be in the states, bordered by distinctly Italian trees that stood black against the dark purple sky.

Nat removed his dress shoes and socks and rolled up his suit pants to submerge his feet in the water. It was temperate, but sobered him too much too soon. He rolled his tongue against itself before taking another swig from the bottle.

"You come here often?" he heard Eleanor say, her voice imitating something vaguely masculine and pervy. She had the bottom of her white dress twisted up into a ball to walk more freely at the expense of exposing a white triangle of underwear.

"Oh shit, are you a vision," Nat said. "Even better than before."

"When before?" She sat next to him and plopped her feet in the water.

Nat took another drink. "The ceremony."

"Will told me I walked too fast." She reached across him to drink from his bottle.

"That was slow for you," Nat said.

"You know me." Eleanor passed back the bottle, which gleamed green from the pool light. "This is amazing," she said.

"The wine?"

"Everything. Almost everything. And your speech? It was spot on."

"It was all over the place," he said.

"No. It was more than anyone could hope for." Eleanor kicked her legs in the water.

Nat could hear "Spinning Away" from the Brian Eno/John Cale split playing back at the party. Eleanor leaned her head on his shoulder, then brought her hand to her chest abruptly as though something had just occurred to her.

"Did you lose your necklace?" Nat asked, noticing she'd only wear this hippy little gemstone when Will was around.

"No. It doesn't go with this dress," she said.

"Why are you twitching then?"

"I'm in awe?" she said.

Nat took in his surroundings again. The vibey pool. The harvest moon shading the high-pointed cypresses and low, crawly vines. Her. "Me too," he said.

"It's like, I couldn't even imagine this before, and now I can't not think about it."

"What? Being in Italy?" Nat asked.

"No. I don't know." Eleanor took her legs out of the water and hugged them. "Look at what we came from, Nat."

"Yeah, your dad's the only one who ever left the country for a fucking war, and now you're a jet setting bridesmaid. So?"

"I mean their marriages. Settling down didn't work."

"Oh." Nat leaned back on his elbows and sighed. "Look... this is tough to say, but none of them probably should've been together. In a way, we're lucky we're alive, you know? If anything, I don't think our or your type of love has to mean settling down, or whatever. You're too smart for that."

Eleanor leaned across his lap again to grab his plate of cake and took a bite.

"You could've asked me."

"Asked you for what?" she said with a mouth full. "For this?" Eleanor smashed the rest of the cake into his face. It was soft and cold. The sweet, whipped taste cut the tannic state of his mouth. He blew icing out from his nostrils, but flecks of white stuck to his eyelashes like fallen snow. Eleanor leaped up, which excited Nat to retaliate.

"It's okay, it's okay." He moved towards her with forgiving arms for a hug, into which she tripped and clung to him, fearfully giggling. Nat supported her while she reclaimed her balance. A string of her dress strap slipped. He skimmed her skin with his fingers to slide it back in place, perpendicular to the perfect line of her clavicle. Eleanor wiped away the icing from his face with the underside of her thumb and licked it. Her eyes mirrored the color of the pool. He wanted to pull her closer, but they kept an innocent rhythm, a Catholic school dance to the sweet melody wafting from afar. Her hands rested on his shoulders, and his palms on her hips. The space between her nose and top lip had curved into an unbearably alluring extra smile above her mouth.

Nat sighed. "You know what happens next?"

Eleanor nodded and winced.

Nat clamped his hands around her waist, giving away his move to throw her in the pool. Eleanor gasped and gripped onto the lapels of his suit jacket to pull him in with her. Nat could've resisted, but at the minor risk of her not clearing the pool's hard edge. So Nat held his breath and let Eleanor take him down with her hysterical scream.

Once they were submerged together, he knew that this was what he'd wanted all along—to be saturated and tangled up with her in the deep end. What was to fear? They knew how to swim.

"You ass!" Eleanor had yelled when their heads emerged. She then jumped on his back to dunk him. Feeling her limbs acrobatically weave with his transported him to those coming-of-age pool parties when un- derwater horseplay was the closest proxy to a sexual encounter. When everyone was weightless and didn't know what they were doing or feeling or if they were the only one.

Nat continued to wade while Eleanor swam over to the shallow end. She stood up and scrunched the water from her hair. The white dress had molded to her, eclipsing the memory of his first wet dream after seeing Jacqueline Bisset scuba dive in *The Deep*.

"You happy now?" Eleanor said, like Nat could ever believe she was as annoyed as she was trying to sound.

"More like painfully bothered." Nat eventually paddled over to the ladder. He felt the weight of the water and its suctioning effect on his suit when he pulled himself out of the pool. He took off his jacket, tried to further loosen the soggy noose of his tie, and sprawled onto the ground. Gravity began to do its thing with all the excess water that had clung to his clothes, soaking into the stone.

"This feels too good," Eleanor said and continued to float gracefully, stirring a fog above her.

The late night sky began to chill his body. He'd already suspected they might've disappeared too long when he heard Nikki and other voices making their way towards the pool. Nat peeled himself off the ground and snuck away to get them towels.

Retrieving the towels presented a challenge. They were inside cabinets behind a candlelit table where Will was telling stories to Frida and Lindsay's sister, Tina. Tina's husband was sitting there too, but had already been bored to sleep.

"What happened to you?" Tina said.

Nat opened the cabinets and sampled each of the towels. He selected the one that felt the thickest, then tossed it at Will. Will was caught off-guard and the towel uncoiled, startling Tina's husband to wake.

"I threw Eleanor in the pool," Nat confessed unapologetically.

"Why are you wet, then?" Tina's husband asked.

"He speaks!" Nat said. No wonder he didn't, though. Tina's husband's pitch was as high as his toddler's. Nat took one of the open bottles of wine from their table to retire to his bungalow.

In his room, Nat shucked off his wet clothes and hung them over the open windowsill. Nat lay on the starched bed sheets that felt like a tablecloth. He could hear his suit drip in the night's stillness. His eyes were heavy, but he felt too much not to grab his pen and let some of those emotions come to the page.

One last kiss to the bottle and he was out.

▶▶

Upon waking, Nat discovered a letter he had written, fueled by sangiovese and now totally stained by it. He laughed at himself and then crumpled the love-drunk words into a ball. Nat opened his bedroom door to the communal kitchen and living space where Frida had her back turned, facing the sink. Nat rushed to hit a buzzer shot into the wastebasket, then shut himself back in his room.

16

JAMIE

INSTEAD OF FLYING FIRST-CLASS to Italy, Jamie was an outburst shy of spending the night in a TSA holding cell. Luckily, some older broads adopted him. They swooped in like hairsprayed angels with leather bag tans, saving him from the gate agents who'd called for backup. They called him "Just J." He coined them "The Babs" because there were multiple Barbaras and they were badass, ripping on everyone they knew with sick burns. These were his people. The Babs offered Jamie a ride after failing to haggle in the duty-free store. But where would Jamie go? Almost everyone he knew was a mile high.

It was drizzling outside in the passenger pickup zone. One of the Babs' daughters picked them up in this big white truck that smelled like upholstered smoke and sour apple candy. The daughter was all right. She knew of Bolero but was more into Mariah Carey and R&B. She didn't talk much during the ride but Jamie and the Babs passed around a bottle of rum leftover from their Caribbean cruise and laughed their asses off.

Jamie gave them Rollins' approximate address in Brooklyn. Rollins would have money, drugs, and someone to get Jamie's passport and travel sorted. But this game plan wasn't enough to stop Jamie from feeling sorry for himself, thinking of everyone laughing at him getting shut down from boarding and missing the first wedding where he wouldn't be a ring bearer or a waiter. He was also missing Frida. He'd been so good since she'd left for fashion week, and for what?

When they pulled up to Rollins' block, Jamie thanked the Babs profusely with sugarcane kisses and told them to call Bolero's tour manager, Old Betty, for tickets to the big show on New Year's Eve at Radio City. They said that was so fancy and then disappeared after a few car honks and water spit up from the truck's back wheels.

It'd been a while since Jamie'd been to Rollins' house. Mary banned him after he raided their medicine closet, but Jamie figured it was because Rollins always gave Mary excuses that incriminated Jamie instead of herself. People had been throwing Jamie under the bus like that forever. Jamie rang the bell several times, hoping Rollins would answer, but Mary opened the door. She looked disheveled in floral pajamas, her red hair wisping out.

"Jamie?" Mary peered her head out the door and did a full scan, like his showing up was part of a prank. "What are you doing here? Aren't you supposed to be in Italy?"

"Couldn't get on my flight."

"I don't understand," she said. "Did you not disclose that you're a felon or something? Because we will sue the shit out of you for breaching—"

"No, Mary. C'mon, it's not like that."

"Well, I'm not going to ask you again," she said, crossing her arms.

Jamie sighed. "I forgot my passport, okay?"

"Oh Jesus, you are a fucking child, aren't you."

Jamie put his head down and switched the hand that held his duffel.

"Well, hurry up then," she said. "I'm already busy taking care of another baby."

Jamie could hear the cluck-like cries of the baby from the depths of the house. Subserviently, he followed Mary through the grand, black-painted rooms covered in crazy paintings. The kitchen was in the back of the house, where the baby was in his carrier thing, squirming. A big TV was playing local crisis-type news on top of the counter. It occurred to Jamie that the last time he'd been in that kitchen, it had a giant pyramid of champagne and a bunch of runway models that had nothing on Frida.

"You certainly packed light," Mary said.

"Yeah. Frida was bringing my suit and some stuff from Milan and we were gonna go shopping once we got to London."

Mary whipped out her tit to feed the baby, whose head also looked like a fuzzy ginger boob.

"So, where is Rollins?" he asked, trying to focus on eyewitness news.

"Don't get jealous now. She's out with a different group of man children that we risk our livelihoods on so they can make records. Call her. It's on the speed dial." Mary pointed to their phone/fax combo next to the fridge. "She might answer that brick we made her schlep around since Desmond was born. Isn't that right, Dizzy?"

This time, Jamie's internal pleading for Rollins to answer worked.

"Hey, hey hun. I said I'd be back in a few hours. Couple more hours. All good over there?" Rollins said.

"Rolls, it's Jamie."

"Jamie Dempsey? What the... Is the phone tripping? Is this inbound really from my house?"

"Yeah, man. I'm at your house."

"You were all flying out for KP's wedding tonight. Right? I know I got that squared, or have I lost my shit?"

"Nah. You're right. I didn't make it."

"Jamie, kid. I don't understand."

Jamie could hear laughter and girls in the background. "Where are you?" he asked.

"I'm ah... I got some action going on. Mostly business."

"So are you gonna fuckin' help me or what?" Jamie said.

"Ha! I can't believe you think I'm the person to help you, kid. Did you tell Mary any of this shit yet?" Rollins said.

Jamie looked at Mary, taking care of her and Rollins' son. Even though Mary kind of looked happy, that didn't make it fair that she had to be the one who stayed home while Rollins was out there coppin' god knows what. Like Jamie's mom, Joanie always took the brunt and never complained. Jamie admired that about her, but Nat seemed to resent it. Jamie thought Nat was too hard on Joanie.

"Can I just come meet up with you? Where are you at?" Jamie asked.

"I'm at The Royalton," Rollins said. "Listen, though, I'm with some people you might know..."

"Okay, whatever man. I'll behave."

"Don't make promises you can't keep, kid."

Jamie smirked and hung up the phone. He knew Mary had been doing that mom thing where it didn't look like she was listening, but probably knew more than anyone even directly involved in the conversation.

"I gotta go meet up with her," he told Mary.

"Is that so?" Mary replied. The baby wasn't feeding anymore, but in a position to burp on her shoulder. "Jamie, do yourself a favor and just go home. That's where your passport is, right?"

"Yeah, but it's early," Jamie said. "And like, all the flights to Italy are only at night, right? So I don't even have to be up early tomorrow."

"Fine," she said. Jamie was relieved that Mary didn't try to fight him. Jamie was uncomfortable when adults raised their voices in front of babies. "Someone will be in touch tomorrow about your flight and travel. Just keep your shit together until you hear from us around noon."

►►

Jamie dropped his bag in a suite at The Royalton. He changed his shirt and rinsed his mouth. Jamie loved these money hotels that had little bottles of mouthwash. He'd remembered begging Joanie to buy him mouthwash when he was a kid. Not even because it had alcohol. He loved its fresh effect, like a swish of minty Slurpee. But back then, Listerine was an unnecessary luxury, something he'd eventually shoplift.

Jamie followed the hotel's blue carpet and snake handrails back to the sunken lobby bar, where he was intercepted by Rollins. Jamie could smell smoky booze on her.

"Listen, kid. Some girlies are here," she said.

"Yeah?"

"One is, uh, one of your old gal pals, Diana... I mean, don't get any ideas that it's got shit to do with me. You know how she is, though... she loves to be in the thick of things." Rollins scratched a swirl of her black hair. "Anyway, I'm here with The Scream tonight so..."

"So?" Jamie said.

"Well, Diana's pretty chummy with Roger, and so that's where we're at with all that. You cool, kid?"

"Yeah, she's gettin' with some old Scottish geezer now? Whatever. Been there, done that."

"Sure, sure kid... just, see..." Rollins pulled Jamie under her arm and whispered, "Rog and these guys are no joke. I mean, you're the odd man out here, you know what I mean?"

"Whatever, man. I don't care. I'm cool. Not looking for trouble, I just wanna get a little tuned up."

"Well, we have a solution for that," Rollins replied, along with a grumbly giggle. She shoved Jamie toward some private bar off the main one. It was a semicircular room with puff-padded walls and a floor that was like a dartboard where Diana Campbell was standing on the bullseye. Diana was the only person Jamie knew who'd compete as hard as him for attention, and tonight was no different. There she was, not wearing a bra under a fuzzy white sweater with a short orange skirt that had a zipper up the front with a little silver loop to stick a finger and pull down.

Jamie pretended not to see her, even when he was in earshot to hear her huff at these two identical-looking tramps she'd brought with her. Diana's sidekicks had streaked hair in pigtails and wore sleeveless turtle-neck mini dresses. One accessorized with a floppy hat. Neither was as hot as Diana. Jamie wiped his mouth to hide his grin. This was classic Diana. A mastermind with a short circuit.

Rollins introduced Jamie to the already lubricated members of The Scream. "This is Roger, Shane, and Sammy. They're as legendary as the Loch Ness Monster and kept Bewilder alive in the dark ages of glam metal."

There were lots of "ayes" and shoulder slapping.

"Is the wee bairn a fuckin' chancer an aw?" Roger asked Rollins.

Jamie was excited to hang out with people who didn't speak his English. It was unbelievable to him that these scruffy grimers with their guttural accents were from the same little island as Frida!

"Jamie's cut from the same cloth," Rollins said.

Jamie nodded with as much reverence as possible for someone who wasn't a fan of their music. The Scream sounded like The Replacements playing Southern rock, but Jamie held back his critique tighter than a fart during fellatio. Rollins wasn't kidding. These dudes were tough. They wore it on their bodies and faces. Even Shane, the guy whose glasses were thicker than a stripper's lucite heel.

Jamie confirmed the band's preference for Tennessee whiskey instead of their ancestral sauce and contributed two bottles of Jack. The gesture entwined Jamie like a new thread on their clan's tartan. Jamie had taken a few shots before Diana approached him.

"Shouldn't you be at the wedding I'm not at because of you?" she said.

Jamie shrugged and looked to find an angle out of their conversation. He wasn't ready for the game she would win outright or by chastising him for not being capable of doing the right thing, which manipulated him into giving up and doing the wrong thing.

Roger mentioned something in his brogue about going somewhere rowdier than The Royalton, so they rambled down the street to a place with a narrow bar and a boxing theme called Jimmy's. Rollins peeled off to talk with the cool old geezer who might've been Jimmy.

"I like seeing all these heavyweights, man," Jamie said to Rog. They clanked pints hard enough to erupt a waterfall down Jamie's fingers. "Fuckin' champions."

"Ah ken thair's nothin' like havin' yir moment with the belt, eh, lad?"

"Yeah?" Jamie replied, not knowing what Rog said. "You ever been on that *Pops* show that films live in London?"

"'89," Rog said stoically.

"When you had the belt?" Jamie said.

"Aye."

Rollins swung in with another round.

Everyone said "*Slàinte*," something Jamie, the Irish, proudly understood.

Bolero's manager, Joe Beck, and his beady eyes weaseled into the pack.

"What's he doing here?" Jamie said.

"You know what I'm doing here. I don't care if you miss the wedding, you've gotta make the *Pops*."

"*Pops* is worth fuck all," said Shane. "Aw lip sync and pantomime. Ave ye seen it even?"

"Nah, we don't get that shit over here," Jamie replied, beginning to catch onto their Highland lingo. The bit about the lip synching gave Jamie an idea about a prank Bolero could pull on the *Pops*.

"Pish," Shane whispered in Jamie's ear. His breath reeked like hamburger meat and relish.

Rollins settled the bill at Jimmy's. She then pulled Jamie aside and said, "Listen. I know you wanna knock off the training wheels, but reel it in."

"Fine, but why's Beck here?"

"That's just fuckin' insurance, kid. Take it easy and consider him your walking bank or bail out."

Rollins left the bar, and they all saluted her.

"Canny lass, that Rolls," Rog said.

"Good polis, bad polis," Sammy said, shoving little Joe Beck to make sure it was known which one they thought Beck was.

Diana stepped in front of Jamie to give Rog a hug and a sloppy double kiss. Jamie watched Rog's beat-up hands firm around her ass.

"The girls wanna go clubbing," Diana told Rog loud enough for Jamie to hear.

Rog laughed. "Fuckin' disco techno n aw tha?"

"C'mon. We'll make it worth your while," she said, turning to grind on Rog before stepping away to let him deliberate.

"Fuckin' bonny, ain't she lad?" Rog said.

Jamie shrugged.

"Ah ken tha look. Smilin' aw coolly at Diana," Rog said.

"What?" Jamie asked, genuinely unsure of what Rog'd said, and not trying to die.

"Ah could fuckin well ken ye bin wi tha burd."

"Been with her?" Jamie asked.

Rog squeezed Jamie's shirt around his chest into a ball and pulled him close enough to see Rog's face morph into a cutthroat. "Ah'm no fuckin dafty, mate."

"No shit. Yeah, we got a history," Jamie admitted. "I'm not gonna step on your fucking toes, man. I swear. I got a girl."

Rog tossed Jamie into Sammy, leaving him susceptible to being crushed by an even bigger dude who was now petting Jamie like a cat. Luckily, Diana put The Scream's biggest hit on the jukebox. This pepped everyone up before they left Jimmy's timeless corner for the Stoplight, a club that probably wouldn't survive another one of the city's crackdowns.

▶▶

The limo was packed, and the ride was bumpy. When they got to the club, Joe Beck ran ahead to talk with the yellow jacket doorman. Beck pointed to Jamie, and then the doorman waved them to the side door.

It was loud and hot and dark if not for the blinking lights. Shane from The Scream's coke-bottle glasses immediately fogged up.

"Too bad getting us in won't make your any dick bigger," Diana yelled over the thumping beat.

"Funny, I don't remember it fitting in your big ass mouth," Jamie said.

"We got a table over there." Joe Beck motioned them to an area behind black velvet ropes. Jamie and The Scream got settled with drinks. They looked like *The Warriors* had bum-rushed the set of a Deee-Lite music video. The girls stayed local to dance to the addictive beats mashed up with sound effects like whistles and buzzers.

An older guy in another VIP section summoned Diana to join his table. She twirled and flashed her ass for Rog and Jamie to see before strutting off, then bent over again like a prostitute into a john's rolled-down car window to chat up the man at the other table. Jamie was confused when Diana glanced back to look at him and laugh smuglike. They didn't speak long, and when Diana came back; she had a message for Jamie.

"For me?" Jamie said.

"Yeah, he says he wants to talk to you," Diana said. "He knows you."

"What the fuck? I don't know him," Jamie insisted. Rog scratched his butted chin.

"Thair a buftie oan yir hands, laddie?" Shane asked.

"I dunno," Jamie said, thumbing the corner of his lip.

"Ye need fir reinforcements, like?" said Sammy, grinding his knuckles.

"Nah," Jamie replied. "They look like a buncha rich wankers."

Jamie approached the other VIP table with his usual long-arm swag of a walk. The guy who'd called Diana over was dark, like Italian or Greek or something. He wasn't ugly except for the way he swirled in the smoke from his fat cigar. His face didn't register with Jamie. He looked serious, like he told the kind of jokes that slapped harder than a belt.

"Are you enjoying yourself?" the man asked Jamie.

"Yeah." Jamie nodded a few times, glancing back towards his Scots. They looked like they were sharpening knives under the table, which gave Jamie a little bit of a shit grin. "Just havin' a good night with some friends."

"Oh yeah?" the man said. His eyebrows looked manicured, and they flattened in this disapproving way when he spoke. "You don't remember me, do you?"

He kinda looked familiar, but now Jamie encountered people all the time that said they'd seen him or knew him. It was disorienting. "Did you come to a show or something?" Jamie asked.

"No," the man said definitively.

"I'm not too good at remembering random dudes' faces," Jamie said. "We've met?"

"Oh yeah, we've met," he replied and placed his cigar on the ashtray to rest.

"Like I said, man, I can't keep tabs on all that," Jamie said.

"Sure, sure. You know what I keep tabs on?" The man jiggled his index finger to summon Jamie close to tell him, "I keep tabs on little mop head shitbags who fuck my girlfriend before the sheets are changed."

"What are you talking about?" Jamie had committed to his position of confused denial even as he remembered it was the goon from Club USA. "I don't know who the fuck you are."

The man stood up and buttoned his suit jacket. Jamie was tall, but he was staggering. "I'm Danny fuckin' Garibaldi," he said, shifting a smile of injurious promise to one side of his mouth. The bass in the club thudded like low blows into Jamie's gut. D GARIBALDI. That name was on every other envelope that slid through the brass slot on Frida's door. Was Jamie fucking stupid? Maybe, but it was New York. People were transient. Why wouldn't it be a previous tenant of the apartment? Why would it be a current fucking tenant of the parts of Frida Jamie now thought of as his alone? He felt a helpless rage.

"Listen, man," Jamie's voice almost cracked. "Frida never told me about you." That was true, but Jamie thought to himself that if he'd known, it wouldn't have mattered. There was nothing that would've stopped him from being with Frida then, or now.

Danny pulled Jamie in by the neck without asking this time. "Kid. I'm gonna pretend to believe you and tell you once, nicely. Take your dirt bag crew and get the fuck—" Danny interrupted himself and released his feverish hand from Jamie's neck to duck from a bottle. The Scream must've been closing in since things looked more heated from afar than they were up close.

Shane tossed Jamie his glasses so he could indiscriminately punch one of Danny's goons who'd stepped up.

Little pistol Joe Beck pulled Jamie by the neck of his shirt. "Out. Now!" Beck barked through his clenched jaw, shoving Jamie toward the side door exit, only to be stymied. The Stoplight's security was blocking them from leaving, and Joe Beck's neck veins were about to blow like geysers.

"This way!" Diana grabbed Jamie's arm, and the two sidekicks huddled around him. The one took off her floppy hat and put it on Jamie's head. The other kissed him to transfer her purple lipstick onto Jamie's lips. Jamie completed his disguise by putting on Shane's glasses, which made him not only blind but so dizzy, Jamie started to dry heave as they were on the run.

They'd escaped to the front of the Stoplight. Jamie removed Shane's fishbowl lenses and ditched the hat. The street was packed with people not waiting to take the party inside. Diana whistled for the limo idling by the door that had blocked their retreat. They hopped inside, and the two girls scurried up the galley to giggle while Jamie and Diana anchored the back. Behind the tinted windows, Jamie could tell that people had seen them. Some ravers gathered around the stretch. Diana found the button to open the moon roof and stood to look out. Not to be outdone, Jamie stuck the better half of his body out with her. Diana blew kisses, and Jamie flipped the bird at some vulture-like paps, who were now in on the action.

"I heard what you said about me to Rollins," Diana said.

"What'd I say?"

"Been there, done that." Diana's expression was a hot mess of angry and horny and wounded, otherwise known as Jamie's exact emotional profile.

"Didn't say I wouldn't do it again," Jamie said under his breath, finding the loop of Diana's skirt zipper to stick his finger through and tug.

"Fuck you," Diana said. Her hand toyed with the buckle of his belt and rubbed down the furry trail beneath his navel.

Jamie thought about how quickly he'd let Diana take him in her mouth again, to swallow his rattled pride.

"There they are!" Diana slapped Jamie's hand away and jumped up and down on the seat cushion to wave.

Jamie could see Sammy was carrying Joe Beck like a sleeping child pulled from a house fire alongside a bloodied Shane and Rog, Rog still drinking a beer.

"Over here!" Diana screamed.

Everyone but Joe Beck appeared calm, if not fucking jovial, once they'd piled back into the car, leaving whatever club carnage behind them. Diana immediately tended to Rog, straddling him right next to Jamie and pressing a bundle of tissues to the cut on Rog's face. Joe Beck let out a wail as he laid arms crossed on the limo floor like he was being waked alive.

Jamie began to belt out laughter. How was he the only one unscathed?

It was then, out of nowhere and years in the making, that Diana wound up and gave Jamie a crack of a slap that blinded him for the second time that night.

17

FRIDA

I T WAS THE MORNING after the wedding. Frida let the water overrun the brim of a pot she'd been using instead of a kettle for tea when she heard Nat's door open and close quickly. She felt relieved, not insulted, that he had avoided interacting with her so early. Frida seemed to have met her match in Nat's desire for privacy. Despite dwelling in the same small bungalow in Castelfiore for days, they'd hardly spotted each other.

Frida's bare foot had stepped on something after pivoting backwards to reach for a mug. She'd squashed what was a wine-splattered ball of paper next to the waste bin. A few visible words lured Frida to lift what had nearly been discarded. She abandoned her tea and tiptoed to read the rest behind the closed door of her room.

Frida spread and flattened the paper. Its texture from the crumples and dried stains gave an archival impression, as though it were of historic consequence. On a held breath, she read the words:

> *ELEANOR,*
> *I DON'T KNOW WHAT THIS IS,*
> *BUT FUCK ME IF IT'S NOT LOVE.*
> ~~*IF WE WERE TOGETHER I'D JOKE*~~
> ~~*AND SAY FUCK ME EITHER WAY*~~
> *WHAT ARE WE WAITING FOR?*

THE OTHER NIGHT YOU DIDN'T WANT TO WAIT ANY-
MORE —
WAS I WRONG TO STOP YOU?
~~*I SWORE THE NEXT TIME YOU LET ME KISS YOU I*~~
~~*WOULDN'T STOP*~~
~~*UNTIL YOU KNEW WE COULD NEVER BE JUST FRIENDS.*~~
WE BELONG TOGETHER IN THE DEEP END
IF YOU'RE READY, I'M YOURS FOREVER —
I MIGHT ALREADY BE.

Frida pursed her lips to exhale her laboured breath, then reread the letter several times until the words jumbled into a complex emotional response that she could not quite categorise. It was as close to thrill as it was to heartbreak. Frida's thoughts returned to the Apex Awards, when she had by chance witnessed Nat gaze with unmistakable bliss at Eleanor from across the room before turning away, having discovered she had come as Will's date. And again, as they stood across from one another during yesterday's ceremony. Jamie had laughed and dismissed Frida's soft enquiry about Nat and Eleanor's relationship. Nat's letter had put to bed whether something had happened between them in the past. Now, Frida begged to wonder if something more would.

Frida crushed the letter again and held it to her chest. She mourned the words that it seemed for now Nat had chosen not to say before carefully returning the balled-up paper to the bin. Only this time, it'd be carefully placed inside.

▶▶

Later that morning, Frida dressed for the pool and brought Marianne Faithfull's recently released autobiography to the veranda where breakfast service was extended to accommodate for the wedding's late night festivities. As such, those lingering at breakfast were those who'd lingered late at the party. Will was sat on the edge with a coffee and a book. Eleanor and Nat were seated at a table in the sun, playing blackjack. Whoever lost the round was charged to swig from various pitchers of water and fresh-squeezed juices to rehydrate from yesterday's alcohol.

Frida picked at a plate of berries from behind her sunglass veil. She could no longer hide the disappointment from her face that Jamie had yet to arrive. Before sleeping last night, she'd even opened the doors to the terrace, as though it would ease his passage to accompany her in dreams. Whilst pretending to read, Frida eavesdropped on Sulky's chat with Nikki's assistant, Dominic. Dominic had promised to bleach Sulky's hair once they returned to New York. Sulky had never been pleasant to Frida, but on this trip, she found he'd come out of his shell and was nearly amicable when not vying for Jamie's approval.

"What did you want to be when you grew up?" Sulky asked Frida.

"What did I want to be?" Frida repeated, as if the question had never entered her mind. "Maybe a dancer?"

"Well, you *were* a back-up dancer before that prima donna kicked you off tour because you got too much attention," Dominic said.

"Oh, that's just gossip." It wasn't, but it was best not to stir a settled pot. "What about you?" Frida asked Sulky.

"What are you guys talking about?" said Eleanor.

"What everyone wanted to be when they grew up," Dominic said.

Nat looked up from his cards. "I know what Miss Huston aspired to be."

Eleanor punched Nat's arm.

"Hey, I didn't say 'Hit me,'" Nat said.

"So stupid. It says nothing about me."

"It says something about you..." Nat replied.

Will put down his book. "Well, now we have to know."

"A boxing ref," Eleanor said. "I don't know. My dad worked a lot of fights at the Garden."

"Now all I can do is picture you with a black bowtie and a whistle!" said Dominic. "Reffing little Jamie and little Nat over whose turn it is to play with the GI Joe!"

Frida laughed along with the group. She felt nearly relaxed when Jamie interrupted.

"Where's my *bella donna*?" He sauntered onto the grounds of the villa and dropped his Burberry duffel in the dirt. Hearing his voice gave her a flutter. Jamie's reception from the others was less friendly. She waited for him to come to her and lift her for a snog. Jamie tasted of an airport smoking lounge and beer. It was unlike him to smell so sour.

"Did I miss anything?"

"Make no mistake, brother. You were not missed," said Nat, shuffling the deck of playing cards one last time before putting them back in their sleeve.

▶▶

Jamie crashed onto the double bed, not having realised it comprised two singles which had rifted them apart. The wooden legs made a horrible sound, skidding against rust-coloured tile.

"Whoa." Jamie popped up to push the beds back together and then laid down a second time, more gently.

Frida stood cold and quiet, like the lizards around the property that froze on shaded walls and stone. But waiting for him to divulge anything about his unaccounted-for days was heating her blood.

"Are you gonna come over here?" he said.

"I've just gotten up."

"You don't want to lay with me? Funny," he said, suddenly flipping the switch of his tone. "I should be the one holding a grudge."

"Pardon?"

"Can't believe I'm here all this way to smooth shit over when you're the one—"

"Are you mad? What have I done?" she asked incredulously, without raising her voice.

Jamie smashed pillows behind him to prop himself up. "You are really fuckin' good at this innocence game."

"Are you in fact taking a piss right now?" she heard herself say and gripped her book to stop her hands from trembling. "I've not a clue what you're implying. In fact, this sounds awfully convenient."

"What's convenient to me? Coming all this way for nothing? Thinking the whole time about you playing me when you're still with that guido rich fuck from the club."

She sat on the corner of the bed and inched towards him, cautiously approaching as though he were a wounded animal. "Why would you think that?"

"Is it true?" Jamie rubbed his eyes. She noticed one side of Jamie's symmetrical face looked swollen. Frida could not tell if it was because he was overly tired, sad, or if it was a consequence of something ill-fated.

"Of course it's not true. Is it more red top gossip? Who's led you to believe this?" she asked, her temperature rising again.

"Forget it. I can't fucking deal with this."

"Forget it?"

"Yeah. I don't even want to know," Jamie mumbled. He took off his blue oxford shirt and trainers and manoeuvred himself to lie down. As he became more resigned, Frida felt more enraged. They both possessed these split extremes, Geminis after all, and now they were working against each other.

Frida stood up again and left their unhappy reunion.

Outside, it had become humid and overcast. Many of the wedding guests were slowly bringing themselves to leave the villa. Those staying one last night remained scattered about. Frida found it unbearable to be in their proximity this fragile. She was much like the weather now, uncomfortable with gloom and capsizing under the weight of tears. She walked up the dust trail to the gate and exited.

Frida followed the unpaved road, battered by both car tires and carriages, bordered thickly by trees and brush. Walking down to where the dirt road became gravel at a crooked fork took several minutes. She veered left, which continued gradually down before plateauing. The tall green brush cleared into a stretch of dormant olive groves, and then a yellowing hayfield. There was a second fork. Each way led steeply down hills, perhaps into the town of Castelfiore or the entrance to the *autostrada*. She stood for the moment, directionless, without vigour. It was as if she'd reached the end of the runway and it was time to pump her shoulders, point her toe, squeeze her waist, and spin around to walk back. She moved more slowly on the return, past the fields and groves. Frida had begun to perspire and resent the frailty of her leather sandals to withstand the inclining trek.

"Hey!"

Frida heard a breathy yell from behind her. It was Eleanor. She was in mismatched athletic clothes and making a fast pace towards her. It oc-

curred to Frida that Eleanor ran more elegantly than she walked, which
was a decidedly endearing physical characteristic. When she reached
Frida, Eleanor caught her breath.

"Woo, that hill sucked! What are you doing out here?" she asked.

"I needed to have a walk." Frida looked down and swirled her dusted
toes around in the gravel.

"I bet. Oh my god, why didn't I bring water?" Eleanor said, keeling
over. "You wanna talk about it?"

Frida contemplated. "I don't know."

She and Eleanor ascended the hill again together.

"I don't blame you," Eleanor said.

"For what?"

"For being pissed off," she said, almost ambitiously matter of fact.

"Thank you," Frida replied with a flattened smile.

"To be honest, I am shocked Jamie found his way here at all," Eleanor
said.

"That sounds rather helpless."

Eleanor laughed. "You've been together long enough to know that
Jamie is basically helpless. Right?"

But it was Frida who felt helpless with the troubles she was climbing
to face again at the top of the hill. She panted to avoid a cry.

"Oh no, Frida. Wait. I mean, he actually got here! He really loves you is
all I'm saying. I mean—he's definitely never said that to anyone before."

Frida trusted the intentions in Eleanor's expression. She had encountered glimmers of Eleanor's sincerity before, yesterday, during the ceremony, admiring Lindsay and Keith, and whenever she and Nat were off
playing their games. In the end, Eleanor disarmed Frida, and she wept
like she hadn't done since her first boyfriend let her drink too much
brandy.

"That's very kind," Frida said after a time during which she had regained composure.

"Do you want me to talk to him? I mean, is it just that he showed up late?"

Frida assessed her risk of involving Eleanor. "That's not all."

"What's going on?"

"He's given in to some rumour about me that I'm still seeing this man, Danny. It's all rather suspect as he's only now arrived with no explanation of his whereabouts and..." Frida petted her temple as if to calm its pulsating. "I can't."

"Oh, shit," Eleanor said. "That sucks."

Frida cackled. "Yes. That sucks."

When they had finally reached the gate to reenter the villa, Eleanor said she'd talk to Jamie. "I need a mission, anyway."

"Now?"

"Sure. Will wanted to go into the village for lunch and to walk around the market, though. Would you go?"

"You're sure?"

"Definitely. You're like the only person Will really likes here, anyway."

►►

The clouds had cleared, and so had Will and Frida's half-eaten plates of cheeses and small salads. They sat outside a café facing a quaint fountain and a few stands of produce and goods. Merchants had begun packing up to honour the afternoon *siesta*. It was only after Will had lit his cigarette that he appeared to remember to light hers. The shy sun had baked into his evenly bronzed complexion. He pushed back his longer hair that had a slight curl and asked for espressos from their plain-clothed server, who had been watching them, or her, rather intently.

"You know quite a bit of Italian," she observed.

"My mother is Italian," Will said.

"Are you two close?"

"I'd say so. I was always treated like an adult. So, we're sort of like friends. There's less of that deferential barrier I've seen with some other parent-child relationships."

Frida had wondered if Will's tone was alluding to Eleanor's relationship with her father, but Frida did not pry and simply said that was interesting.

"Was that the same for you?" he asked.

Frida held her inhale for a moment before answering. "Yes, and no. I was not necessarily treated like an equal. But there were firm expectations to carry adult responsibilities very young... I think it's made me quite serious."

"How so?"

"Well, I know I have a presence. I rarely bring a lighter energy. Eleanor, for example. She has such an ease about her, a comfortable energy." Frida ashed. "I'm not like that."

"I think you're being hard on yourself, not seeing people how they really are. Your energy is enigmatic. Very appealing," Will said.

"It's not that I'm unaware there isn't something marketable about it."

Will perked his brow. He had an elegant profile, with wonderful lines and concave cheeks. Yet he seemed hardened.

The older man acting as server had dropped off their espressos and then walked back to his perch, continuing to ogle Frida.

"Thank you. That's how you take espresso." Will complimented her cultural know-how to drink it quickly. "There are a lot of novices on this trip," he said.

"Very harmless, no?"

He rolled his shoulders. "Here. But can't imagine trying to walk the streets of Rome or Florence."

"You don't mean Eleanor."

"No. She's got that street *savoir faire*." Will pushed the swirl of hair from his face once more. "But she's still green. A little over the top with this London trip for business."

"Well, she should take it seriously, should she not? I'd be very intimidated working for Aja Green." Frida wondered if she had misjudged Eleanor in the past, for perceiving her not to take her relationship with Will seriously. It now appeared it was Will who did not take Eleanor seriously.

Will sat back, stretched his legs to put his hands in his pockets. "Aja seems to enjoy the power trip."

"It can be difficult. To be a woman in that world," Frida said softly. All the while, she could have said that it was challenging to be a woman in any world.

"Fair enough," Will said. "To be honest, this trip hasn't been a good time. I mean, it didn't come at a good time. I need to get back."

"Nothing too serious, I hope."

"That's historically when something nefarious happens," Will said.

▶▶

When Frida returned from the village, Jamie was no longer in bed. Frida drew herself a bath, adding caps of the pantry's olive oil to the clawed tub, a beauty tip she learned from Sofia Loren. Frida spun her weightless hair up into a twist before soaking, occasionally admiring the shade of the orange walls saturate.

She heard the outer door of the bungalow close. Shortly thereafter, Jamie had knocked and requested to enter. When he did, she found his disposition had improved. He looked rested and tidied. Jamie dropped to the ground and leaned his oval chin on his arm, which rested upon the bath's ledge. His eyelashes were like awnings. She felt his stare, not upon her naked curves that taunted above the waterline, but searching her glassy eyes as if to see what might break them and return to his favour.

"Frida, I'm sorry."

Frida held onto his apology before asking him what he was sorry for, since any elaboration would likely destroy the simplicity and ease of accepting it.

"I fucked up," he said.

"I don't understand why you've gone to blaming me." Frida moved her hands from the outer sides of her thighs and pulled them across her torso.

Jamie took her nearest hand from the water and clasped it with both of his to hold while he spoke. "When I heard that shit back when I was stuck in New York, it was like—like you don't love me and it fucked with my head because I know I love you."

She waited for him to say he loved her again and for it to feel good.

"Since the first night I met you. I thought I was gonna get trampled on and fucking die and I didn't care 'cause I was chasing you. I love you." Frida found herself reciprocating the pressure on his hand with hers, but then he pulled away and leaned against the tiled wall. "And then it's like it was some sneaky bullshit game," he said.

"It's not," Frida said, even if it might have been at the start. She turned her body towards him, shifting the water with her movement. Jamie had turned quiet, which made her nervous. "Jamie—" Frida shoved her doubts like fingers down her throat. She stared in his dilated, fair sky eyes shot with thunderous ripples of red while her own eyes slid tears into the water. "Please." She reached towards him.

Jamie crawled back to kneel beside her and then leaned over, submerging his arms to embrace her body in the water. He kissed her, his full lips abrasive against hers until her mouth surrendered. Frida draped her arms around his neck, holding tightly as Jamie moved to lift her from the water.

Once she was stood out on the tiles, Jamie dropped to his knees to caress and lap between the delicate lines below her waist. It felt as if she had entered the warmth of the bath again. She kneaded the lush perks of her breasts as Jamie slid down his trousers. She used his shoulders to dip down whilst he guided himself inside her, filling her with immediacy to thrust upon the floor.

"I love you," she released and cried as they, for the first time, came together.

▶▶

Frida felt as though she was floating since they'd landed in London. She and Jamie had a few days to themselves prior to Bolero's slot on the *Tops* television showcase. They had a royal spree on the King's Road, then hid in North London, where they could stay out all night and in bed all day. Jamie had insisted on caring for her family and hosting a private Sunday roast in Hampstead at the Shepherd's Inn. Jamie played "Wolf", which involved crawling around on the 17th-century floorboards to hunt Frida's niece and nephew. Later that evening, Frida plucked the splinters from Jamie's hands. She couldn't recall the last time her parents had been in the same room together. Jamie had shone by encouraging them to share their fondest memories of the better days.

Bolero's American Invasion went smoothly. A press shoot at The Savoy, a signing at the HMV on Oxford, a taping with Jools Holland. Besides Eleanor's disconcerting absence, there hadn't been a hiccup. Frida suspected Eleanor had left at Will's behest. She kept this to herself, even when Aja Green prodded her about the matter.

The trip culminated at the broadcast for the *Tops*. Bolero's performance was nothing short of a riot. Despite the programme being filmed in front of a live audience, the *Tops* now required bands to pantomime their performances to prerecorded music. Bolero had premeditated to switch roles as a gag. Nat wore shades, clanged a star-shaped tambourine, and stylishly lip-sang in place of Jamie. Nat was smashing—absolutely charming, at ease the way many can only be when acting. Sulky and Greg had swapped their instruments. KP had worn one of Nat's checked Oxfords that barely buttoned on his larger frame. Jamie tapped the drums, flashed KP's borrowed wedding band, and gave abstract stares during the *Tops'* classic filming angles that swooped in for closeups. The crowd devoured their playful attitudes.

The hiccup came at the White Studio afterparty when Jamie made some cutting remarks.

"It's funny even when Nat's pretending to be a frontman."

Nat patted Jamie's chest as though to remind him that the heart is what counts, and warned, "Someday, brother."

"Someday my tit," Jamie said. "Why don't you wish for my fucking voice in one hand and shit in the other and see which fills up first."

"You'd be the first to know what I'd do with that shit," Nat replied.

Attitudes improved after they'd met Nikki Wilshire at the Groucho Club, which was brimming with celluloid loudmouths in equal measures critical and laudatory of one another.

Nat was in rare form since his squabble with Jamie, seemingly decided to continue the charade of behaving as he perceived Jamie to act. He even smoked with Jamie's affectation, as Jamie tended to tilt his head back as if he were deeply contemplative. Nat's behaviour was nearly deviant, toying with—if not reciprocating—Nikki's advances. He hid Nikki's charge card in his trousers; however, Frida realised that even this impolite act showed Nat's gentlemanly nature, as he paid the bill Nikki was typically expected to.

It was a lavender hour when they finally exited the club. Nat insisted his London experience wouldn't be complete without riding in a black taxi. "Look at how much classier they are than our yellow metal beasts!" he nearly slurred. "Come on, Nikki. Let's get you and all those leopard prints back to the zoo."

Nikki gave Frida a priceless look of victory so unexpected that she seemed to be doubting it herself. Nikki's long limbs leaped after him into the open door.

The next morning, Frida had asked Jamie why Nat appeared to be acting out, but Jamie offered little insight. It seemed strange to her that the two brothers who could be so intuitive about so much were likewise so imperceptive, so antagonising, towards one another.

Frida held tight onto Jamie during those last days in England. She'd clutched his hand until her palms sweated, and as they slept. It was as if she knew what trouble would await her when they landed in New York.

18

ELEANOR

B ACK IN MANHATTAN, ELEANOR tugged at the hem of her peri-
winkle polo shirt dress. It was nearly the same length as Nat's
denim jacket that consistently found its way onto her body since he'd
left it at the Rink. This dress never seemed too short before, but she
felt suddenly conscientious, like she was giving ammunition to someone
already pointing a gun at her. Eleanor would have to confront Aja Green
with her legs as exposed as her feelings of shame. Eleanor had canceled her
trip assisting Aja in London for Bolero's events. Her primary excuse was
that Will said he needed her, alluding to vague troubles within his band.
But Eleanor also couldn't face how to move forward when Will told her
she'd only gotten the job with Aja as a favor for Nat. It all gnawed at her
like she wanted to gnaw at the patches of psoriasis she had once chalked
up to changing weather. Her dad would say the patches were evidence
that she was letting the stress win. "Run it off," he'd say.

After an endless ride on the D, Eleanor arrived at a restrained facade
on the Grand Concourse in the Bronx. Eleanor walked through a set
of heavy bronze doors and into a bygone era of the Wonder Theater.
The lobby of the venue was chipping with neglect and overcome by
the smell of standing water. There was a Miss Havisham melancholy
to the dizzying layers of ironwork and chandeliers caked in more dust
than the wishbones at McSorely's. Inside the theater of empty seats,
one could stare up at painted starry skies and the interior walls evoking

the exterior architecture and gardens of an Italian city. The cypresses reminded Eleanor of the last time she felt at peace, night swimming after KP and Lindsay's wedding, when those same trees that looked like wizards with wisdom tipped their hats at her and Nat.

Aja was dusting off her forearms up towards the stage. Eleanor approached her, unsure if she'd been invited to work, grovel, or be fired. She told herself she would make this okay, no matter the outcome. She had the gumption to adapt and some unexpected income. The reproduction rights to photos from her Bolero sessions kept her fed, but that didn't feel nearly as rewarding as getting word from B&M that MTV wanted her back in January. Details forthcoming.

"My grandparents settled up here after immigrating from Ireland," Eleanor said.

"The Bronx gives me a nosebleed," Aja said, beginning to weigh Eleanor down with satchels of equipment, a tripod, portable light, a clipboard, a Polaroid camera, even Aja's wool overcoat. This led Eleanor to guess she was still on for tomorrow's job.

Aja wiped her hands. "It's the last photo shoot that'll ever be here. This place is slated for demolition."

"Really? This place has so much unfulfilled potential," Eleanor said. "Like Shea Stadium."

"They'll tear that down someday, too, child. This is New York, not Paris. No one here surrenders for the cause of preservation. Don't tell me you are actually interested in sports."

Eleanor had gotten savvier at omitting truths about herself to those who didn't deserve to know, and said no. The truth was, the only time she cried when she was in Germany was when the Rangers won the Stanley Cup. She couldn't believe she missed that parade.

"Now, about that stunt you pulled in London," Aja said.

"Aja, I'm so sorry. I think you know me enough to—"

"I don't know you at all," Aja said firmly. "All I know is that most of the girls who get wrapped up in this business are fragile, either like bombs or flowers."

"Right. Well, thank you for the opportunity to apologize. I know I don't deserve it, and you don't need me."

Aja rolled her eyes, which was a physical expression that happened so frequently it might've been a tic. When Eleanor was no longer needed, Aja dismissed her until tomorrow's shoot with a monotonal reminder to wear black.

Back on the subway, Eleanor busted out her Walkman to listen to an old mixtape titled "The Mozical," which contained Smiths songs she'd arranged as an imagined musical. She felt imbalanced, focusing on the failed aimlessness in Morrissey's lyrics, not the equalizing levity and stamina of Marr's chipper riffs. She also couldn't help but acknowledge that she made "The Mozical" in high school to put off her only other big breakup.

Eleanor stopped back at the Rink for tomorrow's change of black clothes, then headed to see Will. He was in a good mood because it would be his last night in The Reverie house. The band had agreed to take a few weeks apart before rehearsals started for their tour supporting Bolero, a decision that confused her. Tomorrow, he'd move back into his apartment in the West Village. That night, Eleanor's sleep only lasted an hour before she woke and attempted to ignore the sounds of delivery trucks and chickens outside the window one final time.

▶▶

The next day, Eleanor returned to the Bronx. The shoot was a clinic, something she could be proud of, but Eleanor resolved it would be her last job with Aja. Aja laughed at Eleanor's formal resignation letter she went through the trouble to type and print at Kinko's that morning.

The next stop on Eleanor's apology tour was the 8th floor of the Music Building. Bolero practiced there most weekdays. After a rattly ride up the freight elevator, she found the windowless door to their space. The door was locked with no sounds reverberating behind it. Eleanor felt defeated to the point of hitting something when an older woman who looked like a gladiator out of Taos with the coiffe of Princess Diana walked towards her with a cowboy gait.

"Excuse me, do you know if Bolero's coming in today?" Eleanor asked.

The woman halted. She then crossed her arms as though she might've been assessing Eleanor's security risk. "Who're you?" she said with a twang.

"I'm Ele, Eleanor."

The woman's smooth, leathered face crinkled into a grin of strange teeth. "Eleanor. The Hillside honey? The boys have been talkin' about yer pop's big birthday plans!"

"What?" Eleanor questioned as she was squeezed into the woman's overwhelming embrace.

"My oh my, I hearda you." She released Eleanor from the hug, but not really. Eleanor still felt herself dangling at an arm's length while the woman got a good look at her, like she was picking out a pup from the litter.

"Really?" Eleanor said, curiously enamored by the woman.

"Bunny's told me all about you. Baby too, but mostly Bunny. I've been dyin' to meet you, Honey."

"Who's—What?" Eleanor asked, now looking down the hallway to see if this was some kind of joke.

"Well, Baby ain't gonna be here today, but you can bet your bottom the rhythm boys'll be here in about an hour—which means Bunny'll be here in about a minute—which is why I'm here about a minute earlier." The woman winked her wrinkled lid.

"Who are you?" Eleanor asked like Inigo Montoya when he encounters the Dread Pirate Roberts.

"I'm Betty, Honey!"

Betty jangled a janitorial keyset and unlocked the room before excusing herself to bring more stuff up from the van. Eleanor had a delightful sense that this lady might become part of the rest of her life.

Perhaps exactly one minute later, Eleanor felt a squeeze to her right side below the ribs. She looked right, but Nat had faked her out and was on her left. He looked showered and alive. They hugged, and he inhaled her in a way that he always had, but she now took to mean something more.

"Look what the cat dragged in," he said into her hair.

"I know," Eleanor said.

Nat stepped back and assessed her black on black ensemble. "Who died?"

Eleanor sighed. "My career."

"Career? I thought that was just something you were doing while you figure out what you really wanted. You know, like you're doing with Will."

Eleanor thrust a punch into the meat of his arm and turned to walk away.

"Hey, Huston—Eleanor, don't walk away. I'm joking."

"You're not joking."

Nat sighed. "No, but I'm poking some fun at the facts. Does that work?"

Eleanor shrugged.

"Also, shouldn't I be the one that's pissed at you for ditching us in London?"

"I know... Are you?"

"No. It's like when parents say, 'I'm not mad, I'm just *disappointed*.'"

"Not our parents," Eleanor replied.

"Pokin' fun at the facts. See? You've got the hang of it."

Eleanor felt a little less shitty.

"Come on in," Nat said, inviting her deeper into their rehearsal space, which wasn't particularly nice except for the band's equipment that had grown in size and prestige since their unsigned days.

"It might not look like we've come that far, but the Garden is four blocks that way." Nat pointed out the wall of windows in the otherwise padded room.

Eleanor moved towards the window. "Heat too," she muttered after pressing her hands on the radiator.

"You look a little shitty, you all right? What have you been listening to?"

"The Smiths."

"Ouch." Nat grimaced. "I don't like to see you like this. Have you heard that song, 'Juicy', yet? Or the new Petty record?"

Eleanor shook her head.

"Oh man. There's some life lessons out there for ya."

"Is that what I need?" she asked.

Betty reentered the room with a stack of binders. She dropped them onto an amp, crossed her arms, then stared at Eleanor and Nat with the creepy adoration of a prom parent.

"Honey and Bunny, together at last," she said.

"Not exactly," Nat said.

"So, You're Bunny?" Eleanor asked Nat.

Nat gave Eleanor a look, expressing something like, 'What can I say?' He had sat down to listen to the whispering strings of an unplugged, red Fender Stratocaster. It looked like it had past lives and mystical properties.

"Course that's Bunny! And like I said, Honey, I've been dying to meet you since Bunny asked me to make that triple-A badge he slipped ya a few months back."

"Is that so?" Eleanor said.

"Oh yeah," Betty said. "Me and Fern came right outta retirement when our gal, Rollins, gave us the buzz. You ever been to the Panhandle? Well, the Panhandle can wait. So, I stepped in to manage the boys out in California for the west coast gigs over summer. And as it turns out—"

"We couldn't live without her," Nat interrupted.

"Takes a woman to get'em off the road to ruin. Am I right, Honey?"

Eleanor just smiled while making various mental notes, like, How do I become Betty? Where is the Panhandle? And, since when did Nat start playing Fenders?

"So, Honey, I thought I'da met you in London. You think you'll be makin' use to join us on the road in '95?"

"I know I'm being stubborn, but I think I'm still a no," Eleanor said.

"Look, the job is essentially made up," Nat said, now kneeling to fiddle with labeled pedals and plugs at Eleanor's feet.

"I feel like you're setting me up to disappoint you either way," Eleanor replied. She could see Betty widen her eyes and back out of the room, having accurately sensed the turn of Eleanor and Nat's conversation.

Nat shrugged.

"You're frustrating me," Eleanor said.

Nat laughed and said something almost inaudible about welcoming her to the club.

"What?"

"Eleanor." Nat stood up to meet her eye line. "You're frustrating yourself. You know you have more potential than anyone. Just follow your fucking instincts."

Eleanor felt stung by bees. "Sorry. Not everyone has it all figured out yet," she said. "Sorry, I don't have a vision and support and piles of money and someone like Jamie I can hide behind."

"Well, you've certainly realized your potential at apologizing." Nat smiled, but she could tell he was annoyed by the way he bit his bottom lip before firming his mouth into a straight line.

"Fucking damnit, Nat. I am really sorry for not following through. Especially to you. For fucking up that opportunity and missing out on London. I just don't know how much more I can grovel today."

"Well. You were missed," he said.

"So we're back to that?" Eleanor wanted to cry and tear off her black poly pants to itch at her legs.

"No. Hey. It's alright," Nat said. "Some good came of it. I had some extra time to get into the studio."

"I didn't hear about that."

Nat whistled the riff from "Eleanor Rigby."

"No way. Holy shit. Bolero recorded on Abbey Road?"

"No, but I did. You know, I didn't want to *hide* behind Jamie and have someone else sing my feelings."

"Oh my god, fuck you. That's amazing!"

"Well, that remains to be heard," said Nat. "But soon enough."

"You're going to release it? With you singing?"

"Don't act so surprised. It cleaned up nice. It's something I've wanted to do for a while," he said. "The timing might never be right, but I know I was in the right place when it all came together."

"Is it gonna be for the second album, or?"

"Nah. It can't wait that long. Gonna be the B-side for the single we're dropping before Christmas."

"Does Jamie know?"

"No," Nat said. "He's got too much going on right now. Not for a normal person, but for Jamie."

Frida had dumped Jamie after suggestive photos of him and Diana and some blowout at the Stoplight made the tabloids. "I sort of feel sorry for him," Eleanor said.

"He's been a miserable piece of shit over it, yeah. But is 'sorry' the right word?"

"I don't know. Diana's moving out of the Rink. Girlcrush got signed to a major."

"Isn't that something," Nat said, not pretending to be surprised. "At least that's great for Lara."

"I had the same reaction!"

"I'm convinced sometimes good things happen to bad people because they involve good people," Nat said.

"Oh! Is that convenient wisdom you've adopted to explain your success?"

"What can I say?" he said, plugging in and sitting back down with the Strat.

"And since when are you playing Strats?"

"The Strat," Nat said. "It's a '61."

"I don't know if that's supposed to mean something to me other than you're rolling in it while I'm grinding it out."

Nat smiled and cooked up something Knopfleresque. "Hey. Don't forget, I've got two years grinding on you," he said. "You can handle it. You're tougher than me."

"All women are tougher than men," Eleanor said.

"Fuckin'-A right. That's why I hired Betty. Plans tonight?"

"Will's moving back into his old place, so eventually heading there."

"Oh. Hawk finally flew that coop?" Nat said.

"Funny... I might even miss those chickens in the alley," she said.

"No, you won't."

"And Frida called for a girl's night."

"Tonight?" Nat asked. "Interesting."

"I can't believe she's moving back to London. I really thought she'd get back together with Jamie."

"Good to see you be such a cheerleader for love," Nat said. "Where are you guys heading?"

"Her place. I guess Nikki is in town and coming over, too."

Nat hit a bad chord and winced.

▶▶

Almost everything in Frida's apartment was some shade of white, except her color-coded racks of clothes. Nikki insisted on rolling them out to the living room to more easily scrutinize while Frida packed and organized her fall/winter wardrobe. Recently, Eleanor had tried to pay more attention to fashion and thought maybe each of them was a study in jeans. Nikki could be Guess. Frida? Calvin Klein. Eleanor, she was probably Levi's or The Gap. Cutoffs.

Frida wasn't drinking, but that hadn't slowed down the power hour of unspoken competition between Eleanor and Nikki to suck down most of Frida's bar. Eleanor prided herself on being a good drinker and thought she'd have a leg up on slinky Nikki. That notion went out the window the second Nikki taught Eleanor how to saber open a bottle of Champagne. Eleanor caught Nikki sizing her up a few times, indirectly through glimpses in mirrors and the reflective glass coffee table.

"Do you want to be bad and get food?" Nikki suggested.

"How is getting food bad?" Eleanor asked.

"Ele, you are too nice or something," Nikki said.

The fizz on an empty stomach had gone to Eleanor's head. "I have a theory about nice. It's like the whole Southern 'Bless your heart,' meaning fuck off thing."

"Ew. I hate the South," Nikki replied.

Eleanor giggled. "Dude. Nikki, a TV show following you around, just like, *existing* in the South, would be a cultural revolution. God, I wish I could make stuff like that happen."

Frida handed Eleanor a zipped white leather booklet of CDs. "Would you pick something out to play?"

"Anything in mind?" Eleanor asked and started browsing.

"Preferably British and sixties."

"That doesn't really narrow it down," Eleanor said.

Frida picked up a cigarette but then looked to reconsider. "I suppose I have a type."

"You are a type!" Eleanor exclaimed, pinching a disc from its clear sleeve.

"We're *all* types, babes," Nikki said as a beast squawked, introducing Jagger to plead for the devil's sympathy. "Okay, okay. That sounded bitchy. But I guess you can take it knowing you work with Aja Green!"

"Oh right, I'd forgotten that you both knew her," Frida said.

"Did Aja give you that whole flower or a bomb bullshit spiel yet?" Nikki asked.

"Something like that," Eleanor replied cautiously.

"Of course she did." Nikki rolled her eyes in a dramatized way that might've been an attempt to imitate Aja. "Yeah, well, I was too much of a bomb for that righteous bitch."

"Oh. Girl power, I guess," said Eleanor.

"And she plays it like she's all professional and asexual? Totally bogus. Can you even believe that Nat had a thing with her and then he plays all bashful with me? Like, what is up with that?"

Eleanor scraped the starry blue Chanel varnish that was brushed onto her thumbnail only an hour ago.

"Well, we don't know if that happened," Frida said.

Nikki hurled her heels towards the foyer and sprawled onto the shaggy white rug. "Whatever. I just can't believe that we didn't bone."

"That's crazy," Eleanor said, sliding onto the floor to join Nikki. "I mean, you could be on *Baywatch*."

"Her screen tests did not go well," Frida whispered to Eleanor.

"Ugh!" Nikki kicked her feet up onto the cream sofa. "You all saw Nat at the pool in Italy. Those forearms, back definition? I can tell from that physique. Like, his type just works harder, babes."

"That's true," Eleanor said mid rug petting, trying to suppress what she'd wanted to do with Nat after they'd thrown themselves into the deep end.

Frida gasped.

"Excuse me? Is this chick kidding me? Where do they sell what makes your girl-next-door vagina so special?" Nikki sprang up and huffed some of the additional white decor she'd brought to Frida's up her nose.

"Nikki. Please," Frida said.

"I just mean you're right that Nat's a hard worker! Sorry." Eleanor excused herself to pee.

Frida's bathroom was calming and immaculately clean, even nicer than some hotels she'd stayed in with Will. There was a vase of dried pink petals and a candle burning a peony scent. Eleanor wished she could hide in there for the rest of the night, thumbing through magazines and the seafoam cloth copy of Marquis de Sade's *Bedroom Philosophers* that was on a tray by the bath. She wished her friends Adele and Robin could replace the two perfect supermodels that'd somehow both been slighted by the Dempsey brothers outside the door. When Eleanor returned from the bathroom, at least Nikki was gone.

"She has a date," Frida said.

"I hope she grabs dinner first, otherwise she'll eat him alive," Eleanor said.

"Oh, that's bad." Frida simpered. "It's been a while since I've had a laugh."

"Oh man, you too? I'm definitely hurting these days."

"Shall we spill our guts or our throats?" Frida asked.

"Do you have a VCR?"

"In the bedroom," Frida replied.

"Can we go, like, rent a movie at Blockbuster or whatever?"

"Do you not have to see Will?"

"I don't think he cares. I have to see him, but... I just want to do something normal before I have to deal with another gut spill."

▶▶

90 minutes later, they were braless in Bolero t-shirts—the only relaxed cotton clothing Frida owned—under Frida's luxury covers, chugging

Evian, and watching *When Harry Met Sally*. Frida had never seen it, and it took Eleanor every bit of restraint not to quote and provide her own commentary.

"Can I be bold and ask if there's messaging behind your selection?" Frida said.

"Can I be bold and guess this is the first time you've had snacks in your bed?"

Frida tossed a half-popped kernel at Eleanor exactly as daintily as she would've predicted.

"I know you said Jamie's reached out a million times... do you think you'll call him back?" Eleanor asked.

"It's too soon, though I've been ill about it nearly every waking day."

"Can I confess something?" Eleanor asked while looking at the screen.

"All right," Frida said.

"I just want to say I'm sorry. That day in Tuscany, when we hiked back up to the villa together, and you were upset."

Frida removed cucumber slices from underneath Eleanor's eyes. "Go on."

"Well, I really meant what I said. That I believe Jamie loves you. But I'm sorry if I encouraged you to get back together without really knowing the situation," Eleanor said.

"You've no need to apologize for that," Frida said.

"I'm not trying to say Jamie is innocent, but I lived with that girl... Diana, from the pictures... They have history and—"

"Eleanor, please. I can't be bothered by some stranger's agenda."

Eleanor felt her face crease.

"What's wrong, then?" Frida said.

"I don't know how you have it so together." Eleanor took a deep breath. "I just feel so lost."

"Patience, love." Frida leaned over to push Eleanor's hair back and gave her a soft kiss that felt maternal. Frida then pulled the beaded cord on her bedside lamp, which, along with her eye mask, seemed to instantly power her down into total sleep.

Eleanor stayed up until Harry finally put it on the line, and he and Sally got their hard-earned happy ending. Maybe by the new year Eleanor would find the same courage to get her coconut cake and chocolate sauce on the side.

19

WILL

WILL'S FIRST MORNING BACK in his apartment felt comforting but a bit ominous, like his coffee darkening the water in the press. He hadn't planned to be alone, but wasn't surprised when Ele was a no-show. She might've tried to call, but he had yet to reconnect his landline. To be fair, Will's efforts were elsewhere. He recently met with his lawyers and the accountant. Booking the support slot for Bolero's world tour would finally absolve The Reverie of their debts. This gave Will permission to move out. He was establishing a soft bend before his complete break from the band.

Nearly on time, Andy and Dasuki yelled up from the street to his open window. Will took their help to move out the rest of his things as the band's blessing on the issue.

"Looks better without Cath's weird art shit," Andy said, leaving the door open behind him.

"Where's Dave?" Will asked.

"Dunno. We've been out since last night. Say, where's Ele, man?" Dasuki said.

Will shrugged.

"Bolero boys had a mad party last night. You think she was with them?" Dasuki said.

"I'd give it a 50/50 chance," said Andy.

"You think?" Dasuki said.

"Oh, I'd be wrong." Andy keeled over haughtily.

"I'm done betting after last night anyway," Dasuki replied. "Done cold."

"You two hit AC again?" Will wicked his hair from his face.

"Chill, dude. We were blowing off more steam than money," Andy insisted.

"So I'm buying breakfast?" said Will.

"Yeah, man. Dying for a short stack," Dasuki said. "We waiting on Ele?"

Before Will could say no, Ele appeared through the open door.

"Hey, you guys double parked? You know you're getting towed," she said.

Andy rushed over to the window and then emitted a sigh of relief.

"Always the joker," said Dasuki, sharing his high-five-low-ten combo handshake with Ele.

"The real joke is that shirt you're repping." Andy tugged at the Bolero shirt underneath Ele's open jacket. "Does Will not give you enough Reverie merch?"

"Well, no, actually." Ele walked the periphery of the room as if she were testing the soundness of the floorboards. "Wow, this place is so nice."

Will backed up and leaned against the windowsill as she approached him.

"I'm sorry about last night," she said softly to him. "It got late. I tried to call."

Will kissed the corner of her mouth. She smelled unlike herself, like fresh-cut roses. He noticed her nails were painted, her hair styled softer. He also noticed, likely to his own detriment, that he didn't always pay this much attention to her. It was only when she'd been distant.

"Where've ya been, Ele?" Dasuki asked.

"Would you believe me if I said I was at a supermodel sleepover?"

Will lit a cigarette.

"I'd believe you, but only if you told me every gory, naked detail," Andy replied.

"Can we talk?" Ele asked Will.

"I gotta get out of here," Will said.

"I know. I mean, I didn't mean it has to be now. Where are you going?"

"Breakfast, then getting the rest of my stuff."

"I'll help."

▶▶

When they got back to the Reverie house, the energy was strange. Will's feet felt heavy as they entered the door. And then they felt wet. His rubber soles squeaked on the wooden stairs as water eerily cascaded down. Ele nervously chuckled, as if this was a prank.

Dave.

Will pushed past Andy's cursing to run up the stairs and heaved the unlocked apartment door. It cut like an ore through the slow-rising gloss coating the floor.

When Will's fingers felt the resistance from the lock on the knob of the bathroom door, his blood rushed faster. He could hear the shower pounding. "Dave!" he screamed and threw his body against the door. And again. "Dave!"

Eleanor handed Will the bat they kept around in case of a break-in. Now, Will was using it to break in. Will took a measured breath with the bat over the brass knob like the head of a nail and hammered down. And again. And again. When the handle dangled limp, Will slammed the bat laterally into the jamb and forced the door open to a burst of steam and a fountain pooling water over the subway tiles.

Dave was in the bathtub, his face bent on its side with wet clumps of hair that looked to be leeching life away from the half of his head still above water. Dave's naked body was cocooned in the shower liner that he must have pulled down when he'd either fallen or attempted to stand up. Will skidded onto his knees. They thudded against the tiles. Will was now in range of the fat droplets from the shower's downpour. He pulled Dave's head up by the hair. His eyes were closed and mouth gaping.

"Dave, talk to me!" Will yelled, slapping his hollowed cheek. Will then submerged his arms into the bathwater to position Dave to pound his back to instigate vomiting. Breathing. Anything.

Will coursed his fingers down Dave's arm to find the pulse on his wrist, then stepped into the hot water, displacing waves of it. He bent his knees and scooped his arms under Dave's torso, attempting to dredge Dave from the tub. Ele ran in, turned off the faucet, and then grabbed from under Dave's shoulders. With Ele's help, they could get Dave onto the floor.

"Get him on his back," Will ordered her.

"Oh, fuck!" Andy said from behind Ele in the hallway. She shoved him and told him to call 911.

Will leaned on his elbow and scooped his hand under the back of Dave's neck, tilting his head. He pinched Dave's earlobe, something he'd remembered from lifeguard training but like everything else he was doing, had never had to do. Will put his ear close to Dave's mouth but heard no breath, felt no breath on him. Will looked down and saw Dave's slick, yellowed chest neither rise nor fall.

Will inhaled, pinched Dave's nose, and then exhaled a deep breath into his thin mouth. And again. And again. And twice more with prayer and pressure.

When the rescue breaths weren't enough, Will forced the heel of his right hand to the bottom of Dave's breastbone and locked it with his left. On the first compression, Dave's eyes shot wide as he croaked gargles of rotten liquid. Will felt Dave's bones crack under his force.

"Thank god," Ele said, falling to her knees beside Will. She placed her hand on Will's soaked back.

"Dave." Will took a deep breath and rocked Dave, whose legs began to respond. "Dave, are you with us, man?"

Dave nodded and attempted to crouch. Will assisted Dave onto his side, which caused Dave to groan. Ele pulled a bath towel from the back of the door to cover him. Will sat silently on the edge of the tub. He watched Ele console Dave. It was like a long, numb blur of time and sounds until the ambulance came and went.

Ele stayed outside and saw them off. Will went back inside to find Dasuki had turned the power off and was attempting to clear out the flood. Andy was nursing his right hand.

"What happened to you?" Will said.

Andy said nothing, but Will could see Andy had popped the sheetrock of the kitchen wall with his fist. There were red-stained clumps of white crust in the dent.

"Good thing you don't need your hand to play guitar or anything. How many times am I going to bail you out, man? Since college I've been bailing you out! It's over," Will yelled.

Andy shoved Will into the wall. "It already was fuckin' over! You've just been too much of a pussy caught up in your god complex to say it to our fucking faces."

Dasuki intervened, checking his body between Andy and Will. "That's enough."

▶▶

After they borrowed Satan's wet vac from Noodle Garden and Andy's temper cooled, Dasuki drove Will and Ele back to his apartment.

"I'll call Cath..." Will promised.

"We gotta keep this between us, though, right?" Dasuki said. "I mean, with the label and the press and shit, we can lose the tour, right? Like, I don't want Dave surviving this just to crack again if all this crashes down on us."

Will agreed.

"Ele, can we trust you?" Dasuki asked her.

Ele nodded. Her eyes looked bloodshot with emotions that, like her place in the car, had taken a backseat to everyone else's.

▶▶

Ele took Will's neighbor's old newspapers to shove inside their shoes while Will stripped down. He went into the bathroom to run the water to take a bath. He adhered to the belief that it was never too early to get over something, face whatever was upsetting, and move on. Will climbed into the tub and stared at the flow gushing out of the spout as the water slowly rose around him.

Ele came in shortly after he'd turned off the faucet and removed the clothes stuck to her body. She stepped into the tub and sat across from him with her legs tucked up to her chin and held tight. For a while, they sat in silence, warming themselves back up to life, maybe even to each other.

"Here," he said, helping her legs relax between his when he noticed the red scabs on them.

"Stress," she said.

"I hadn't noticed."

"I noticed," she replied.

"This is pretty different from our first shared bathroom experience."

"Yeah. Well, this is better than our last bathroom experience together."

They both shared a brief, painful laugh.

"I thought he was dead," she said. "Dave would've died if you weren't there."

"Or maybe he wouldn't have broken ribs." Will lapped a handful of warm water to comfort his face. "I don't know."

Their silence resumed. Will appreciated that Ele seemed to be waiting patiently before they talked again, but part of him would have preferred if they didn't need to speak at all.

The sun set early that night. The times were changing. Will sorted through his records and put on Bob Dylan's *Blood on the Tracks*.

"This song reminds me of you," he said. "You're a Big Girl Now."

"We're not on the same page," she said.

"I think we are for this breakup."

"Ouch," she said.

"Any parting words?" Will said.

"Just London."

"Really, you want to bring that up? Clearly there's been a lot going on."

"Still. It was a big deal for me to cancel like that to come back with you, like you needed me. Then I didn't hear from you for a week and didn't even know what was going on. You didn't need me at all."

"Does anyone really need anyone?" he said flippantly.

"Then why did you ask me to come back with you?"

"Those weren't my exact words."

"Wow! Mixed messages," she said.

"Mixed messages? Come on, Ele. You're like the girl who wants to be chased but doesn't want to get caught."

The look on Ele's face after his remark was conclusive. Will struck a match to light what he knew would be their last shared cigarette. He watched Ele take a deep breath after a shallow drag.

"So you stopped chasing me," she said in a tone Will interpreted as relieved.

"Well, it didn't seem like you wanted to be caught," Will said. "Not by me, anyway."

20

ELEANOR

"TAKE A BREAK BEFORE you break" was one of the life lessons Bolero's tour manager, old Betty, wafted out more frequently than the smoke circles from her Virginia Slim. Eleanor idolized Betty and adopted her twangy ism just in time to honor the breakup with Will that was kept secret to protect Dave.

Eleanor's break took the form of a reverse commuter train home for her dad's birthday. This year, it fell on the eve of Thanksgiving. The conductor gargled "Hillside" with the same intonation that guys used to sell ice cream at the beach as the train came to that familiar rattling halt.

Outside, Eleanor felt the crisp air flush her cheeks as she ran across the overpass to get in line for a breakfast sandwich at the hut next to the station. She'd left the city early to savor what she'd argue Long Island did best, the BEC. The Holy Trinity of factory cheese blanketing oozy eggs and chintzy crisp bacon between a kaiser roll. Eleanor peeled the warm foil back, globbed a half with a packet of ketchup, and sank her teeth into something worth more than it cost. In short order, her breakfast sandwich was as satisfying as the fallen leaves on the walk home.

▶▶

Everything in her dad's house seemed the same, but for a deeper indentation in his armchair. She could see that Mick was still in the habit of making a whole pot of coffee but only drinking two cups. Dust stuck to Eleanor's fingertips when she opened the window to air out her tiny bedroom. She and her dad painted it blue and orange after the Miracle of '86. The room was like an exhibit of her adolescence. Pippi Longstocking books. Track medals. Photos she'd taken of Bolero, other local bands, and the skateboarders under the Unisphere at Corona Park. Music documentaries, mostly taped from VH1. She pulled out the box with her green Doc Martens, then cut herself on a wire hanger while perusing the rest of the relics in her closet.

Eleanor found bandages in the bathroom behind the ICE-HOT, the same old jar of blue jelly she once smeared on her freshly scraped knee when she was eight, mistakenly thinking it would help. Her mom freaked out and made her take a bath, which escalated Eleanor's pain into extreme panic. Eleanor usually laughed off these memories of incompetent caregiving, but there were times she was too tender for them to feel funny.

Later that afternoon, Eleanor connected with her girls from the German job. Adele was spending the holiday with Robin's family. Being so close in Floral Park, the three of them planned a late night reunion in Hillside at Eleanor's beloved local, Down the Hatch.

▶▶

Eleanor and her dad made it ten minutes into their conversation before he gave a curt smile and slapped the armrest. That was his signal, like an automated warning when you had under a minute left on your phone card. She wished she'd paced their chat better and said more. She'd prepped to avoid binary questions, to probe the way good producers got more meaningful material from their cast interviews in the confessionals.

"What are you drinking these days, kiddo?" he asked.

She almost said everything, but that wouldn't go over well. "I had a lot of cool beers in Germany. I loved this sour style called *gose*, and there was this great cheap stuff called Maternus in plast—"

He was already halfway to the kitchen. "I got some Buds in the fridge."

Eleanor tried to enjoy the beer, but the offer had given him permission to turn on the MSG network and stare at scores and highlight reels. This validated her decision to involve Nat and Jamie in her dad's birthday plans. The Dempsey brothers loved her dad, and vice versa. They were like the sons he never had and could only love because they weren't actually his sons. Mick Huston was too much of a hardass. Eleanor found Nat and Jamie's take on her dad being a hardass darkly comical because the Dempseys came from a household where getting in trouble guaranteed physical injury. In that way, they were lucky their dad, Nathan, wasn't around often. He'd disappear, usually claiming it was for an "investment opportunity." Once, Nat called the Hustons when someone was trying to break in. Eleanor watched her dad run down the street in his robe with a bat in hand to scare off the assailant. The next day at school, Nathan (junior) told the whole school to call him Nat from now on. For the first time, Eleanor experienced deep admiration for someone her own age because they were brave.

On his better days, Nat and Jamie's dad seemed cool. Everything was over-the-top. He was handsome and wanted to go by his first name, something her dad would never entertain. But as Eleanor got older, even the memories of Nathan's good side distorted, or maybe sharpened. Once, Nathan was driving them home from Carvel. She, Jamie, and Nat were all sugarhigh rolling around the "way back." He was singing along to "Stuck in the Middle with You," zigzagging the car from one side of the street's parked vehicles to the other. It was a game until he smashed more than a side mirror and sped off. When he saw there was no damage to their station wagon a few blocks from the scene, he laughed like it was a game he'd won. The kids were sworn to secrecy, or he'd throw their Brown Bonnets in the trash. Eleanor had buried this incident until recently, when she saw a movie called *Reservoir Dogs*. What about that Stealers Wheel song made sense to associate with diabolical scenes?

It had been at least a year since anyone had heard from Nathan, and longer since either of his sons had spoken to him.

"Is that a circus horn?" her dad asked.

Eleanor's face went red. Not because she heard the horn, but because she heard it in addition to a three-word phrase. Eleanor and her dad opened the front door and stepped out onto the stoop.

There they were, the sons no one wanted, announcing their arrival while hanging out of a moon roof. Half the block had come out to watch their stretch limo complete a 15-point turn onto their narrow street. Nat took the megaphone away to stop Jamie from chanting, "Big Dick Mick."

Once the limo found a lopsided position on the curb to idle, Jamie climbed out of the moon roof like Ace Ventura.

Big Mick's face looked disapproving, but amused. Of their few genetic crossovers, this was an expression Eleanor knew she'd inherited. "Jamie, let's get two things straight. No amount of money will earn you the option to call me by my first name, and two? You aren't gonna be rich long if you keep pulling stunts like this."

"C'mon, old man. Can't blame me for trying," Jamie said.

"Sorry, Mr. Huston," Nat said and Mick reached out for them to exchange a solid handshake. "All the bad ideas were Jamie's. But once we'd heard Eleanor was coming home for your 50th and Thanksgiving, there was no stopping us."

"Oh yeah?" Mick said. "What if it was last week when you booked Letterman?"

"Did you see us?" Jamie asked him.

"Past my bedtime," Mick said.

Eleanor didn't believe for a second that her dad didn't tune in, but enjoyed witnessing that Nat and Jamie actually let something go.

"Hoping you'll make an exception to go to our big show at Radio City," said Nat.

"After the ball drops into 1995. How cool is that? Never been done," Jamie said.

Nat admitted, "I don't know if that's true."

"I'll go if your mom needs another adult present," said Mick.

That seemed to remind them to do a quick drop in with Joanie. Her excitement to see everyone wore off quicker than a whip-it. She was in holiday prep mode and shooed them out.

Eleanor freaked at the Mick-specific decor inside the limo on behalf of her father's slim show of gratitude. Semper Fi and Irish flags. Bottles of Jameson in every cup holder. A silver flask engraved, "Not Protestant Whiskey." Van Morrison crooning from the speakers. By the time "Domino" played through, a bottle of Jamo was ready for the orange recycle bin, and they'd pulled up to the best restaurant in town. Mick told the limo driver to drop them off down the street, not to embarrass him. Dinner at Saint James was reserved for significant achievements, like cheating death or making a holy sacrament. Nothing confirmed one's faith in Hillside like a New York strip with sides of creamed spinach and french fries.

Everyone transitioned to Guinness after they were seated. Their perfect pours blended into the atmosphere of the restaurant's black-paneled walls and sepia-tone photographs of bare-knuckle boxers. The steaks were great, but the main course was a roast. Eleanor watched her dad pick Nat and Jamie apart on everything from their haircuts, music, childhood phases, and past girlfriends.

"And what's with this flashy gym class shit you're wearing?" Mick said.

"What're you talking about? It's top!" Jamie said, proudly zipping up his track jacket.

Eleanor could tell where her dad was going once he started aiming at youth athletics. Her father had never been prouder than the year she beat everyone in the mile. She was nine.

"I mean, we can expect she'd beat Nat since he forgot to grow until he hit about 17, but you, Jamie? Pitiful!" he said.

"I could beat her now," Jamie insisted.

"That's ridiculous," Eleanor said.

"I thought Eleanor would run in the Turkey Trot tomorrow, but I guess she only runs other people's errands these days," said Mick.

Eleanor squeezed her silverware.

"C'mon, Ele. I'll fuckin' run it tomorrow if you do." Jamie egged her on, "5K? I don't give a fuck."

"You're delusional," Eleanor said to Jamie, though she was thinking it'd feel good to run and shift her thoughts—to vanish into that mindless top gear. "We'll see how I feel in the morning."

"That's a no!" Her dad got up to use the bathroom, which dictated that the meal was over.

Nat perused a rainbow of plastic credit cards and seemed to randomly choose which one to pay. The clock was nearing ten. Eleanor tried to be evasive, suggesting that she'd find her own way home, but Jamie and Nat were not having it. Once they cracked she was going to the Hatch, it was on.

"That's my fucking former employer, after all," Nat said. The head bartender, Connor, had always thrown Nat bar back jobs when nothing else was panning out. "Plus, there's no way I'm missing out on meeting the German job crew. I've got a lot of questions."

"You know they're not German," Eleanor replied.

"But are they hot?" Jamie asked.

▶▶

To Eleanor, stepping into Down the Hatch felt like slipping into her best worn sneakers. On slower nights, the older regulars and commuters would post up to the bar with enough vacant stools between them to maintain being alone while drinking together. But on hot nights before holidays, the bar swelled up with the next generation like Ellis Island. They narrowly passed some contrarian cool kids playing darts, clogging the pathway connecting the bar to the billiards table and barroom.

"That was us," Nat whispered what she was thinking as they made their way to approach Connor O'Donnell, the dashing Irish vampire behind the stick.

It was the busiest night of the year, but Connor still handed Eleanor a ten-spot out of the register and winked hello amid his refilling. He was as timeless as that perfect pour of Guinness, with his slicked-back hair and know-all-say-nothing bartender's grin. Eleanor took the bill and dashed off to the jukebox with his blessing, leaving Nat and Jamie to applaud the novelty bar tap they paid for Connor to have made with one of Bolero's Apex Awards. It was the tap and toast of the town, and by far the coolest thing she'd seen anyone do with their fame.

First she played New Order's "Temptation" for seven minutes of runway to make the rest of her selections. She'd jumped back to the beginning of the alphabet when Nat and Jamie slid next to her to oversee the operation.

"Where the fuck is *Light Up & Shine On*, man?" Jamie yelled back at Connor.

"If you're still alive in '95, we'll change it straight out!" Connor's brogue hadn't broken in the twenty years since he'd fallen down the hatch.

Eleanor felt the brisk gusts of Robin and Adele's arrival before turning to see their rosy cheeks. "Holy shit!"

"We're like pilgrims here to claim your homeland," Robin said.

"You kind of look like sexy pilgrims," Jamie said. Compared to the girls after Bolero, Eleanor's friends were from another planet. Adele was like a fresh-faced nun who wandered out of the convent and ended up in Tangier. Robin resembled a corn-fed Elizabeth Taylor disguised to tour with The Grateful Dead.

"You must be Jamie," Robin and Adele said in unison.

"I'm so happy I could kiss you guys!" Eleanor said.

"Wouldn't be the first time," Robin replied.

"What's that now?" Nat's slug of an eyebrow raised incredulously.

"Nothing," Eleanor and Robin said in unison.

They were less than a drink in before the questioning began. "What was little Ele like in school?" Adele asked.

"Ele was a total tomboy," Jamie said.

"I was not," Eleanor said.

"C'mon, you were on the handball side of the gym during those fuckin' school dances," said Jamie.

Robin turned to Nat. "Nat, will you settle this?"

"She did wear gym shorts, almost year round for a while." Nat gulped his Guinness. "I mean, not that she was flying under the radar with those legs," he said, wiping away his stout mustache.

"Wow." Eleanor shoved him. "These legs are going to kick your ass."

Connor dropped them shots and said, "How they haven't yet is a mystery to us all."

Eleanor noticed that Adele and Robin both made eyes at Connor, and she wondered which of them might try to climb that Celtic tree.

"So tell us some Eleanor stories in Germany," Nat said.

"She was like a baby deer," said Robin.

"I fell in love with her on day one." Adele put her arm around Eleanor. "She was all business, but then by the end of the day just... luminous! Drunk jumping over this massive bonfire and singing me to sleep."

"What did you sing?" Nat asked her.

"I don't remember," Eleanor said.

"'Once in a Lifetime,'" Adele said.

Nat admitted that was very fucking endearing. Eleanor thought she felt him rub her lower back.

"Boo! That's so PG," said Jamie.

Robin alluded to more R-rated adventures, but Eleanor signaled to put the kibosh on it. Robin pivoted to a terrible decoy story about filming themselves on a mission impossible to find air conditioning.

"If our second album is as boring as that story, we'll never end up in the jukebox," Jamie said.

"Ladies Room?" Adele suggested.

The three girls crammed into the single use.

"I love you guys, but I do not understand why we need to be in here together. It's not like we're saving time," Eleanor said.

"Ele. Relax. We're young," Robin said.

"Where else could we talk business?" Adele said.

"Excellent point, Adele. Like, dude. Ele. What is your life? *The Reel World* should film you instead of the other way around."

"Now that I've met Nat, I totally get it. You two... it just makes me want to cry!" Adele rolled out extra toilet paper, not because she was crying, but because she was correctly expecting the bar would run out by the end of the night.

▶▶

A few drinks later, Robin decided she didn't want to contain some of their R-rated times and Eleanor no longer cared. Jamie couldn't take it anymore.

"You were making out with Ele?" he said.

"So what? Haven't you kissed those sweet little pillows?" Robin taunted Jamie and squeezed Eleanor's blushing face, smushing her lips into a pucker.

"No, that was me," Nat said.

Eleanor gasped at the drop of their PG bombshell. She flung her leg at Nat, which connected, but Nat caught it, causing her to hop on the foot still grounded before falling into him.

"And, she's finally done kicked his arse!" Connor shouted from behind the bar.

"That was one stupid time years ago," Eleanor said. "That kiss doesn't count."

"Whose fault was that?" Nat said. He spread his hand across his heart like he was holding fondly onto the memory, even though it mortified her.

Once upon a time, Nat showed up at a party after she took ecstasy for the first time. According to the recap, she was all over Nat and allegedly begged him to take a hit so they could go into the pool together. By the time Nat got hold of the E and the E got hold of him, Eleanor was already coming down hard. It was, in the end, a pathetic, amateur misalignment of drug use that ended in dry mouth and getting chased off the tennis courts by Arrow, the rental cops that patrolled the school grounds. Nat met Karen, what might've been days later. It made the most sense to bury the humiliation.

"I'm fuckin' flabbengasted!" Jamie said. "Is that even a real word? *FLABBERGASTED!*"

Eleanor couldn't tell if Jamie was jealous or looking for an excuse to be consoled between Robin and Adele's chests.

"Finally, a song I like," said Robin.

"I played this one for you," Eleanor said.

"Is this a Clash cover?" Jamie said.

"Big mistake." Robin started schooling Jamie on The Maytals. Meanwhile, Adele had meandered over to Connor at the bar.

Nat followed Eleanor to re-up the tunes. "Sorry that slipped out before, about the kiss," he said.

Eleanor might've given away that her knees felt weak by the way Nat pitched his head to say 'kiss.' "No, it was funny," she said.

"I'm loving Adele and Robin, by the way. I feel like I'm getting to know you more."

"Really?"

"Yeah. Earlier you were all moody, but now that your girls are around—"

"They make me so happy," she told him.

"I know most men need women, but I'm learning women need women," Nat said.

"And women don't need men," she said.

"Ha. You can say that again. I mean, no one needs me." Nat rubbed his chin. "Except Bolero, and that's fucking too much to handle as it is."

"But you like to be needed," Eleanor said.

"I'm not sure you have the right Dempsey," Nat said.

"No! Jamie needs to be *wanted*."

"No argument there." Nat stepped closer to her, tilting his head again and said, "I'd argue, though, it can be nice to be wanted."

"Mmm hm," she replied through a tight smile, rubbing her shoulder against his. Her emotions made setting the musical mood this flip of the discs more challenging. "This is too hard."

"Let's talk it through," Nat responded without an air of dismissal towards her most trivial problem.

"Do you ever find it interesting what music you hate or love because of your associations? Like, I love Springsteen because my dad—"

"No, you don't." Nat stopped her. "You love Springsteen, even though it's adorably unfashionable, by the way, for far less wholesome reasons than his arena rock for the forgotten working man."

"You don't know what you're talking about." Though it was entirely true that she would've let the Boss do all sorts of things to her in his glory days.

"Fine, but if you think about playing any Bruce tonight, I'll tie you up," he said.

Eleanor pretended she wasn't listening, and that he wasn't exciting her. "At the same time, I think I kind of hate Van Morrison, even though my dad loves him."

"Also, not a fact!" Nat said. "You only hate Van Morrison 'cause he was rude to Lindsay when he came into that fancy restaurant she worked at."

"Yeah, Springsteen would never do that," she said.

"Oh, Miss Huston."

"Uh oh, I can tell how drunk you are when you start calling me *Miss Huston*," she said.

"There's something naughty about the etiquette," he admitted.

"It's just your thing for older women, and I'll always be younger," she said.

"But you'll always be too old for my shit." Nat grinned. "Really, though. Don't act like you can hate on the Van when I know you used to lie around that year you were away at school, rolling strawberry joints, listening to 'Tupelo Honey' and 'Sweet Thing' and imagining someone thinking about you..." Eleanor hung on his words as her teeth lost grip on her bottom lip and slipped her mouth shut. "You just didn't think it'd be me," Nat said.

"No—I mean, I did," she said.

"Yes, you imagined it'd be me?" Nat leaned in as if he expected she would share a secret, which made her feel uneasy about the secrets she was keeping.

"Time out," Eleanor said. "This is too much right now. You pick the rest."

After last call, Connor allowed them to stay until their final song played, signaled by a drum riff lifted right from the Ronettes, which melted into The Jesus & Mary Chain's shoegazy slow dance, "Just Like Honey."

Robin linked hands with Jamie and they flopped around, their arms like rogue fire hoses.

Adele partnered up with Eleanor to seek permission to go home with Connor.

"Immediately. You've never picked a better notch for your bedpost," Eleanor said.

Adele kissed her and then summoned Nat by using the same tone as a preschool teacher to pluck the wallflower, which worked, leaving Eleanor and Nat to each other.

"There's no pool for you to throw me in tonight," Eleanor said.

Nat said nothing, and she was glad that he didn't. Instead, he placed her arms around his neck, pulling her to dance against him. She closed her eyes and felt his lips lightly rest on her cheek while they swayed.

Then the Hatch was closed to everyone but Connor and Adele.

Nat instructed their limo to take Robin home. "If you're going home alone, do it in style," he said, tapping the roof to send her off.

"Yeah, Nat would know. He does it all the time," Jamie said.

On the walk home, Eleanor caught a whiff of fresh bread from the Italian bakery in town. It was a rite of passage for Hillsiders in drunken revelry to duck under the bakery's propped, slatted door, which seeped yeasty steam, and beg in Spanglish for a loaf straight out of the oven. Nat tipped the bakers a wad of cash, payback for their years of generosity and tolerance with the custom. The three of them broke bread and continued to walk home under the yellow glow of street lights crossed by shoelaces and power lines.

Once they were back on their block, Jamie made no ceremony of goodbye. He wobbled up the front stoop, checking under each plant pot for the spare key while giggling.

Nat released Eleanor's hand which she hadn't noticed he was holding.

"Jamie looks ready for a run in a few hours. Don't you think?" he said.

Eleanor gave Nat a hug, warmer than the center of the bread she consumed, before crossing the street to go home. She knew Nat was watching her until she got through the door. They were *compadres*. No, they were *simpatico*? Betty would say they were something that sounded Spanish and saccharine and accusatory and true.

Eleanor was too tempted by the television to go right to bed. Infomercials. Click. Hairband videos. Click. *Silk Stalkings.* Hmm. She wished she could watch Nickelodeon's *Guts*. She wished she had more guts. The Turkey Trot was in a few hours. It was no race for a piece of the Agro Crag, but...

21

NAT

NAT CARRIED UP ONE leaf for the dining table. It was a practiced skill to avoid denting the walls or wood. Everywhere was narrow, much like his escape from the shotgun house where he'd grown up. Joanie was in the kitchen. They usually talked in the mornings. That's when he'd call from the road. This morning she was preoccupied, taking inventory of her serving ware and produce. Nat looked forward to Thanksgiving. He liked the plainness of his mom's cooking and Eleanor's "dirty smashed" potatoes that were never fully peeled or mashed. Jamie was always brutally hungover, which made it the quietest meal of the year, unless their dad made an appearance. Nat waited until he heard motors starting up from the street to hop back upstairs to wake the golden child.

Jamie whined in response to Nat's knocking, which he took as permission to enter.

Nat pulled the string on the window, which slapped up the plastic venetian blinds. Jamie rolled over indignantly.

"You're late," Nat said, because it'd be true if he didn't frequently repeat this lie. Nat kept Jamie on time by constantly letting him think he was at least 30 minutes behind.

"For what?" Jamie groaned.

"Turkey Trot, shitbird."

Jamie budged from his horizontal state into a seated hunch. "Nah, fuck that."

But Jamie's action spoke loudly, even accounting for how loudly Jamie spoke his words. Jamie was preparing to be swayed.

"Eleanor's expecting a race," Nat said.

"Ele doesn't care," Jamie said.

"Yeah, but think of all the people at the finish line, right? Rooting for Jamie Dempsey, the hometown hero. Think of the press."

Jamie stood up with some hesitancy and belched. "Huh?"

"Never know. You could score points after the whole Frida-Diana triangle and brawl bullshit." Nat walked away to give his brother space to mull over the angle.

A minute later, Nat heard Jamie curse through a short and probably cold shower.

▶▶

Nat made his way down Second Avenue, passing some tables set up for volunteers to hand out water and oranges to the runners, and others collecting canned goods for the food drive. All of Hillside's former athletes took part in the Turkey Trot, even those white heads from the Tenement generation that first settled here after the war, making the upgrade to share two walls instead of all four.

Nat thought he'd been pulling Jamie's leg about a crowd. In fact, there were a few hundred Hillsiders standing around, sipping coffees, smoking cigarettes, anticipating food comas, football on the couch, or working time-and-a-half later. Nat found Eleanor's dad a head above the rest, even over some kids on their parents' shoulders. Mick had scouted the optimal spectator spot, right by the finish line, where the exit of the bus loop split between the Ave and the parking lot of the grammar school.

Mick shoved a coffee into Nat's hands as if to say he'd been expecting Nat to report for duty. Nat bit into the styrofoam cup, creating an indentation before taking a sip. And that was that for chat. Mick was one of Nat's favorite people to be around, but not to talk to. Eleanor's dad intimidated a lot of people, it was like the intro to Bad Company's "Burnin' Sky" preceded his entrance to a room.

Some preppy couple in matching red tracksuits crossed the finish line first to golf claps. What was becoming of this town? They looked like they hadn't broken a sweat. Nat realized he could relate, his having a #1 record and saying, "The songs wrote themselves." Sure, those 12 mostly did, but that didn't account for the hundreds that were too derivative, incomplete, overworked, and terrible.

Soon after the frontrunners, Nat heard a chatter spread among the Hillsiders.

There they are, Mick didn't say, but gestured to Nat with a nudge.

Jamie was wearing a bucket hat and blathering to Eleanor in tandem stride, only 100 yards away. Nat made a quick run to grab some dentist office cones of water.

Jamie pointed towards Nat and Mick, then punched the sky with his fist a few times. He pulled a cigarette from behind his ear, lit it, and took a few theatrical drags.

"What a knucklehead," Mick said.

Eleanor shoved Jamie, which he clearly took as permission to ditch her and sprint the final straightaway while smoke trailed from his Popeye sneer. This further incited the crowd's curiosity and cheering for Jamie after he passed through the painted finish line.

Nat trailed in Mick's wake through the crowd towards Jamie, and they arrived at the same time as Eleanor. Nat stayed back so Mick could greet her first. Mick then turned to heckle Jamie, who looked pretty green after his stunt.

Eleanor approached Nat. "Well, I'll be damned to see you at this wholesome community function," she said and thanked him for the water.

Nat let her lean on him while they observed the unfolding mess. Jamie was keeled over with this combative, ashamed expression. He had tried to stand upright to sign some autographs and chat with some surrounding girls. But as soon as Jamie talked, Nat could see his dopey, hungover eyes turn blue to volcanic. Jamie began to pant, hacking air like Morse code. Then, in an act of desperation, Jamie MacGyvered his bucket hat to collect what was no longer a dry heave. Jamie's projectile eruption was uncontainable. His barf overflowed from the hat, splattering onto the barely legal bystanders. Their squeals of endearment had turned as sour as the bread, beer, and bile that'd spewed out of Jamie's mouth.

A riot of laughter ripped from those outside the splash zone.

Nat and Eleanor weren't among those humored by Jamie when he was this much of a gong show.

"You ready to go, kiddo?" Mick said to Eleanor, likewise unenthused.

"See you later," she told Nat.

After they left, Nat turned back towards Jamie. It was unsurprising and baffling that his brother was now being consoled with Gatorade and fresh towels by fresh girls amnesiac to Jamie's antics. They were happy to step around his watery barf that ruined the sponsored ad on the blacktop.

Nat twitched when he felt a meek tug on his arm. He tracked down the tiny perpetrator's long pigtails as she ran back to her mother. Karen's daughter Julia was now bashfully clinging to her mother's leg. A taller guy with a short beard and a high-collared peacoat stood with them.

The man said, "I'll go get the car," as Nat approached them to say hello.

"Well, now. How lucky am I to run into you two?"

"It doesn't look like you were running," Karen said.

"You look great," Nat said, admiring her wide-brim hat and how her thick brown braid showcased over her shoulder like a sash.

"You too," Karen replied.

"Well, I'm looking better than Jamie, for once." Nat glanced back towards his brother's mess. "Happy Thanksgiving, by the way." Nat reflected on years past, when he had to carry up two leaves from the basement to account for them.

"New traditions this year," Karen said. "Go on to the car, Jules."

Nat kneeled to grab a heatbox hug from Julia through her puffy yellow coat to say goodbye. "Damn, you're getting strong," he told her.

Karen sighed at his PG-13 language.

"So who's the fella?" Nat asked.

Karen crossed her arms. She didn't answer, but Nat saw a glint in Karen's Swiss-neutral eyes when she turned her attention back from overseeing Julia's safe passage to the car. The Turkey Trot hadn't been a relay race, but there was something in their exchange that felt like the successful passing of a baton.

"So, have you done any growing up in Bolero world?" she asked.

"Not as much as Julia," Nat replied.

"Well, it's been good to see you back in Hillside. With old friends."

Nat puffed his shoulders from their sockets to agree without being too conspicuous. "Ah, c'mere," he said, and she reticently accepted his farewell embrace.

Her scent of jasmine faded when she walked away. He'd never really loved the smell as much as he'd appreciated its pleasant consistency.

▶▶

Later that afternoon, Nat was staring at the popcorn maze on the ceiling above his bed when Eleanor barged in. She never knocked. He didn't know if that was an only child thing or an Eleanor thing. She brought with her the warmth of the oven that'd been at 400 degrees all day. Eleanor's hair was wet and tied into two braids. She wore an Irish oatmeal sweater that fell to her thighs over shorts, tall socks, and green Doc Martens.

"Dusted those boots out of the back of your closet, I see." Nat remembered her wearing the boots right out of Trash and Vaudeville. They must've blistered the shit out of her feet by her pace and the walk up Broadway back to Penn, but she was too proud to stop or admit it.

"Shit. I always forget to take my shoes off by the door," she said.

"It's okay. Joanie expects you to break the rules." Nat enjoyed watching Eleanor angle for space on his boyhood bed. He sat up so she could sit beside him against the wainscot wall.

"I can't believe you're wearing jeans and a belt in bed." Eleanor wrinkled her nose.

"Did you ever think it's because I'm used to being interrupted?"

"Maybe," she said, playfully rubbing her leg against his.

Nat moved his hand onto her knee to calm it from jerking. She let his fingertips tuck under the top of her ribbed sock, and he felt the smooth skin on her leg beneath it. Eleanor's cold hair and warm face nuzzled into his neck, sending him an unignorable invitation to ravage her when Jamie barged in the door, shirtless, still looking like hell.

"Ele—You bring them taters?" Jamie asked.

"See what I mean?" Nat said to her.

Eleanor fell into Nat, laughing.

"What'd I do?" Jamie whined.

▶▶

True to tradition, Jamie passed out before it was time to do the dishes. Nat did more than his fair share while Eleanor dried beside him. Occasionally, Nat caught his reflection in the window above the sink and maybe, for the first time, recognized the person he was becoming and liked it.

Afterwards, Nat slipped two tall boys into his jacket pockets to prepare for a stroll with Eleanor. A few blocks away, they hopped a fence into the school fields. Most nights there'd be Arrow patrol, but there was usually a stalemate on holidays. Eleanor led them back to the same tennis courts where they found themselves fucked up and unsatisfied so many years ago.

"Choice pit stop." Nat's lips pressed a smile on the frosty aluminum can as he took a drink.

Eleanor sat up on the backrest of the perforated bench. "Hey. I know I said it at the dinner table when we were doing the rounds before, but I can't thank you enough for last night, making that happen for my dad's birthday and everything. I needed that more than you know."

"Happy to help—happy to be home, surprisingly."

"Sidenote. Robin's sisters freaked about her showing up home in a limo. They all came out and took pictures in it."

"Your buddies are a riot. I would've liked to have seen you during some of your German shenanigans," he said.

"Well, it wasn't all great," Eleanor admitted.

"It never is." Nat sat next to her on the bench.

"I hate to say I'm glad you weren't there, though. I kind of needed something of my own," she said.

"Ironic coming from an only child," Nat replied.

Eleanor frowned, and Nat felt bad that she'd taken offense.

"Hey, I'm sorry. I didn't mean that like it's a character flaw," he said.

"It's not like I had a choice, just like you had no choice of Jamie being your brother..."

"Yeah, no. I think it's given you a sensitive spot for knuckleheads, and I love that about you." Nat coughed. "I mean, I probably benefit from that."

"'Treat others the way you want to be treated,'" she quoted.

"The Huston family motto."

"That and the Folger's jingle."

"Yeah, I don't know about you, but I'm missing that Italian coffee," Nat said. "I'd give up beer for espresso."

"I miss everything about Italy," she said.

"I could've done without a certain guest being there."

"Lindsay's sister?" Eleanor joked.

Nat coughed again, this time unintentionally. "So, where is Will on this fine holiday?"

"Things are weird," she said. Nat watched Eleanor pull the arms of her jacket and poke her fingers in the fraying holes around the cuffs. "I don't want to talk about it."

"You don't want to talk to me about it, or you don't want to talk to him about it?"

"I want to talk to you, but I can't," she said.

Nat got up and walked over to grip onto the chainlink facing the courts. They felt so iced that with enough pressure, they'd snap. "That doesn't tell you something?" he said.

"Yeah, believe me. It tells me a lot, Nat," Eleanor said a little loudly. "But I don't think it's right to share with you yet."

Nat glared at the netless green courts until the lines blurred. He felt Eleanor come up and hold him from behind, tightly clasping her wrists around his chest. He closed his eyes and meditated on patience, timing, and the words he'd only shared with her in trashed letters and a song she'd yet to hear.

"It's like the laws of math," she explained, rubbing her head against his back like a cat. "It's against the order of operations or something."

"This is feeling pretty close to out of order, Eleanor."

"Fuck, I know. I'm sorry." She withdrew, and then her tone shifted to alert. "Oh, shit."

"What?" Nat said as a spotlight suddenly hit them like a target.

"Run!" Eleanor said excitedly and pushed Nat to retreat.

Nat took off behind her, not because he feared the consequence of trespassing now that he had some clout, but because it made him feel like a kid again. In the distance, he could hear the verbal threats from the rent-a-cop behind them. "It's just a matter of time!"

Nat agreed more deeply than the air that filled his lungs to run. It was a matter of time before he'd catch up to Eleanor and they could run together at the same pace.

22

JAMIE

Pretty soon, Jamie would be high on permanent markers from signing his blobby initials on jewel cases, maybe even some supple skin. Bolero's "Whatever Tomorrow" was beating expectations on the Modern Tracks List. Meanwhile, "Muse Box" was still holding in the Top 10. These were things to brag about, and today he was in rare form to need a reminder.

The press photographers were like a human blockade keeping back fans who'd overcrowded every aisle of Tower Records' flagship store. Nat and Jamie were here to promote the release of the "Whatever Tomorrow" single. Two and done. Jamie was dissatisfied. He'd barely broken enough sweat to wipe from his philtrum. He didn't like to sing sitting down, but standing during an acoustic set looked stupid. Now that his singing was done, Jamie fidgeted about the wires entangling him and his brother in the tight performance area to find the maracas. Jamie felt even more stupid now, waiting to shake these baby rattles while Nat adjusted a second mic to his mouth. Jamie stared down at the watch Frida had given him, which was suspended in time. He tried to prevent his disappointment from being caught on camera.

"I'll do one now, I guess," Nat said, repositioning himself. What was this guess bullshit? Since rejoining the band in Vegas, Nat seemed certain about everything. "This is sort of a new song about old feelings, or maybe it's an old song about new feelings." Nat cleared his throat. "If you get the 'Whatever Tomorrow' 7 inch, this one's on the flip side."

When Nat played his song, Jamie emptily grooved on the black and white shakers. The pair of maracas were kind of like him and his brother, opposites with all this kinetic shit springing inside them. Nat's song had evolved from something they'd laid down at Lochstock that didn't make the record. Nat made the song better and kept it for himself, something he told Jamie he wouldn't do. It wasn't just the mood of the song. The lyrics were different, too. Or maybe they only sounded different because Nat had never sounded like this before. His delivery wasn't soft and spare, like when he was teaching Jamie a song to sing back. Jamie prized his ability to dig deep and make Nat's songs great. But with this song, Nat had accomplished great without him, and that made Jamie feel like a limp dick. Jamie examined his brother's performance. Nat's face stretched with his eyes shut. His neck strained to croon like the lyrics were a key, unlocking a secret.

It then occurred to Jamie that they were.

▶▶

After the set and subsequent signing, Nat and Jamie hit the Americana for another press conference. Jamie was not having it. The day had started too early, and they had their party at the Palladium later that night. Jamie sat with his hands jammed up against the seams in his pockets. Bolero's PR rep Lisa was moderating the media while Old Betty was manning the perimeter as if Brad Wesley's goons from *Roadhouse* were gonna show up with boot knives out.

First Nat singing, now Nat having a fuckin' gas, bantering with reporters? It was like *Freaky Friday*, the Dempsey edition. Nat was conversationally holding the mic instead of stiffly leaning over it, saying, "People are fuckin' bored, and that includes the lot of you writing up nonsense. It's like you're looking for Bolero to fill the void without sports rivalries because of the strike and the lockout. Bolero against The Reverie. Bolero against pederasts and corporate pigs... I mean, even me versus Jamie! You've all picked your sides, though, right?"

"All right, sorry guys," Lisa said. "The boys are on a really tight schedule and have to get going."

"You know. Actually, I'll take a few more," Nat announced. This was unprecedented. Jamie pulled a cigarette to take the edge off. Nat called on some lady journo from Billboard. "We fuckin' love Billboard, don't we?" Nat questioned Jamie, who nodded but kept his mouth fiercely squeezed around the filter of his Camel.

She asked about Nat's B-side. "Is 'Always Home' to test the waters? Are you planning to sing more Bolero songs in the future?"

"Well, by your standards, 'Whatever Tomorrow' will probably top the charts with that mope singing. So, I don't think we're gonna sideline him anytime soon. But 'Always Home'—it's been on my mind for—for years I've been hung up on it." Nat scratched his chin.

"Sideline." Jamie stubbed out his smoke in the hotel's clean ashtray.

Nat continued. "So, I was recently at our drummer KP's wedding in Italy. You know this because the papers all had the scoop on Jamie missing it."

Jamie looked over at Lisa. "Can we fucking get out of here already?"

"Anyway," Nat said. "The potential—or something beyond what I initially thought was possible with this song occurred to me, as it does. I blame being just soaked in wine and night swimming and love."

Jamie's brow furrowed as Nat's inversely raised.

"So I ended up rewriting this outtake called 'She's Leaving' into 'Always Home.' A few days later, we were in London for the *Tops*, and I conned someone down on Abbey Road to roll the tapes for me."

About every hand flung up. When Nat asked for the next question, Jamie kicked his chair back in contempt and stormed out of the room.

▶▶

Jamie hid out the rest of the day playing *Street Fighter II* and killing a case of Heineken with Sulky until the car rolled up to take them to the Palladium.

A few paparazzi were lurking outside the club. Jamie avoided them by hopping over the sawhorse barricade. The wood felt mushy from the sleet that began to fall from the early December sky. Underneath the marquee was almost steamy with all the lights, which made it even brighter than the club's marquee itself. Jamie saw Rollins talking to a slick-looking guy with an eye patch.

"Jamie boy! C'mere!" Rollins hustled Jamie into a headlock. Jamie could feel her feverish blood through her suit as her arm coiled around his neck. "I gotta introduce you to our host. This is Peter." Jamie strained to stare up from Rollins' hold. "Shit, man, are you a pirate?"

"No, I'm Canadian," the man said.

"Listen kid. I've got Nat talking to the guy from Supreme about doing a campaign, you know? Those skaters in the 'Whatever Tomorrow' video are Supreme. I mean, this guy, this guy made Stussy *Stussy*! Pinnacle shit!" Rollins said. "And wait'll you see the footage Peter's got playing inside. I mean—How many fuckin' TV monitors are stacked in there?" Rollins turned to ask the one-eyed Canuck who'd already walked away.

Jamie was half-wasted but had yet to take any digs to match Rollins' whiteout energy. As a rule, Jamie shouldn't have anything illegal on him, not after the shit the mayor tried to pull. Holding was an undocumented job responsibility for hired Bolero entourage. But tonight Jamie reasoned he could break the rules, since it wasn't more than he could handle himself. Jamie told Sulky to go bag them three tall boys from the bodega when he saw Ele arriving alone.

She flicked the mist from her hair and leather blazer once she was under the marquee. "Congrats on the new single!"

"Whatever," Jamie replied.

"You mean 'Whatever *Tomorrow.*'"

"Funny," he said and sneered at one of the paparazzi flashing at him.

"Funny?" Ele repeated. "What's up with you?"

"Nah, nothing. Where's Will?"

"I don't know. Where's Nat? He's been calling me all week, but we keep missing each other. He's all jazzed up. Do you know what that's about?"

"Oh, you haven't heard that fuckin' song then?"

"Still in cellophane. Haven't had a chance yet. I was up at my old producer's about doing this *Reel World* London job. Things are happening really fast with that... Is Nat here yet?"

"Yeah. He's here." Jamie hesitated. This was his opportunity to switch gears hard and fast, the same way he caused the chain to break off a bike he failed to steal as a kid. "He probably just wanted to go on about the tour. Pretty sure he brought Nikki tonight." Ele's smile, along with her eyes, looked to wilt. He almost felt bad. "Look." Jamie thumbed the corner of his lip. "I'm not doing this shit tonight. Fuck this party. You gonna come with us or what?"

"Us?"

Jamie nudged his chin toward Sulky, who was shuffling back towards them.

"Ugh," Ele said.

"What the hell?" Sulky handed out the bagged beers.

Ele took hers reluctantly, appearing to long to be inside the Palladium doors. "I don't know, Jamie."

"Seriously? You're never around anymore. And you went and saw Frida? And now she's gone. I never ask you for anything."

"Fine," she said. "But I want to come back later."

"Whatever," Jamie replied.

Sulky led their misfit trio away from Bolero's big party. The last thing Jamie, Sulky, and Ele shared was a joint graduation party from high school. If tonight went half as well, someone was gonna lose a tooth.

They were three empty High Lifes away from the Palladium when Sulky slipped them underground into a place he loved called Iggy's. Some geezer was singing, "Who re You?" from a small stage encircled by tables.

"Yeah dude, exactly," Ele muttered. "Karaoke? Jamie, who are you?"

Sulky went to work, clearing out the best seats at the bar, moving them away from the stage, and then brokered their order. The bartender brought over three rocks glasses, a bowl of yellowed limes, and a rule-bending bottle of tequila so they could over serve themselves. No salt because it made Jamie's fingers swell. After they downed a first round, Sulky left to entertain himself with some regulars, a rowdy table of older broads wearing tinsel crowns.

Jamie caught Ele people watching and became annoyed that she wasn't smiling. He poured three finger-widths up the glass and shoved her to take it back with him. She took a gulp and then rolled her neck and shoulders around to give the effect that she was composing herself.

"Okay. What are we doing?" she said.

"I don't know. Tell me something juicy and fucked up," he said.

"Are you fucking kidding? You're an idiot. I'm not here for that. There are plenty of other options." Ele flung her hand around the female-dominated room. But as Jamie looked around, he decided he wanted Ele more than anyone else there.

"You are so fucking uptight," he said.

"Don't insult me," she said while gnawing lime pulp.

"Don't get pissed at me just because Will can't loosen you up," he said.

"You need to be examined," she said.

"Okay, okay. I care is all! You know I love you," he said.

"Not that it's any of your business, but we're not even—" Ele shook her head a few times like she was arguing with herself over what to say next.

"What?"

"Forget it. Can you just respect some fucking discretion? At least with Frida you were more protective of her and what happened between you two... not to mention you actually tried to avoid or at least minimize whatever else went on outside of that."

"Alright, alright, but I don't wanna be thinking about that broad right now. Nothing but trouble," he said.

"Hello, kettle black." Ele bumped his glass like a shuffleboard puck and again they upped the ante on the agave.

"It is different, though," Jamie admitted. "Or it was."

"What?"

Jamie twisted the watchband around his wrist, feeling his clammy skin underneath it. "Frida," he said. "Not even sex, but like, being together. Feeling like a puppy at her feet under the table, trying to catch scraps." Jamie stopped, but he wanted to say more, to tell Ele that he'd been looping on this idea of asking Frida to marry him just because it was the biggest gesture he could equate to how he felt.

"I swear I believed this was going to happen to you someday, but I can't remember if that's true or not... I think that there's hope that—Oh shit." Ele'd dribbled the bottle's contents into and around their glasses, which excited him.

"You spilled!" Jamie used a pretend voice like a tattling kid. "Now you gotta spill something," he commanded, leaning into her. Ele smelled like cotton candy and spearmint.

"Ah fuck you, that is such a good rule." Ele shoved his arm, but instead of releasing her hand, she kept her grip on it. "Okay. What?"

Jamie glanced around and located Sulky's bleach-tipped head by the stage with Dominic, Nikki's assistant. Why was he here? But as long as Sulky was preoccupied, Jamie told Ele they should slide into the bathroom.

Iggy's dank bathroom was tight. Single occupancy to use the toilet. Double occupancy to use the imagination. Jamie showed off his dexterity and generosity to prep Ele a nice bump—like he'd learned for a quick one—on the hammock of skin that linked the thumb.

"Jesus, that's too big!" Ele declined his offering while clumsily balancing her body between his legs around the toilet.

"That's what all the ladies say," he said, skimming her dose and rubbing the excess across his chompers.

"That's not what I hear," Ele joked while taking up her heap.

Jamie laughed, but wondered who the fuck would say that trash? He dispensed another dash for himself, then lit a cigarette to up the buzz.

He shared the smoke with her from his hand and supported them against the slippery tile wall so they could watch his smoke circles dissipate like stars in the mirror. It was the closest he'd been to anyone in weeks. For the moment, they stayed quiet, ignoring the muffled melodies and discordant clanks penetrating outside the confines of their space.

"We're lookin' menacing, if you ask me," he said at their shadowy reflections.

"You kinda look like Nat right now," she whispered, tilting her head back.

Jamie felt threatened, as if his awareness was now heightened to see what Nat saw in her and what Jamie didn't know they saw in each other. "What are you afraid of?" he asked.

"Right now?" Ele looked surprised. She peeled his arm off and turned her back to the mirror to sit on the sink and face him. "Nothing. I mean. My mind's too busy feeling like it's in a Mexican Colombian air show," she rambled.

"Bullshit. You ain't fooling me," Jamie said while chomping on the smoke between his teeth. Ele looked down to smooth the hem on her black shorts, which she'd layered over thick black stockings. Jamie swept the hair away from her ear and put his mouth to it. "You're all wound up with inhibitions," he whispered while squaring up their hips.

"This isn't happening," she said when he took her neck in his hands.

"It doesn't have to mean anything," he told her, close enough to shotgun, but heavy pounds on the door became unbearable. Ele pulled away from him and stormed out of the bathroom.

It was Sulky and Dominic who'd been knocked into each other's arms.

"What the fuck is her problem?" said Sulky.

"She's cool," Jamie said, preoccupied with watching Ele, who'd gone up to talk to the karaoke emcee. "Let's get more of that tequila."

Ele returned with a fuck-me grin like nothing had happened, which relieved Jamie. Like she knew he didn't mean what he'd said.

"Get ready for a 'Fairytale of New York' duet, you maggot," she said after launching at Jamie, roughnecking his collar.

"You signed us up for karaoke? Hell no."

"Come on, Jame." She puffed out her lips to pout, proving she was trashed. "It's almost Christmas!" She pounded the bar top and poured herself another bruiser from their second bottle.

"I get paid too much," Jamie said.

"Psh. I slipped that dude a TEN-DOLLAR BILL to play The Pogues! Paid too much? You pampered twat." Ele refilled his glass. "I think you owe me to go down up there tonight."

Jamie leaned close enough to feel the warmth of her breath. "For what?"

Ele stared him down with her eyes like Christmas wreaths on the nicest doors in the neighborhood. "Your pushy bathroom etiquette."

"I'd sooner push you back into that bathroom," he said.

"Stop messing with yourself," she said. "You're not messing with me."

Her eyes were glassy now, like the last one had finally tipped her to a point of no return. Jamie suspected he was there, too. Even though he couldn't feel anything, he was still throwing every kind of shit to see if they'd fuck.

"Can a Shane and Kristy please come to the stage?" Iggy's karaoke guy announced.

But "Shane" wasn't going to the stage and "Kristy" had made a run for it. Jamie saw Ele stammer her way up the steps, using her hands as a second set of feet to leave. Jamie fought his way to chase after her, yelling at Sulky and Dominic to stay put with a lie that he'd be right back.

A wintry mix jarred Jamie's exit out onto the wet concrete. Ele was out balancing on the curb. "Fuck you goin!" Jamie mixed command and question. He reached to grab Ele's wavy arm, which had yet to catch a cab. His grip skid on the black sleek of her leather sleeve.

Ele's face turned stunned. Their legs split, initiating a blackout burst of both heads on their trip to the curb. Jamie's left eye smacked Ele's face, backed by the studs of her jaw. His brow pulsed to alert to future pain sensed from less accidental collisions. Now there were only hot tears. Ele'd broken most of his fall. Jamie used his adrenaline rush to scrape her yardsaled limbs up from the pavement. The blood bloomed from her mouth, cut by his head. Holding her surrendered body in his arms, she seemed serene.

"Now I'll never get a cab." Ele's disheveled smile sped up her lip's crimson drip. They laughed, and he squeezed her tighter to feel anything, everything.

"Nah, rag doll. Nothin' to worry about." Jamie propped her arms around his neck and hid her face against his chest. "I seen that *Taxicab Confessions* show."

Seconds later, they were on the pleather seat of many a sin before them. In the shadows, Jamie envied Ele's tongue, primally licking her wounds.

"Take me home," he heard her whimper like it was an invitation to plunge and suck from her mouth. The taste of an iron kiss would be the last memory lost to the night.

▶▶

The first time he woke, it was not with his eyes. They were still crusted shut. His tongue moved first. It slowly darted from behind his teeth that felt loose, piercing between the seal of his lips. His mouth was dry and his lips too, adhered by blood rust. He was now attuned to his icy breaths that came in slowly and out quickly through his nose. He did not know why he had bled. He was not yet to the point of knowing how or what to ask. He was not subconscious but in a state of subhuman.

His second stage of waking was knowing not only that he was human but also which specific human he was. Not yet did he know why or where he was, other than he was suspended in something sinister, like a cage. It was dark and still, but for gusts of cold air that were without pattern and unwelcome. He felt the weight of another human clinging to him and the dampness of the clothes that stuck to his body. Why were they like gutted fish wrapped in yesterday's news?

Jamie released the clench of his fingers. His nails had been dug deep into the edges of a filthy rubber and felt mat he must've pulled up from the floor to cover them. His hands were bruised and so cold they now felt burned. He touched his left eye and could tell by its throb and size that it must be pink or green, on its way to the black shade of the box he was in. "Where the fuck are we?" he said.

"We're stuck." Ele sniffled. "In the elevator in my building. I never take it, but you made me."

Jamie was freaked out, but released a cackle demoted by his physical condition into a dehydrated cough. "Do you remember what happened?" The last thing he could remember was them being in the bathroom at some basement bar.

"Not really. I remember we were at Iggy's and some guy was singing The Who. I remember when you were shaking the elevator so hard I thought the cables were going to snap and we'd fucking die."

Jamie could hear in her voice that she had started to cry. "I miss Frida," he said, maneuvering to sit in Indian style and hang his head heavily between his hands.

"Then stop being such a piece of shit and go fucking do something about it," she said.

"Like you? You're the same fucking tease playing all sides."

"I hate you, Jamie," Ele said, her words echoing through the shaft. There were other sounds now too, mechanical, electric. Men talking.

"Hey!" Jamie spat out with debilitated anger. "We're fucking stuck in here!"

The caged elevator cab started to climb slowly, now passing a line of light, a drafty gap from the bottom of an industrial door to the floor they'd been jammed up from approaching for a time unknown. Jamie began yanking at the elevator's retractable door grate, which wouldn't unlock until the cab settled in alignment with the floor.

Finally, the building's steel door swung open to the unbearable brightness of daylight, a jumpsuit repairman, and Nat.

23

FRIDA

NEARLY FIVE YEARS AGO, when the world had just turned into the 1990s, Frida was consuming a layer cake of fashion magazines and sharing a not-quite first-rate hotel room with some long forgotten rival. That was when she had read the now infamous declaration that Linda Evangelista wouldn't get out of bed for less than $10,000. This valuation had spurred Frida to more carefully assess herself as a commodity and to plan for retirement. She'd become vigilant not to be defeated by the biological clocks winding down on the ways in which she had to utilise her body.

On a rainy December day in Soho, Frida had surpassed her financial goal and unofficially retired. This decision was kept private. It was hardly the most important secret Frida had been carrying.

Frida's last contractual commitment was at the promotional launch of Dior's new fragrance in Paris. Her advert, which contained a sealed, scented sample, would permeate every January 1995 issue. Frida was featured sumptuously beholding the perfume's bulbous, canary-tinted glass bottle. Shot on location during a chilling evening in Rome, her feet had pruned whilst shuffling atop wished coins in the Trevi Fountain. They dressed her in an *haute couture* gold gown with a scooped bustier and a handkerchief hemline that was both leggy and mimicked water flow.

She remembered the night she met Jamie. From then on, he never missed an opportunity to say gold was her colour. When Frida saw the photograph they'd selected for the campaign, she nearly cried. Steven Meisel had immortalised her body at its pinnacle and captured her personal objective, to invoke Jamie's desire for what could be their *dolce vita*.

If an agreeable reaction to the perfume had been a condition of her hire as ambassador, Frida would have lost the job. When renowned perfumier, Pierre, had so pridefully described to her the intricate notes of magnolia, rose, and sandalwood for his *eau de toilette*, Frida had to excuse herself to wretch. She nearly missed *les toilettes*. Frida apologised more profusely than the aromas to Pierre, then left him among the vials which reminded her of a home pregnancy test she had taken once before, and would urgently need to take again.

▶▶

"The Sixth of June."

Frida had finally revealed the news to someone outside her closed circle of relatives and doctors. The more she shared, the less she felt bouts of nausea, the more she experienced a fluttering sense of desirable anticipation.

"You're freaking kidding me." Nikki yawned. Their time difference reasonably explained that she was waking up for the day. Frida had been staying at Nikki's flat, a gift Nikki received on her 21st birthday, around the time Frida and she had first met through old boyfriends.

"If you don't mind, to keep it between us for the time being," Frida requested. Nikki, a self-proclaimed gossip, might seem an unlikely confidante. But Nikki was of a dynastic surname, and being of a prominent family required sweeping much larger secrets under the carpet.

"Of course," Nikki said. "Babe, if it's a boy, I will take him to Raffles for his 21st and flirt with all his friends." Nikki cackled.

Frida smiled nervously through the receiver, recalling how scandalously someone had found Nikki with KP's teenaged brothers after the wedding in Tuscany. "You're mad," Frida told her.

"*You're* mad. You're having a baby. I'm having a spa day. Anyway, I'll be bouncing between Palm Beach and Palm Springs all winter. So you can stay as long as you want."

"Thanks, love."

"Now that I know, I'm going to spoil you rotten with gifts and have them stock the house. You have to take Polaroids of how fat you're getting," said Nikki.

"You're too much," Frida replied as she was tenderly smoothing the front and back of her hand down her belly.

"So, are you telling Jamie?"

"You're implying that I haven't," Frida said.

"Duh."

"If it comes up..." Frida said.

Nikki repeated her. "If it comes up? What the heck does that mean?"

Frida meant that while Jamie had been persistent about winning her back, she was not yet prepared to test his determination under the condition that she was carrying their child.

"Look, if you take him back, tell him he needs a new publicist," Nikki said.

"Is that your endorsement?"

"Girl. You know you know best," Nikki said. "I don't worry about you. I only worry about you being cheap with this house hunting. Don't disappoint me after being a frugal bitch all these years. *Especially* if you take Jamie back. He might end up richer than I am. I mean, not really! But whatever."

"We'll see, then."

"Oh. And after you lock down a house, you absolutely must hire Duarte. He's a freaking genius," Nikki said.

Frida looked about the black deco-patterned walls as she sat upon an oversized metallic chaise and felt as though she had met enough of Duarte to know their tastes were wildly incompatible. "Well, that's a lovely gesture," Frida replied.

►►

If there was something Frida coveted as much as gestures, it was aesthetics. Playing to both, Jamie had found her the following day. He was waiting outside Nikki's flat, looking as idyllic as the property Frida had just viewed in Primrose Hill.

Jamie knelt on the wet pavement. Clutching onto Frida's hands, he said, "I didn't know where to get flowers, but I just wanna be with you. I'll leave the band and do whatever. I don't wanna fuck around anymore."

Frida looked into his beautiful, welling eyes. Blue, sober, and truthful in this moment. She was touched. Yet she could not help herself but to uncharacteristically and haughtily laugh from the bottom of her not quite visible belly.

►►

Frida felt like cold butter on toast that first night of their reunion. She would melt in time if she wasn't forced to spread too soon. Jamie's gentle gaze and touch suggested he was undeterred by the weight she had gained, or oblivious to its implications. In the morning, he had not so much as enquired how to prepare her eggs. He'd waited until after serving them at her bedside to mention that he'd like to pay Nikki's bill for a long distance call.

"That's lovely, but I doubt Nikki has ever seen a utility bill," Frida said.

"I called Joanie on how to do the eggs," Jamie confessed.

"As if she didn't dislike me already. Now to be receiving middle of the night calls about soft-boiled eggs?"

"Nah, Joanie thinks you're classy. She was just bent out of shape because you called our house 'homely.' But at Thanksgiving, Ele said that's like a compliment in your English. So it's all good now."

"Is Eleanor well?" Frida asked, even though they had been in touch. Frida knew she was planning to take a job filming in London that following month.

"I dunno. Last time I saw Ele, we got so loaded and I ended up helping her get home. Nat still hasn't talked to me like I did something wrong." Frida listened carefully to Jamie's puzzling words and wondered about the missing pieces. Jamie rubbed his head. "I was meaning to tell you something about that."

"Oh?"

"Yeah. Me and her got stuck in the elevator overnight, pitch black. It was so cold and fucked up. To be honest, we were both crying by the morning, and it hit me hard..."

"What did?" Frida said.

"Life and what not. Like, I knew I needed to be with you. That's why I flew out. I'm missing rehearsals. I'm definitely fucking pissing everyone off, but I don't care. I'll quit everything and be your fucking house cat. Whatever."

Frida sensed his hopelessness and hopefulness all in one winded breath. She let him hold and kiss her to empathise with Jamie's noble but horrid idea. This Jamie beside her now was docile and loving. But he could only exist temporarily, so long as the other versions of himself existed elsewhere. Otherwise, she knew he would become cantankerous, intrude on her space, and act out desperately for attention. "I'd love that," she shared. "But it'd be best for you to keep your other commitments."

"So come back to New York and go on tour with us," Jamie suggested as flippantly as leaving the band. "Six months around the fuckin' world. Tour ends in June, right after our birthdays. Then we can go tear it up on whatever fucking riviera you love the most."

But of course, it was the Sixth of June that Frida was due to give birth to their child. And so Frida confessed to him that she'd become pregnant.

Jamie's eyes had never been wider. They appeared to droop with wonder. "You're gonna have it?"

"Yes," she said. "Another Gemini, bound to be dreamy and dreadful, just like us."

Jamie seemed relieved, and then very quiet. He lay in her lap and caressed the parts of her designed to recreate. After they made love, Jamie asked her if she'd ever been pregnant before.

"No. Just a scare once, when I was younger," she told him.

"I got someone pregnant before." Jamie wiped his brow with the back of his hand. "Way before I met you, before Bolero got signed. I told her I'd help her, and she said she already got rid of it. Blamed me for why she got an abortion. Like if it'd been with someone else, she'd have kept it. I never felt worse in my life." Jamie's long arm spread across her belly, and she could feel his body radiate pain while he attempted to soothe hers. "Couldn't even tell anyone, but she could sell me out about it any minute."

"Diana?" Frida guessed.

Jamie confirmed, burying his head under her arms.

"Well, that's cruel, but it is her right," Frida said.

"I know. I don't blame her and I'm fucking lucky because then I wouldn't have even met you but like, I want you to have our kid." Jamie lifted his head and wrapped her arm around his neck so he could smell and kiss her forearms and wrists. "You're so fucking perfect and sharp like a tack. No one deserves you. But this is fate like, it's gotta mean something, right?"

▶▶

Over the next week, Frida took seriously the compartmentalised way in which Jamie could be in her life. He was intuitive and attentive to her, and his touch on her body was a tonic. She adored his sunny disposition. He took her as sovereign, as if no one could know or do anything better than her. This was, of course, the best of Jamie. And so she decided that as long as he was at his best with her, she might bear the ugliness of his world that was likely to exist when they were apart. Frida's greatest ally to minimise Jamie's worst elsewhere was his brother, Nat. Frida needed to deliver Jamie back to Bolero so Nat and Jamie could carry on with their tangled fates.

Days before Christmas, Jamie and Frida were walking through the wilds of the Heath after a morning of promising appointments. Her house on a cobbled lane was under offer, and Frida had healthily carried into her second trimester. With clearance to fly, she suggested they go to New York for the holiday. Jamie smothered her with his approval.

"We'll bring loads of gifts," she said. "Throw a dinner. Share our news. You can get on with rehearsing. I'll stay through New Year."

"Then?" he said.

"After the tour, you'll return to England and take time off to be with us," she said.

"Us..." Jamie wiped the crease of his mouth into a cheeky grin that faded when he shared his dread about facing his brother back in the states.

"You'll have to mend things," Frida said firmly. "Though I may have an idea to improve your odds."

24

WILL

WILL WATCHED CATH AS she rose, led by the bones of her hips, towards the windows to seal out the chill it added to the room.

"How do you explain that?" she said and pulled on her shapeless smock dress.

"Tell me you're asking rhetorically," Will replied nonchalantly, lighting a cigarette from beside his low platform bed.

"Validation?"

"Or your basic trauma bond."

"Your exaggerating is a little traumatic," she mumbled.

"We're hitting the road for the tour two days after Dave's out of treatment. This is real, Cath," Will said.

"He'll be in a good headspace." Cath layered on a large knit sweater. "It was an accident." Observing Cath so relaxed had made it clear why Will had wandered to Ele, someone who could be emotionally invested in a conversation with a cab driver.

"Either way. This is it, Cath. I'm one foot out the door." Meanwhile, Cath had put her coat on to leave. "You know I don't need this," Will said.

"So Dave, The Reverie, they've become your charity case?"

"Why else would I agree to support Bolero on the North American leg of their tour? They'll have some cushioning and then I'm done."

"That fulfills another one of your grand metamorphoses?"

Will searched for his breath to let his anger go. He wanted to curse Cath out for being obtuse and enabling, which was useless. Instead, he pulled his jeans on and walked to the bathroom to piss. He owed it to himself to shed his skin of this band. They were lucky to be alive, but had outlived their potential.

Cath was still lurking at the door when he returned to the room. "Well, um, do you want to visit Dave later?"

"Not today. I need some space. I'll check in on Christmas," he said before Cath left the apartment like a drafty apparition.

As immediately as the door closed, there were knocks at it again, too aggressive to be Cath's. Nat Dempsey appeared to be seething through the peephole. Will opened the door shirtless, which seemed to have further aggravated Nat's demeanor. Will noticed one of Nat's eyes was discolored, like a torch.

"I'm guessing Eleanor isn't here right now."

"Nope," Will responded, leaning his body on the threshold.

Nat's slack brows flattened, and he tucked his top lip into his mouth. "Really fucking casual."

"All due respect, Nat, you have no idea what you're talking about."

"Whatever. Keep playing that self-righteous shit."

As Nat turned to leave, Will considered Eleanor's conflict of allegiance and her kindness to protect The Reverie. Will called after him. "Nat, wait. Are you hungry?"

"Not really," he said.

"Me neither. Just, hang on."

▶▶

Gold tinsel hung from the greasy, fake garland that decorated their booth. The smells from the griddle validated Will's position against eating meat. Nat looked exhausted since switching locations to the diner across the street. Therefore, Will found it odd when Nat put his hand over his mug to halt the waitress from topping off his half-drunk coffee.

"So what's this about?" Nat said.

Will exhaled. "Look, man, it's against everything in me to trust you. But I've gotta do Ele a solid and level with you now." Will warmed his throat with coffee and opened up. "We almost lost Dave a few weeks ago, before Thanksgiving. Ele was there when we found him. So, we've all been lying low while he does his 28 days. And—"

"And you thought I'd get you fired from the tour?" Nat said.

"I wouldn't put it past you. But that's just the half of it."

Nat folded his arms across himself. "And the other half?"

"If Dave can't keep it together, Bewilder's going to drop us, which would be devastating."

"Look. I'm sorry about Dave, but I haven't seen you give a shit about anything since I've known you, man."

"I have no interest in disputing that. I'm a little checked out," Will admitted, then filled his lungs with a fresh smoke. "But it's not just about me. Look, I know I'm not like you and don't know what it's like to have a brother like yours. But Dave, Dasuki and Andy—they're my brothers. I'm telling you in confidence that I've been digging us out of a financial and legal chasm. We're on the hook to pay back the label for rerecording *Neon Plane*. We don't repay it, we lose the rights to our music as collateral. We're barely making a dime beyond *per diem* for this tour. I'm paying for Dave's treatment out of my own pocket."

"That's tough, man," Nat said.

"I'm just doing the tour to get them—us—out of this mess, and then I walk away." Will sat back against the booth cushion and felt the mood shift in their shared silence.

"I need another cup," Nat said.

"She was just around to pour you one."

"Yeah, I mean, it's a ridiculous system, though. Why would I want her to dump scalding black coffee to imbalance my preferred ratio?" Nat explained this like it was the most obvious and reasonable position, and everyone else was crazy for heeding such a stupid, standard practice.

"Are you okay?" Will asked.

"Yeah, no," Nat said. "This is great and all—you going on about your shit. If you need me to be fucking explicit, I'm not gonna rat you out to Rollins or anyone."

"I appreciate that."

"Yeah, well." Nat coughed. "You're not gonna appreciate why I came to press you this morning." Nat thanked the waitress for refilling his emptied mug, then continued. "I mean, what the fuck is it with rock'n'roll where every time you go looking for someone, you end up seeing something you weren't supposed to see?"

"I don't know how this morning is any of your business." Will held some more silence before speaking again, knowing this was all coming down to Ele.

Nat rattled a sugar packet.

"Look, I don't know what's going on with Ele," said Will. "She was a bit of a mystery to me."

"Is that your excuse?" Nat said.

"For what? Ele and I aren't committed to each other—and I don't mean that in a 'bohemian' way, I mean at all. We haven't been together for a while now." Will stubbed out his cigarette and then narrowed his eyes. "Otherwise, quite frankly, Nat? I'd be knocking on *your* door to 'press' you about crossing lines. Especially after this new song. Come on, man."

Nat released what Will interpreted to be a shameless laugh, like Nat was honored to have been called out for his flagrant encroachment. "Oh man, I'd have liked to seen that," Nat said.

Perhaps Will finally understood the friendly nature of Nat's antagonizing. The weirdness of the whole situation made Will feel a bit lighter. He emitted a few laughs himself.

"Will, man. You're a better person than I wanted to believe. As much as I'd like to prolong our unholy communion—" Nat stood up and threw a twenty down. "Well, you know what I've gotta do."

"I can't wish you luck," Will said, accepting Nat's hand for a stare-down shake.

"Oh, I get it. Luck is the furthest thing I've ever wished for you." Nat smirked. "But that's all done now. I'll see you all on the road."

"I'll try to look forward to it," Will said, which was true.

25

NAT

"THERE'S NOTHING LIKE SITTING in church and thinking about sex," Jamie once tried to whisper too loudly into Nat's ear during midnight mass on Christmas Eve at their local parish. Nat had punched his brother back into the pew. Not because Jamie was wrong, but because he was breaking Nat's concentration on the matter. Even tonight in St. Patrick's Cathedral, with all its glowing candles, cascades of poinsettias, and opulence to hold one's holiest attention, Nat's mind was still stuck in the gutter acts of love.

The mass had reached the part in the liturgical structure where everyone shook hands for peace to be with them. Nat accepted his brother's offering of peace. He was bound to forgive Jamie again and again. Being that it was approaching the alleged son of God's birthday, Nat decided he should pray for Jamie's children. God knows how many he might end up having. Nat had no faith that having children would make someone a fundamentally better person, but a kid might prevent someone like Jamie from becoming a worse person. Nat also knew that children were expensive, and that might incentivize Jamie to be more driven and cooperative within the band to succeed.

At this point, neither Frida nor Jamie had confirmed that she was pregnant, but Nat had no other explanation for their reconciliation or Jamie's charade of good behavior. Since returning from London with Frida, Jamie had been focused and on time for every rehearsal. Not staying out too late or getting into fights. Shopping for furniture. Now this? Jamie and Frida were hosting this extravagant, traditional night in New York. A band familyish affair of the Dempsey and Sullivan brothers, along with their moms, Joanie and Peg. Their fathers, who once spent Christmas Eve at an OTB with money stolen from their sons' sock drawers, were not invited.

At the end of the mass, Nat lit two candles. The first was for him and his brother to see it through with Bolero together. The second was for the person he'd always held a candle for—that no matter what, she'd find her way and, just maybe, they would find their way to each other.

▶▶

After the mass, it took about twenty minutes to go two blocks in the limo. The car reeked like burnt chestnuts Greg bought on the street.

"It's too bad KP and Lindsay couldn't be here," Frida said.

"I don't know, man. Jewish Jamaican Christmas sounds pretty good to me," Greg said.

Jamie pointed out Frida's giant perfume ad in a window at Saks.

Sulky bemoaned, "Mr. and Mrs. Billboard."

When they arrived at Jamie and Frida's hotel for dinner, Jamie hugged Joanie and said, "Can you believe it, ma? From Astoria to the Waldorf."

Their dinner party was led like the reversal of the scene in *Goodfellas*, away from swanky blueblood dining rooms, down service steps, and through musty corridors of glassware and seasonal platters before being settled into the private cellar room, surrounded by cedar and bottles waiting to peak.

Jamie pushed several outfacing corks like they were control room buttons. Nat let him take the head of the table. Frida sat between Nat and Jamie. The moms scolded Greg for lighting his cigarette with the candelabra at the center of the table. Everyone's festive clamoring grew in anticipation for the poor waiter tasked with getting them drinks.

"They're lucky none of us has a corkscrew," Nat said.

"Or a saber." Sulky mimicked the motion he'd seen Nikki do like a karate chop across a giant bottle of Champagne he'd pulled from the shelves.

Jamie reached down the table to grab what he must've thought was a tray of cheese stabbed with miniature silver sabers. When he popped a cube into his mouth, Nat watched Jamie's eyes bug and jaw concave into the same expression of a little kid who'd prematurely transitioned out of diapers and realized he'd shit his pants.

"Ew!" Jamie spewed.

At least he used his linen napkin instead of a bucket hat to spit up what was not cheese but unsalted butter, a whole other type of crime. It became clear to Nat that their party's exclusive basement dining room was less of a VIP situation than it was the restaurant's solution to quarantine them from their more civilized patrons.

Everyone was at the tail end of their first round when Jamie and Frida held hands and stood up.

"We're having a baby!" they said in unison.

Other than some high-pitched cooing from the moms, the boys took in this information rather neutrally, which Nat knew probably pissed Jamie off, that they didn't find this particularly provocative or noble. Nat felt relieved that he was not surprised by what was a surprise for Jamie and Frida. Part of Nat also softened to the whole idea when he saw that sharing this news brought pink tones back to Frida's highly defined cheekbones.

When the waiter came around for their dinner orders, each of the guys started fucking around by ordering Beatles songs. Nat asked about the "Savoy Truffle."

The diplomatic waiter apologized, as the Peacock Alley only had Périgord winter truffles available this evening. Once the orders were in, Nat bummed a cigarette from Greg as an excuse to be alone outside. Soon after, Frida joined him under the gilded awning.

"I can't in good conscience give you more than a drag," Nat said, holding out his cigarette.

"God no, thanks," she said.

"I'm just testing you," said Nat.

"Isn't that typical," Frida replied.

"Look who's getting to know me." Nat stepped out from the awning to admire the hotel's place in the skyline. "Did you ever see that old photo of the two guys dining on a fucking beam on top of this hotel?"

"I don't think so," she said.

"It's a good one. These steel workers or something. Cool as cucumbers, enjoying a meal at the top of the world. Kind of like Jamie and me—we're just pulling this stupid stunt. But it could end up being a fucking classic."

"Nat." Frida touched his arm. "If it hasn't been clear, I'm glad he has you."

Nat shook his shoulders and tossed the cigarette, which was immediately swept up by the uniformed hotel staff. "You know what, Frida? Same. I know I give you, or everyone, a hard time."

"No more than you give yourself," she said.

"Tell me what else you know."

"Actually, I do have something I've been meaning to tell you," she said. "About Eleanor."

"Please don't tell me she's pregnant," Nat nervously joked, which caused Frida to belly laugh, something Nat had never heard. Maybe because she'd only recently developed a belly.

"Well, I know she's been on your mind." Frida wrapped her beige scarf tighter around her neck. "And, well, she and Jamie've both told me about the night they were caught in the lift. I'm not naïve to believe Jamie's account, but I believe Eleanor that—"

"Whoa, wait. Hang on," Nat said. Frida's attempt to divulge this information was a tooth pull. "It's all right. This might sound fucking weird, but I don't care as long as she's okay." Nat sighed hard breaths to cut through the December air. "I just need to see her but her dad was saying—"

"That's the thing," Frida said.

Nat clamped his teeth into a deep bite.

"She's home now."

"Hillside?"

Frida nodded.

Nat grabbed Frida by her buttery leather gloves and pulled her in for a quick hug. "I swear to god, most of the time I know money is bullshit, but then there's times I've never been luckier to have a wad of cash in my pocket."

"Why?"

"Because I need a fucking taxi!" Nat shouted and ran out towards the street.

He couldn't wait for the concierge to arrange things. He couldn't wait to cross the East River and get to her.

26

ELEANOR

E LEANOR FIGURED SHE HAD slept in more places this past year than in her prior life combined. Some were memorable. The bunk above Nat at Lochstock. Her room in Leipzig with the view of a humble river carved through trees. Hotel suites, hiding with Will before their flame blew out like a birthday candle. Alone by the pool, under towels and the Tuscan sky the night of Lindsay and KP's wedding. Then there was her stint at the Rink, where she could only hope to work or party hard enough to fall asleep unbothered by its shifty walls and people. Now, after a week spent in a St. Louis motel by the racetrack to shoot in one of the new *Reel World* castmate's hometowns, Eleanor was back in her first bedroom and preparing to move on to her next. From January to June, while Bolero toured the world, she'd be sharing a flat with the rest of the PAs in Notting Hill to film the first international season of the show. Only the feeling of a dwindling opportunity to share a bed with Nat before, or perhaps ever, tempered Eleanor's enthusiasm.

Packing was easy, mechanical by now. Eleanor was in the zone of fold-and-rolls. She had to retire a few favorites, such as jeans with threadbare thighs and t-shirts that were too gray and stiff with soap residue from sink washes. As much as Eleanor had been raised militarily to avoid getting attached to things, this exercise reminded her that she was a sentimental person and that was okay. Emotions did not always have to be qualified or put to some higher practical purpose. They could just be felt, even if they felt useless. She didn't have to avoid pain or fear of loving or losing like deadweight in a backpack. She could carry it, or let it go, or slow down and take a break. Things didn't have to work out. Old Betty summed it up best when she said, "Things don't work out when they're not supposed to work out."

As soon as she heard one hard knock, followed by two softer taps, Eleanor sprinted to the stairs. She slipped on the top step and overextended her arm, which caught her from taking the entire flight on her ass. Twice her stomach had plunged by the time she reached the front door.

Eleanor answered the knocks and stood temporarily frozen as if it'd help her freeze this frame of Nat on her stoop, cupping his hands together in the cold as if he'd been pleading for her to answer. A smile had augmented her pebbled cheeks into boulders. Eleanor reached out to smooth her hands through his hair, which flicked like grass with morning dew, and then dove in to hug him.

"Did I just hear you fall?" Nat said.

"Yes!" She clutched onto him with abandon. "I fucking fell for you!" Their embrace felt like a great stretch, deepening with every shared breath. Eleanor could feel his eyelashes flutter on her neck, leading her to believe that he might be crying. Her body felt secure in the hold of his arms.

"Besides falling for me, you need to stop falling so goddamn much," Nat said.

"But actions speak louder than words." She let out a cackle. Eleanor invaded his open coat to feel his body more intimately and dug her chin above his collar to nuzzle below his fresh stubble. "But you're right. I need to slow down."

Nat held her face in his palms. "Yeah, but not yet," he said and coated her lips with a wholehearted persistence that made her entire body beg to marry his tongue with hers.

Nat pulled his arms around her to bring them in from the cold, but they didn't make it much further. It was like every part of him that touched her was an awakening. His imperfect nose and perfect lips swept her while she melted, stupefied, and was pinned with pleasure against the jangling frames and coats hooked on the wall of her father's house.

"Oh my God," Eleanor moaned when Nat caressed her breasts over her shirt and down her ribs before swooping under her backside to pull her firmly against him. "Wait—stop." She dropped to her knees.

"Fuck, is Mick home? I just assumed cause he's not in the chair, and fuck," Nat whispered, introducing to her his manner of being disheveled and giddy.

"No, he's working."

"Then why are you whispering?" Nat said.

"I don't know!" She sprang up and squirmed back into his arms. "He'll be home any minute."

"Joanie is staying in the city. Do you want to come over? I mean—"

Her heart raced, and she started to run in place. "I want to come over. Let me just—" Eleanor looked down at herself in her oversized Champion t-shirt. "I have to grab some clothes and hygiene stuff."

"Hygiene?"

"I'll be right over!" she said and shoved him out the door.

Eleanor ran upstairs to brush her teeth and hair, wash her armpits, then threw on her Adidas breakaway pants. She left a note for Mick along with two cookies to sweeten that, between the lines, she was definitely across the street having sex with a Dempsey.

►►

Eleanor entered Joanie Dempsey's house, which was freshly Windexed and decorated for Christmas morning. Eleanor remembered for the first time to pull her shoes off by the door before going further inside. Upstairs in Nat's room, Eleanor saw copies of Bolero's new single with "Always Home" stacked on his dresser.

"Oh, can I have your autograph?" she said in a breathy, waifish pitch.

"Where do you want it?" Nat asked, and she shoved him onto the bed. "I refuse to ask if you liked the song, by the way."

"I refuse to ask if it's about me."

"Don't tell Jamie, but they're kind of all about you, even when they aren't... The good ones, anyway."

"Shut up," she said, and he did shut up because she leaned over and his mouth was on hers again, vibrantly coloring between the lines of every encounter that led to the depth of how she felt about him. Eleanor could taste that he brushed his teeth too, which made her lips temporarily stretch thin into a smile. She loved him. Eleanor understood what Nat meant in his song, that she was always home to him, even when neither of them was home. But they were home together now, and their chemistry and momentum overrode any chance or need to discuss this.

"Are you sure you don't want to go to a hotel or whatever?" Nat asked.

"No," she said, proving her insistence by straddling him on his twin bed with mismatched flannel sheets.

Nat returned her intensity, locking eyes like he needed to tell her through his gaze alone how good it was going to feel for him to slide his hands up her ankles to the back of her thighs, which it overwhelmingly did.

"Good, because I can't think of anything better than this," he said.

"Then what?" she said on his neck.

"Being with you... Being inside you in the first place I dreamed about it."

She felt Nat firm his grip under the elastic at the top of her breakaway pants, and with welcome force, he tore them apart to a titillating symphony of snaps.

"Is that what you want?" he asked.

"God, yes," Eleanor shrieked and surrendered herself to the blur of fantasy and reality and coming undone.

White light shone through the small window above their locked feet. Eleanor had woken up laughing. She grazed the dark hair on Nat's arm and tightened it around her body. They were a perfect pair of spoons, the heirloom kind that their ancestors crossed oceans with to start a new life. She felt his breathing pattern change and his body stiffen to stretch to know he was awake now, too. Eleanor turned around, their faces slightly obscured by the middle of the pillow they shared. Nat's eyes had never looked so relaxed. She smoothed the follicles that rebelled against the strong shape of his eyebrows during sleep back into place, something she hadn't realized she'd always wanted to do.

"Are we dreaming?" she said.

"I don't know. Let me check." Nat pinched her tush as if to confirm. She twitched her body against his, which increased her heart rate.

"What does ass pinching remind you of?" she asked him.

Nat maneuvered so he could bury her arm underneath his head. "Your dad's sadistic lawn chairs. No question. Sitting on the back patio, not paying attention to Mets games on the radio with you."

"Dreaming of what we were gonna do someday," she said, smoothing his hair.

"You were dreaming," he corrected.

"What were you doing?"

"Already living the dream," Nat said.

"I love how you try to sound sarcastic when you're telling the truth," she said.

"I love you knowing that about me," he said.

Eleanor smirked. "I know a lot about you."

"Yeah? And I know a lot about you." Nat returned the smirk and looked down, showing that he was impressed by her naked body pressed against his.

"What do you know?" she asked, swaying to entice him.

"I know you are efficient. Like dangerously efficient."

"What the fuck!" She chortled.

"Yeah," he said. "You're always carrying, like, five too many things—sometimes I think you'd walk a tightrope because it'd be the shortest distance between two points."

"Only because it'd be a challenge," she said. "Well, that's not exceptionally romantic."

"Oh, exceptionally romantic?" Nat's firm hand rocked her hip. "In that case, I love how everything has an effect on you. When I can smell a static chill on your hair and coat when you've been outside," he said. "And you always hug me for so long—you just cling onto me and everyone has to stand around waiting, and I have to hide the fact that I just want to bury myself in you."

"I feel like you're just trying to tell me I smell."

"That's your takeaway?" Nat gently pushed back the hair from her face. "You smell like a mint julep most of the time, but I'm very into all those parts of you that aren't sweet."

"Prove it," she said.

Nat put his money where her mouth was. Only once did he detach his lips from her dragonish morning breath to ask, "Do I have to be efficient?"

▶▶

Hours later, the reality of Christmas interrupted Eleanor and Nat. Jamie, Frida, and Joanie returned home in a stretch car filled with presents. Eleanor couldn't have felt worse about being empty-handed, especially after Frida gifted her a Burberry trench, shearling gloves, and rubber boots she called "Wellies" to be properly outfitted for the rainy British winter.

Frida gave Nat and Jamie white gold Claddagh rings. Eleanor tried not to laugh.

"This isn't the most subtle way to encourage us to have a loyal and amicable brotherhood," Nat told her.

Eleanor noticed that Nat seemed more touched by Frida's other gift to him. It was a framed, black-and-white photograph of two men fine dining on an iron beam above the city, similar but lesser known than Charles Ebbets' "Lunch Atop A Skyscraper." Frida gave all the credit to Waldorf's tireless hotel concierge.

Giving basis to abhorrently capitalistic Christmas commercials, Frida and Jamie gifted Joanie a red Lincoln Town Car with a ribbon bigger than a Slip'n'Slide. Joanie seemed underwhelmed, if not burdened by the idea of parking it on their narrow block, until she learned it was for transport to the second part of the gift from Nat.

"No, you didn't!" Joanie slapped her boys' arms and squealed. "A beach cabana at ABC? I gotta call my sistah!"

Back at the Huston house, Eleanor and her dad's traditions remained modest. They listened to Bing Crosby and exchanged stockings with things like travel toiletries, calling cards, playing cards, and wool socks. Mick made Shepherd's pie. For dessert, they ate apple pie *à la mode*, which her dad loved to say. Then they watched *A Christmas Story*, even though she hated it, because he loved it.

The whole holiday had been the best kind of torture. Festive with loved ones while yearning to disappear and catch up on years of not being with Nat. That night, she exercised restraint by staying at her dad's, knowing she would join Nat in the city tomorrow. Then they would fulfill their gift, a promise to give each other as much as they could to hold on to after the year's end.

Eleanor had been snooping through Nat's room at The Gibson with his blessing, while he read NME with his legs crossed over the arm of a deep-set chair in the sitting area. She perused his piles of endorsement clothes still tagged, shoes, and sunglasses in boxes. Bins of fan mail. CDs. Contracts. Tour binders. Coasters and napkins and notebooks scribbled with things that might become songs.

Nat said he loved her more in the last three days than Eleanor had ever heard from anyone in her life. She rolled her eyes, even though she believed him. She loved him, too. But every time Eleanor intended to say it, she choked up, interrupting moments when they held each other, and during conversations that felt more honest and liberating than confessionals.

"I'm sad I'm going to London," she said one morning when they were naked under covers.

"Why? Do you think you're running away?"

"No. I'm sad this is going to end," she said.

"Oh, I'm expecting it to crush me to a paralysis I can only write my way out of."

Eleanor invited him to crush his face between her bare chest. After coming up for air, he told her, "Just so you know. When the time comes, that would be my preferred way to die."

"Don't die yet," she said, climbing on top of him.

"You're telling me."

After Eleanor ended up on his side of the bed, Nat caught her staring too long at the cigar box under the table on his bedside.

"I've been waiting for you to lift the lid on that," he said.

The box was one of the first things she'd noticed after occupying his suite, but had been unwilling to look inside, even when Nat wasn't around. She had mostly written it off as storage for condoms, maybe phone numbers of girls to use them with. Nat kissed the beauty mark on her shoulder and told her to open it. Instead, she ended up back on the other side of the bed.

Eleanor stubbornly waited until the next day, when Nat was at rehearsal. The box was filled with treasures. A photo of him, Jamie, and his parents, cheesing as big as the Cyclone behind them at Coney Island. Nat looked eerily similar to his father, except for the mustache and the sneer. There were picks and ticket stubs. The AAA badge when he was a guitar tech on the tour he worked with KP. A chain with a medal for St. Anthony. A strip of negatives from Eleanor's photos used for the cover of *Light Up*. A 4x6 of the whole tired crew at Lochstock posed like a class photo in the mess hall, she and Nat laughing at the center of it all. There were matchbooks from the Hotel del Coronado, the Rainbow Room, the Groucho Club, and the Belgian restaurant she'd taken him for his birthday. A Rosso di Montalcino cork. Photos from KP and Lindsay's wedding, one of her walking down the aisle. There was a folded crayon drawing of Nat with a guitar signed by Karen's daughter, Julia. A yellowed postcard Eleanor had sent him with a covered bridge after her mom died. A much older letter made sepia by age, marked "Soldier's Mail" across the stamp zone. In November 1943, Jack wrote to Dorothy that he loved her but didn't expect her to wait for him. It ended with, "If I'm alive after this is all over, meet me at Sunrise Diner and I'm yours forever. I might already be!"

It was just like Nat.

This was his muse box.

▶▶

The last day of 1994 hit like a bittersweet rush of bubbly between the temples. Eleanor planned to moderate her drinking, knowing the first day of 1995 was going to be tough enough without a legendary hangover. Nat'd be on a bus to Boston, and she'd be on the redeye to London.

The Rockettes had barely finished high-kicking through their final holiday show before the stage underwent a reset for Bolero's midnight concert to kick off their "Alive in '95" tour. All access at Radio City Music Hall was surreal. The energy radiated from both sides of the golden contour curtain that dripped in shapes, like nothing else she'd seen. Eleanor moseyed around before hiding all the way up in the viewing room to watch soundcheck.

Guitars jam. Full instrumentals. Drums only. Then Jamie. "Cha check, check. Helloooo. 1-2." After a run-through of their set, Eleanor returned to the stage where everyone but the band was still scattered, including Aja, who was staffed to cover the event.

"You're packing light," Aja said, pointing to Eleanor's Contax T2 slung around her hip.

"It's nice to be a civilian," Eleanor said.

"Oh, I don't know, Ele. Seems like you've always been a little more than just that," Aja said.

"You're the boss."

"Well, not of you anymore," Aja replied.

Eleanor took the jab with her mouth closed, knowing she deserved it and was also in too good a mood to wish Aja anything other than a happy new year.

At 10, there was a pre-party on the seventh floor in the Roxy Suite. Though Eleanor and Nat hadn't been able or interested in hiding their affection until this point, Nat promised her he'd try to resist during the pre-party, which would be stacked with snap-happy reporters. Awkwardly, Will and the rest of The Reverie would also be there. Nat and Eleanor agreed to abstain temporarily from one another while making out in a coat closet. Old Betty caught them. She crossed her Floridian forearms and shook her head, saying, "Bunny and Honey, *simpatico* at last."

Back in the Roxy Suite, Rollins made a cryptic toast about her dead predecessor and a fool's errand that turned to gold. Everyone became distracted by Jamie, whose sticky fingers had found a toy soldier's hat from the *Christmas Spectacular*. Eleanor went over to the boys in The Reverie to wish them luck on the tour. Dasuki was all seven feet of enthusiasm, "ready to rip." Andy's hand had healed. Dave looked more like himself, not the one Will had broken back to life. Eleanor was relieved to see no trace of vacancy or gauntness in Dave's kind face when he thanked her for her help that day.

Will paused his cross-armed conversation with some publicists when he saw Eleanor wave at him. They both walked to meet in the middle of the distance between them.

"Happy New Year," Eleanor said, once again feeling lucky she had this occasion to lean on for words when she wasn't sure what to say.

"You know it," he said.

"Well, you're on the final stretch now. Try to connect and enjoy it."

Will scratched the hair she'd once cut in a bathroom in Berlin.

"That hair's getting long again," she said.

"I know. I need a new hairdresser," Will replied.

"I'm sure you'll find a better one."

Will looked back to the women he'd been chatting with and gave an amused shrug.

►►

Eleanor skipped watching The Reverie's set at 11 to party in Bolero's dressing room. Unlike the quasi-formality of the party in the Roxy Suite, this one was packed to the gills with everyone Eleanor would ever want to see reflected infinitely through rows of mirrors lit up by vanity bulbs. The shared mindset was overt—all they had was one power hour of their lives left before the ball dropped into a new era. Eleanor introduced her dad to Old Betty. He was impressed, nearly excited by her security protocols. Joanie was telling everyone about Atlantic Beach Cabana culture. Lindsay was validating Frida's analysis about Jamie and fatherhood while protectively shooing away smokers. KP was in awe that the wine he requested on their rider was fulfilled. "Can you believe these bozos got us Brunellos?"

As a complete surprise, Nat had invited Eleanor's buddies from Germany. Adele was still with Connor from Down the Hatch, and Robin was busy showing Lara from Girlcrush her new tongue ring. It was joyful chaos, grounded by Nat's playful gropes and glances. Eventually, Bolero was being directed to stand by. This began a frenetic series of goodbyes as everyone was ushered to various Very Important places.

Eleanor swallowed the unfamiliar heartbreak creeping up her throat. She was comforted by Frida and Lindsay. The three of them linked arms and followed the sound of "This is the One" by The Stone Roses over Radio City's PA system. It was getting louder and louder as they approached their destination, stage left anchored by a high-top table with complimentary earplugs, 1995 tiaras, Frida's Evians, and buckets of Champagne and Guinness. When the recording faded out, Eleanor looked over to center stage. Even this close, it was all darkness eclipsed by a projected display with the live broadcasting of the ball and all of its 180 white lights from Times Square.

Finally, the sold-out crowd began the countdown from 10.

On one, Nat emerged from the stage and grabbed Eleanor. They kissed each other over the passage of time, through a squall of sweet perspiration, happy nerves, and confetti.

The rest of the band simmered in formation. The cheering for the new year had become a growing, restless chant for Bolero. "Alive in '95! Alive in '95!"

"Let's do this!" KP shouted over to Nat and threw his chin up.

Eleanor freed Nat to join them. "Now the hard part starts?" she yelled.

"Nah," said Nat. "The hard part was thinking this might never happen."

ACKNOWLEDGMENTS

Endless gratitude to the community that grew out of the will to learn how to write this book.

Early on, I found my characters and voice in Alison Hicks' Center City Philly Wordshop, and continued on with the Salon. Those encouraging, humbling, curious, and talented writers have "stayed with me." Extra special thanks to Rob Wright, Lynne McMahon, Tammi Markowitz, (N)Ash Humienny, and Carolyn Clarke.

Annie Liontas, your Novel Writing Intensive through Blue Stoop and early mentorship got me from draft 1 to 2. Anna Dorn, your critique, questions, and margin 'lol's helped me revive this project. Thank you both for your brilliant books and brains.

So much love to my family, including my parents who told me I could be anything I wanted to be (except an asshole). To my siblings, May May and Broseph—I am grateful for our bond and that we are our biggest fans, not rivals. To the remarkable rest of my family and friends, thank you for your wisdom, support and our experiences that show up in all kinds of ways on and off the page.

The path to publication made me reflect on coming up an angsty, proud and blissfully irrelevant part of the NYC/LI music scene as a teenager in the late nineties. I will forever strive to live up to those formative lessons in authenticity, a DIY spirit, and generosity to uplift others.

Lastly and mostly to Pete. Thank you for encouraging and challenging me to share this story. None of this would've happened without my love for you.

ALIVE IN '95 DISCUSSION GUIDE

To offer reading groups or individuals more insightful and specific questions, this guide includes details that may reveal "spoilers." We kindly recommend finishing ALIVE IN '95 before reading further.

1. Being set in 1994, what cultural references, historic events, and social mores felt super nostalgic? How do you think the era shaped the plot of *ALIVE* and its characters' belief systems?

2. There's a lot of attraction and tension among many of the characters. Were you surprised by some of the connections, or curious if things were going to go in a different way? Who were you rooting for and did this change?

3. Discuss Eleanor's early decision to take the PA job in Germany and her time abroad. What do you think she got out of that experience, and can you relate to an opportunity you've taken?

4. How did the women characters in *ALIVE* navigate male-dominated industries and power dynamics? In what ways were they influential to the success of Bolero?

5. How would you describe the dynamic between Nat and Jamie as brothers and as bandmates? How consistent were you sided with one or the other throughout their conflicts? For those with siblings, what rang true about their tensions and rivalry?

6. Which characters led you to question their intentions and felt unreliable? Did any of your feelings change by the story's conclusion?

7. There's a limited presence of parental figures—Why do you think that is? What did you learn about characters by what was revealed of their relationships to their parents/childhoods?

8. What did you make of Eleanor's indecision and professional struggles? How were her frustrations and missteps relatable? There are a few instances where we see glimmers of ideas and excitement towards her future. What direction do you predict her career could take down the line?

9. What did you make of Nat's decision to leave after the "bust" at Santa Monica Pier Fest. Do you think he intended to come back? What do you think shifted during his AWOL and when he returned to the band?

10. Chances are, you are not like Jamie Dempsey. What did you learn from his point of view? Could you empathize with his perspective? What do you see as his redemptive qualities?

11. *ALIVE* takes us on a rollercoaster—Lochstock! NYC! Eastern Germany! So Cal! Vegas! Tuscany! London! Nat, Jamie and Eleanor's hometown on Long Island! Which transported you? How did the locations influence the story development?

12. Which characters do you think changed the most over the course of the year? How so? What events contributed to those changes?

13. In the final chapter, Eleanor finds sentimental treasures in Nat's cigar box, including various keepsakes from the past year. What did you make of this collection or her reaction to it? Do you have anything similar? What's inside your "Muse Box"?

14. How did you feel about the ending? What could the future look like for Nat and Eleanor, Jamie and Frida, or Will?

15. What were the most memorable scenes or lines from *ALIVE*? We'd love to hear from you! Please share on IG and tag: @alive_in_95 / @brinesociety or email: hi@bewilderpress.com

ABOUT THE AUTHOR

Jennell McHugh was born a bridge-and-tunnel New Yorker. Growing up, she hustled on the periphery of the music scene, interviewing bands on a Talkboy. Along with degrees from Temple and Columbia University, she continues to apply those early surveying skills to support libraries and education research. After decades of urban dwelling, she is now open to hosting you in Lancaster, PA, where she lives with her honey and two dogs. *ALIVE IN '95* is her first novel.

▶▶

PSSST…

VISIT
BEWILDERPRESS.COM
FOR LINKS TO THE
ALIVE IN '95
"MIXTAPES"
ON SPOTIFY